This Book Belongs To:

_____

_____

The Arabian Nights

pictures by René Bull

CHILDREN'S CLASSICS

This unique series of Children's Classics™ features accessible and highly readable texts paired with the work of talented and brilliant illustrators of bygone days to create fine editions for today's parents and children to rediscover and treasure. Besides being a handsome addition to any home library, this series features genuine bonded-leather spines stamped in gold, full-color illustrations, and high-quality acid-free paper that will enable these books to be passed from one generation to the next.

The Arabian Nights

with illustrations by Rene Bull

CHILDREN'S CLASSICS

NEW YORK

A Note to the Reader: There are racial references and language in this story which may be offensive to the modern reader. He or she should be aware, however, that these do not reflect the attitudes of the publisher of this edition.

This 1986 edition is published by Children's Classics, a division of dilithium Press, Ltd., distributed by Crown Publishers, Inc., 225 Park Avenue South, New York, New York 10003, by arrangement with Dodd, Mead & Company.

CHILDREN'S CLASSICS is a trademark of dilithium Press, Ltd

Printed and Bound in the United States of America

Library of Congress Cataloging-in-Publication Data

Arabian nights. English. Selections.
   The Arabian nights.

   Summary: An illustrated collection of twenty-six stories from the "Arabian Nights," including those of Sinbad, Ali Baba, Aladdin, and lesser known characters.
   [1. Fairy Tales.   2. Folklore, Arab]   I. Bull, René, ill.   II. Title.
PZ8.A85   1986   398.2'2   86–13650
ISBN 0–517–61934–2

 h g f e d c b a

CONTENTS

THE ARABIAN NIGHTS

LIST OF ILLUSTRATIONS

THE ARABIAN NIGHTS

LIST OF ILLUSTRATIONS

ix

THE ARABIAN NIGHTS

LIST OF COLORED PLATES

FOREWORD

THE tales from *The Arabian Nights* have a unique place in Western literature because of their exotic qualities. With genies instead of witches, scimitars instead of swords, dust and sand in place of dirt and forests, viziers in place of knights, they are an education in Eastern culture and customs, conveyed with excitement and color. Through them, we are vaulted over the walls of forbidden cities; allowed to peek through crevices in secret caves; learn passwords and methods of invoking magic powers; and become intimately acquainted with a people whose customs, language, and attitudes have changed remarkably little in the more than ten centuries that the stories are said to have existed.

Handed down orally for centuries before they were written down, some translations have filled as many as sixteen volumes. The twenty-six tales in this volume include all the outstanding favorites and provide an excellent introduction to the vast number of stories that have been told over the ages. Here we find Ali Baba, Sinbad, Aladdin—all household names—together with tales that roam from Persia to China, down to Africa and back to Arabia, in a translation that retains the accuracy, energy, and intrinsic appeal of the originals.

The illustrations of René Bull that accompany the stories transport us great distances, to places where not only the clothing is different, but also the physical characteristics of the animals, the people, and their belongings are unlike any we are used to seeing or could hope to see. Here are delightful drawings of puffy-cheeked genies, scrawny old men who dance like dervishes before our eyes, enormous jars, monstrous sultans, strangely shaped buildings, arches, minarets, mosques, windows, ships, fish, gnarled trees, bejeweled cyclopses, ornate bottles, baskets, and rugs, together with a selection of paintings in the most exquisite colors, as befits our images of Eastern opulence.

THE ARABIAN NIGHTS

The stories cover a broad range of styles and subject matter—now whimsical, now mysterious, now sinister—but they have a common thread: a betrayal of trust deserves immediate and appropriate punishment. This theme first appears in the introduction, where the framework for the tales is laid. A sultan, finding that his wife is betraying him, takes his revenge by having her executed and, resolving never to be betrayed again, insures this by marrying a maiden every night and having her killed the following morning. The vizier's daughter, Scheherazade, devises a scheme to put an end to the killings. She marries the sultan, and, on their wedding night, begins to tell him a story that cannot be completed until the following night. Each night she finishes the former night's story and begins a new one, and this continues for a thousand and one nights, until the sultan's need for vengeance is exhausted.

The framework serves its purpose well, and the advocacy of punishment for betrayal is a recognizable universal ideology. What is peculiar to these stories are the methods of carrying out punishment and revenge which often will seem to us excessive and barbaric. A thief is "quartered," a deceiving pet is dashed to death, a wicked genie bottled up and thrown into the sea. Although we are accustomed to folk and fairy tales that pit good against evil and evil against evil with witches, curses, wicked step-parents, or cannibalistic giants, these tales introduce us to a different cast of characters and strange methods of operation. Unlike our Western folk and fairy tales, which are pure fantasy, the Arabian Nights tales are closer to the reality of a people we are only beginning to become acquainted with today. Severe punishment, even death, for trifling offenses was almost as common as it was for severe offenses, not only in the Arabian Tales, but in Arabian life.

With the world changing from moment to moment and scarcely anything remaining constant, it is surprising that the Eastern countries have maintained so much of their ancient heritage. Only a generation or two ago, reading *The Arabian Nights* provided a magic carpet ride to a land and a people most of us would never see or know. Today, when one reads the stories, we not only enter this fascinating and exotic world, but also are better able to understand a land and people who are as close as our

xiv

FOREWORD

television sets. What better way to breach the cultural gap than through their literature? *The Arabian Nights* has belonged to the world's literature for over a millenium, and to English literature for a century. With this new edition, our young people may profit to a greater extent than any of their predecessors in understanding the differences and recognizing the similarities of Eastern and Western peoples.

PATRICIA BARRETT PERKINS

Baltimore, Maryland
1986

THE ARABIAN NIGHTS' ENTERTAINMENTS

THE chronicles of the Sassanians, ancient kings of Persia, tell us that there was formerly a king of that potent family who was regarded as the most excellent prince of his time. He was as much beloved by his subjects for his wisdom and prudence as he was dreaded by his neighbours on account of his valour and well-disciplined troops. He had two sons : the elder, Schah-riar, the worthy heir of his father, and endowed with all his virtues; the younger, Schah-zenan, a prince of equal merit.

After a long and glorious reign, this king died ; and Schah-riar mounted the throne. Schah-zenan, being excluded from all share in the government by the laws of the empire, was so far from envying the happiness of his brother, that he made it his whole business to please him, and in this succeeded without much difficulty. Schah-riar, who had naturally a great affection for the prince his brother, gave him the kingdom of Great Tartary. Schah-zenan went immediately and took possession of it, and fixed the seat of his government at Samarcand, the metropolis of the country.

After they had been separated ten years, Schah-riar, being very desirous of seeing his brother, resolved to send his vizier to invite him to his court. When he came near the city, Schah-zenan was informed of his approach, and went to meet him, attended by the principal lords of his court, who, to show the greater honour to the sultan's minister, appeared in magnificent apparel. The king of Tartary received the ambassador with the greatest demonstrations of joy, and immediately asked

1

him concerning the welfare of the sultan his brother. The vizier, having acquainted him that he was in health, informed him of the purpose of his embassy. Schah-zenan was much affected, and answered: Sage vizier, the sultan my brother does me too much honour; nothing could be more agreeable to me, for I as ardently long to see him as he does to see me. My kingdom is at peace, and I want no more than ten days to get myself ready to return with you. There is therefore no necessity for your entering the city for so short a period. I pray you to pitch your tents here, and I will order everything necessary to be provided for yourself and your attendants. The vizier readily complied; and Schah-zenan, having made his preparations, at the end of ten days took leave of the queen his wife, and went out of town in the evening with his retinue. He pitched his royal pavilion near the vizier's tent, and conversed with him till midnight. Wishing once more to see the queen, whom he ardently loved, he returned alone to his palace, when, to his inexpressible grief, he found her trafficking with his enemies for his betrayal. Before the conspirators were aware of his presence, the unfortunate prince, urged by his just resentment, drew his scimitar and slew them, and then pitched their bodies into the fosse which surrounded the palace.

Having thus avenged himself, he returned to his pavilion without saying one word of what had happened, gave orders that the tents should be struck, and before day began his march, with kettle-drums and other instruments of music, that filled every one with joy, excepting the king. He was so much afflicted by the disloyalty of his wife, that he was seized with extreme melancholy, which preyed upon his spirits during the whole of his journey.

When he drew near the capital of Persia, the Sultan Schahriar and all his court came out to meet him. The princes were overjoyed to see one another, and having alighted, after mutual embraces and other marks of affection and respect, remounted, and entered the city, amidst the acclamations of the people. The sultan conducted his brother to the palace provided for him, which had a communication with his own by a garden. It was so much the more magnificent as it was set apart as a banqueting-house for public entertainments, and other diversions of the court.

Schah-riar immediately left the king of Tartary, that he might give him time to bathe, and to change his apparel. As soon as he had done, he returned to him again, and they sat down together on a sofa or alcove, and the two princes entertained one another suitably to their friendship and their long separation. The time of supper being come, they ate together, after which they renewed their conversation, till Schah-riar, perceiving that it was very late, left his brother to repose.

The unfortunate Schah-zenan retired to bed, but although the conversation of his brother had suspended his grief for some time, it returned again with increased violence; so that, instead of taking his necessary rest, he tormented himself with the bitterest reflections. All the circumstances of his wife's treachery presented themselves afresh to his imagination, in so lively a manner, that he was like one distracted. Not being able to sleep, he arose, and abandoned himself to the most afflicting thoughts, which made an impression upon his countenance it was impossible for the sultan not to observe. Schah-riar, distressed at the melancholy of his brother, endeavoured to divert him every day by new objects of pleasure, and the most splendid entertainments. But these, instead of affording him ease, only increased his sorrow.

One day, Schah-riar having appointed a great hunting-match, about two days' journey from his capital, in a place that abounded with deer, Schah-zenan besought him to excuse his attendance, for his health would not allow him to bear him company. The sultan, unwilling to put any constraint upon him, left him at his liberty, and went a-hunting with his nobles. The king of Tartary, being thus left alone, shut himself up in his apartment, and sat down at a window that looked into the garden. In this place, where he could see and not be seen, he soon became a witness of a circumstance which attracted the whole of his attention. A secret gate of the sultan's palace suddenly opened,

3

and there came out of it several persons, in the midst of whom walked the sultana, who was easily distinguished from the rest by her majestic air. This princess, thinking that the king of Tartary was gone a-hunting with his brother the sultan, came with her retinue near the windows of his apartment, and the prince heard her hold treasonable conversation with some of her companions.

The baseness of his brother's wife filled the king of Tartary with a multitude of reflections. How little reason had I, said he, to think that none was so unfortunate as myself? It is surely the unavoidable fate of all in power and high position to have their honour and estate conspired against. Such being the case, what a fool am I to kill myself with grief! I am resolved that the remembrance of a misfortune so common shall never more disturb my peace.

From that moment he forbore afflicting himself. He called for his supper, ate with a better appetite than he had done since his leaving Samarcand, and listened with some degree of pleasure to the concert of vocal and instrumental music that was appointed to entertain him while at table.

He continued after this very cheerful; and when he was informed that the sultan was returning, went to meet him, and paid him his compliments with great gaiety.

Schah-riar, who expected to have found his brother in the same state as he had left him, was overjoyed to see him so cheerful: Dear brother, said he, I return thanks to Heaven for the happy change it has wrought in you during my absence. Pray do me the favour to tell me why you were so melancholy, and wherefore you are no longer so.

The king of Tartary continued for some time as if he had been meditating and contriving what he should answer, but at last replied, You are my sultan and master; but excuse me, I beseech you, from answering your question. No, dear brother, said the sultan, you must answer me; I will take no denial. Schah-zenan, not being able to withstand these pressing entreaties replied, Well then, brother, I will satisfy you, since you command me; and having told him the story of the queen of Samarcand's treachery, This, said he, was the cause of my grief; judge whether I had not sufficient reason for my depression.

Oh! my brother, said the sultan, what a horrible event do you tell me! I commend you for punishing the traitors to your state and person. None can blame you for what you have done. It was just; and, for my part, had the case been mine, I should scarcely have been so moderate. I now cease to wonder at your melancholy. The cause was too afflicting and too mortifying not to overwhelm you. O Heaven! what a strange adventure! But I must bless God, who has comforted you; and since I doubt not but your consolation is well grounded, be so good as to inform me what it is, and conceal nothing from me. Schahzenan was not so easily prevailed upon in this point as he had been in the other, on his brother's account. But being obliged to yield to his pressing insistence he related to his brother the conversation he had overheard. After having heard these things, he continued, I believed all women to be naturally treacherous. Being of this opinion, it seemed to me to be in men an unaccountable weakness to place any confidence in their fidelity. This reflection brought on many others; and, in short, I thought the best thing I could do was to make myself easy on my own account, and warn you to anticipate the sultana in her designs upon you.

On hearing the dreadful tidings which his brother imparted to him, the sultan fell into an incontrollable rage, and instantly gave instructions for the execution of the sultana and her fellow-conspirators.

After this rigorous measure, being persuaded that no woman was to be trusted, he resolved, in order to prevent the disloyalty of such as he should afterwards marry, to wed one every day, and have her strangled next morning. Having imposed this cruel law upon himself, he swore that he would put it in force immediately after the departure of the king of Tartary, who shortly took leave of him, and, being laden with magnificent presents, set forward on his journey.

Schah-zenan having departed, Schah-riar informed his grand vizier of his vow, and ordered him to provide him with a new wife every day. Whatever reluctance the vizier might feel to put such orders in execution, as he owed blind obedience to the sultan his master, he was forced to submit. And thus, every day, was a maid married and a wife murdered.

The rumour of this unparalleled barbarity occasioned a general consternation in the city, where there was nothing but crying and lamentation. Here, a father in tears, and inconsolable for the loss of his daughter; and there, tender mothers dreading lest their daughters should share the same fate, filled the air with cries of distress and apprehension. So that, instead of the commendations and blessings which the sultan had hitherto received from his subjects, their mouths were now filled with imprecations.

The grand vizier, who, as has already been observed, was the unwilling executioner of this horrid course of injustice, had two daughters, the elder called Scheherazade, and the younger Dinarzade. The latter was highly accomplished; but the former possessed courage, wit, and penetration infinitely above her sex. She had read much, and had so admirable a memory, that she never forgot anything she had read. She had successfully applied herself to philosophy, medicine, history, and the liberal arts; and her poetry excelled the compositions of the best writers of her time. Besides this, she was of perfect beauty, and all her accomplishments were crowned by surpassing virtue.

The vizier passionately loved this daughter, so worthy of his affection. One day, as they were conversing together, she said to him, Father, I have one favour to beg of you, and most humbly pray you to grant it. I will not refuse, answered he, provided it be just and reasonable. For the justice of it, resumed she, there can be no question, and you may judge of this by the motive which obliges me to make the request. I wish to stop that barbarity which the sultan exercises upon the families of this city. I would dispel those painful apprehensions which so many mothers feel of losing their daughters in such a fatal manner. Your design, daughter, replied the vizier, is very commendable; but the evil you would remedy seems to me incurable. How do you propose to effect your purpose? Father, said Scheherazade, since by your means the sultan makes every day a new marriage, I conjure you, by the tender affection you bear me, to procure me the honour of his hand. The vizier could not hear this without horror. O Heaven! he replied in a passion, have you lost your senses, daughter, that you make such a dangerous request? You know the sultan's vow; would you then have me propose you to him? Consider well to what your indiscreet zeal will expose you. Yes, dear father, replied the virtuous daughter, I know the risk I run; but that does not alarm me. If I perish, my death will be glorious; and if I succeed, I shall do my country an important service. No, no, said the vizier, whatever you may offer to induce me to let you throw yourself into such imminent danger, do not imagine that I will ever consent. When the sultan shall command me to strike my *poignard* into your heart, alas! I must obey; and what an employment will that be for a father! Ah! if you do not dread death, at least cherish some fears of afflicting me with the mortal grief of imbruing my hands in your blood. Once more, father, replied Scheherazade, grant me the favour I solicit. Your stubbornness, resumed the vizier, will rouse my anger; why will you run headlong to your ruin? They who do not foresee the end of a dangerous enterprise can never conduct it to a happy issue. I am afraid the same thing will happen to you as befell the ass, which was well off, but could not remain so. What misfortune befell the ass? demanded Scheherazade. I will tell you, replied the vizier, if you will hear me.

The Ass, the Ox & the Labourer

A VERY wealthy merchant possessed several country-houses, where he kept a large number of cattle of every kind. He had the gift of understanding the language of beasts, but with this condition, that he should not, on pain of death, interpret it to any one else.

He kept in the same stall an ox and an ass. One day, as he sat near them, he heard the ox say to the ass, Oh, how happy do I think you, when I consider the ease you enjoy, and the little labour that is required of you. You are carefully rubbed down and washed, you have well-dressed corn, and fresh clean water. Your greatest business is to carry the merchant, our master, when he has any little journey to make, and were it not for that you would be perfectly idle. My condition is as deplorable as yours is fortunate. Daylight no sooner appears than I am yoked to a plough, and made to work till night, which so fatigues me, that sometimes my strength entirely fails. Besides, the labourer, who is always behind me, beats me continually. By drawing the plough, my skin is all flayed; and in short, after having laboured from morning to night, when I am brought in they give me nothing to eat but poor and insufficient food; so that you see I have reason to envy your lot.

The ass did not interrupt the ox; but, when he had concluded, answered, They that called you a foolish beast did not lie. You are too simple; you suffer them to conduct you whither they please, and show no manner of resolution. But they

8

would not treat you so, if you had as much courage as strength. When they come to fasten you to the stall, why do you not resist ? why do you not gore them with your horns, and show that you are angry, by stamping with your foot ? And, in short, why do not you frighten them by bellowing aloud ? Nature has furnished you with means to command respect ;

'. . . made at the labourer, as if he would have gored him.'

but you do not use them. They bring you sorry beans and bad straw ; eat none of them, only smell and then leave them. If you follow my advice, you will soon experience a change, for which you will thank me.

The ox took the ass's advice in very good part, and owned he was much obliged to him.

Early the next morning the labourer went for the ox. He

9

fastened him to the plough, and conducted him to his usual work. The ox, who had not forgotten the ass's counsel, was very troublesome all that day, and in the evening, when the labourer brought him back to the stall, and began to fasten him, the malicious beast, instead of presenting his head willingly as he used to do, was restive, and drew back bellowing ; and then made at the labourer, as if he would have gored him with his horns. In a word, he did all that the ass had advised him. The day following, the labourer came, as usual, to take the ox to his labour ; but finding the stall full of beans, the straw that he had put in the night before not touched, and the ox lying on the ground with his legs stretched out, and panting in a strange manner, he believed him to be unwell, pitied him, and thinking that it was not proper to take him to work, went immediately and acquainted his master with his condition. The merchant, perceiving that the ox had followed all the mischievous advice of the ass, determined to punish the latter, and accordingly ordered the labourer to go and put him in the ox's place, and to be sure to work him hard. The labourer did as he was desired. The ass was forced to draw the plough all that day, which fatigued him so much the more, as he was not accustomed to that kind of labour ; besides, he had been so soundly beaten, that he could scarcely stand when he came back.

Meanwhile, the ox was mightily pleased ; he ate up all that was in his stall, and rested himself the whole day. He rejoiced that he had followed the ass's advice, blessed him a thousand times for the kindness he had done him, and did not fail to express his obligations when the ass had returned. The ass made no reply, his strength was so much exhausted that he fell down in his stall, as if he had been half dead.

Here the grand vizier addressed himself to Scheherazade, and said, Daughter, you act just like this ass ; you will expose yourself to destruction by your erroneous policy. Take my advice, remain quiet, and do not seek to hasten your death. Father, replied Scheherazade, the example you have set before me will not induce me to change my resolution. I will never cease

10

THE ASS, THE OX AND THE LABOURER

importuning you until you present me to the sultan as his bride. The vizier, perceiving that she persisted in her demand, replied, Alas! then, since you will continue obstinate, I shall be obliged

'...he could scarcely stand when he came back.'

to treat you in the same manner as the merchant whom I before referred to treated his wife a short time after.

The merchant, understanding that the ass was in a lamentable condition, was desirous of knowing what passed between him and the ox, therefore after supper he went out by moonlight, his wife bearing him company, and sat down by them. After his arrival, he heard the ass say to the ox, Comrade, tell me, I pray you, what you intend to do to-morrow, when the labourer brings you food ? What shall I do ? replied the ox ; I shall continue to act as you taught me. Beware of that, replied the ass, it will ruin you ; for as I came home this evening, I heard the merchant, our master, say something that makes me tremble for you. Alas ! what did you hear ? demanded the ox ; as you love me, withhold nothing from me. Our master, replied the ass, addressed himself thus to the labourer : Since the ox does not eat, and is not able to work, I would have him killed to-morrow ; therefore be sure to send for the butcher. This is what I had to tell you, said the ass. The interest I feel in your preservation and my friendship for you, obliged me to make it known to you, and to give you new advice. As soon as they bring you your bran and straw, rise up and eat heartily. Our master will by this think you are recovered, and no doubt will recall his orders for killing you ; but, if you act otherwise, you will certainly be slaughtered.

This discourse had the effect which the ass designed. The ox was greatly alarmed, and bellowed for fear. The merchant, who heard the conversation very attentively, fell into a loud fit of laughter, which greatly surprised his wife. Pray, husband, said she, tell me what you laugh at so heartily, that I may laugh with you. Wife, replied he, you must content yourself with hearing me laugh. I cannot afford you satisfaction, and can only inform you that I laugh at what our ass just now said to the ox. The rest is a secret, which I am not allowed to reveal. What, demanded she, hinders you from revealing the secret ? If I tell it you, replied he, I shall forfeit my life. You only jeer me, cried his wife ; what you would have me believe cannot be true. If you do not directly satisfy me as to what you laugh at, and tell me what the ox and the ass said to one another, I swear by Heaven that I will no longer live with you.

THE ASS, THE OX AND THE LABOURER

'. . . cried there all night.'

Having spoken thus, she returned to the house, and, seating herself in a corner, cried there all night. Her husband, finding next morning that she continued in the same humour, told her, she was very foolish to afflict herself in that manner; that it concerned her very little to know, while it was of the utmost consequence to him to keep the secret: therefore, continued he, I conjure you to think no more of it. I shall still think so much of it, replied she, as never to forbear weeping till you have satisfied my curiosity. But I tell you very seriously, answered he, that it will cost me my life if I yield to your indiscreet solicitations. Let what will happen, said she, I do insist upon it. I perceive, resumed the merchant, that it is impossible to bring you to reason, and since I foresee that you will occasion your own death by your obstinacy, I will call in your children, that they may see you before you die. Accordingly he called for them, and sent for her father and mother, and other relations. When they were come, and had heard the reason of their being summoned, they did all they could to convince her that she was in the wrong, but to no purpose: she told them she would rather die than yield that point to her husband. When her children saw that nothing would prevail to draw her out of that sullen temper, they wept bitterly. The merchant himself was half frantic, and almost ready to risk his own life to save that of his wife, whom he sincerely loved.

Now, my daughter, continued the vizier to Scheherazade, this merchant had fifty hens and one cock, with a dog that gave good heed to all that passed. While the merchant was, as I said, considering what he had best do, he heard his dog tell the cock of the sad perplexity which assailed their master.

What, has our master so little sense? exclaimed the cock; he has but one wife, and cannot govern her, and though I have fifty, I make them all do what I please. Let him take a stick and thrash her well; and I will answer for it, that will bring her to her senses, and make her forbear to importune him to discover what he ought not to reveal. The merchant took up a stick, went to his wife, and belaboured her so soundly, that she cried out, Enough, husband, enough ; forbear, and I will never ask the question more. Upon this, perceiving that she repented of her impertinent curiosity, he desisted ; and opening the door, her friends came in, were glad to find her cured of her obstinacy and complimented her husband upon this happy expedient to bring his wife to reason. Daughter, added the grand vizier, you deserve to be treated as the merchant treated his wife.

Father, replied Scheherazade, I beg you would not take it ill that I persist in my opinion. I am nothing moved by the story of this woman. I could relate many, to persuade you that you ought not to oppose my design. Besides, pardon me for declaring, that your opposition is vain ; for if your paternal affection should hinder you from granting my request, I will go and offer myself to the sultan. In short, the father, being overcome by the resolution of his daughter, yielded to her importunity, and though he was much grieved that he could not divert her from so fatal a resolution, he went instantly to acquaint the sultan, that next night he would bring him Scheherazade.

The sultan was much surprised at the sacrifice which the grand vizier proposed to make. How could you, said he, resolve to bring me your own daughter ? Sir, answered the vizier, it is her own offer. The sad destiny that awaits her could not intimidate her; she prefers the honour of being your majesty's wife for one night, to her life. But do not act under a mistake, vizier, said the sultan; to-morrow, when I place Scheherazade in your hands, I expect you will put her to death; and if you fail, I swear that your own life shall answer. Sir, rejoined the vizier, though I am her father, I will answer for the fidelity of my hand to obey your order.

When the grand vizier returned to Scheherazade, she thanked her father for having obliged her; and, perceiving that he was overwhelmed with grief, told him that she hoped he would never repent of having married her to the sultan; and that, on the contrary, he should have reason to rejoice at his compliance all his days.

Her business now was to adorn herself to appear before the sultan; but before she went, she took her sister Dinarzade apart, and said to her, My dear sister, I have need of your assistance in a matter of great importance, and must pray you not to deny it me. My father is going to conduct me to the sultan; do not let this alarm you, but hear me with patience. As soon as I am in his presence, I will pray him to allow you to come early on the morrow, that I may enjoy your company for an hour or two ere I bid you farewell and go to my death. If I obtain that favour, as I hope to do, remember, shortly after your arrival, to address me in these or some such words: 'My sister, I pray you that, ere I leave you, which must be very shortly, you will relate to me one of the entertaining stories of which you have recounted so many.' I will immediately tell you one; and I hope by this means to deliver the city from the consternation it is under at present. Dinarzade answered that she would with pleasure act as she required her.

The grand vizier conducted Scheherazade to the palace, and retired, after having introduced her into the sultan's apartment. As soon as the sultan was left alone with her, he ordered her to uncover her face: he found her so beautiful, that he was perfectly charmed; but, perceiving her to be in tears, demanded the reason. Sir, answered Scheherazade, I have a sister who loves me tenderly, and I could wish that she might be allowed to come early on the morrow to this chamber, that I might see her, and once more bid her adieu. Will you be pleased to allow me the consolation of giving her this last testimony of my affection? Schah-riar having consented, Dinarzade came an hour before dawn on the next day, and failed not to do as her sister had ordered. My dear sister, cried she, ere I leave you, which will be very shortly, I pray you to tell me one of those pleasant stories you have read. Alas! this will be the last time that I shall enjoy that pleasure.

Scheherazade, instead of answering her sister, addressed

16

herself to the sultan : Sir, will your majesty be pleased to allow me to afford my sister this satisfaction ? With all my heart, replied the sultan. Scheherazade then bade her sister attend, and afterwards addressing herself to Schah-riar, proceeded as follows.

The merchant & the Genie

THERE was formerly a merchant who possessed much
property in lands, goods, and money. One day being
under the necessity of going a long journey on an affair
of importance, he took horse, and carried with him a wallet
containing biscuits and dates, because he had a great desert
to pass over, where he could procure no sort of provisions. He
arrived without any accident at the end of his journey; and
having dispatched his affairs, took horse again, in order to return
home.

The fourth day of his journey, he was so much incommoded
by the heat of the sun, that he turned out of the road to refresh
himself under some trees, where he found a fountain of clear
water. Having alighted, he tied his horse to a branch, and,
sitting down by the fountain, took some biscuits and dates out
of his wallet. As he ate his dates, he threw the stones carelessly
in different directions. When he had finished his repast, being
a good Mussulman, he washed his hands, face, and feet, and said
his prayers. Before he had finished, and while he was yet on
his knees, he saw a genie of monstrous bulk advancing towards
him with great fury, whirling a scimitar in his hand. The genie
spoke to him in a terrible voice: Rise, that I may kill thee with
this scimitar, as thou hast killed my son; and accompanied these
words with a frightful roar. The merchant, being as much
alarmed at the hideous shape of the monster as at his threats,

18

answered him, trembling, Alas! how could I kill your son? I never knew, never saw him. Did not you, when you came hither, demanded the genie, take dates out of your wallet, and as you ate them, throw the stones about in different directions? I did all that you say, answered the merchant; I cannot deny it. When thou wert throwing the stones about, resumed the genie, my son was passing by, and thou didst throw one into his eye, which killed him; therefore I must kill thee. Ah! my lord! pardon me! cried the merchant. No pardon, exclaimed the genie, no mercy. Is it not just to kill him that has killed another? I agree it is, replied the merchant, but certainly I never killed your son; and if I have, it was unknown to me, and I did it innocently; I beg you therefore to pardon me, and suffer me to live. No, no, returned the genie, persisting in his resolution; I must kill thee, since thou hast killed my son. Then, taking the merchant by the arm, he threw him with his face on the ground, and lifted up his scimitar to cut off his head.

As soon as she had spoken these words, perceiving it was day, and knowing that the sultan rose early in the morning to say his prayers, and hold his council, Scheherazade discontinued her story. Dear

'. . . he found a fountain of clear water.'

sister, said Dinarzade, what a wonderful story is this! The remainder of it, replied Scheherazade, is more surprising, as you will allow, if the sultan will but permit me to live this day, and allow me to proceed with the relation on the morrow. Schahriar, who had listened to Scheherazade with much interest, resolved not to put Scheherazade to death that day, intending to execute her when she had finished the story. He arose, went to his prayers, and then attended his council.

During this time the grand vizier was in the utmost distress. Instead of sleeping, he spent the night bewailing the lot of his daughter, of whom he believed he should himself shortly be the executioner. As, with this melancholy prospect before him, he dreaded to meet the sultan, he was agreeably surprised when he found the prince entered the council chamber without giving him the fatal orders he expected.

The sultan, according to his custom, spent the day in regulating his affairs; and, when the night had closed in, retired with Scheherazade. The next morning before day, the sultan, without waiting for Scheherazade to ask his permission, bade her proceed with the story of the genie and the merchant; upon which Scheherazade continued her relation as follows :—

When the merchant saw that the genie was going to cut off his head, he cried to him, For Heaven's sake hold your hand! Allow me one word. Have the goodness to grant me a respite of one year, to bid my wife and children adieu, and to divide my estate among them. But I promise you, that this day twelve months I will return under these trees, to put myself into your hands. Do you take Heaven to be witness to this promise? said the genie. I do, answered the merchant, and you may rely on my oath. Upon this the genie left him near the fountain, and disappeared.

When the merchant, on reaching home, related what had passed between him and the genie, his wife uttered the most piteous cries, beat her face, and tore her hair. The children, all in tears, made the house resound with their groans; and

20

the father, not being able to resist the impulse of nature, mingled his tears with theirs.

At last the year expired, and he was obliged to depart. He put his burial clothes in his wallet; but when he came to bid his wife and children adieu, their grief surpassed description. Affected beyond measure by the parting with his dear ones, the merchant journeyed to the place where he had promised to meet the genie. Seating himself down by the fountain, he awaited the coming of the genie, with all the sorrow imaginable. Whilst he languished under this painful expectation, an old man leading a hind appeared and drew near him. After they had saluted one another, the old man inquired of him why he was in that desert place.

The merchant related his adventures, to the old man's astonishment, who, when he had done, exclaimed, This is the most surprising thing in the world! and you are bound by the most inviolable oath. However, I will be witness of your interview with the genie. He then seated himself by the merchant, and they entered into conversation.

While the merchant and the old man who led the hind were talking, they saw another old man coming towards them, followed by two black dogs. When he was informed of the merchant's adventure, he declared his resolve to stay and see the issue.

In a short time they perceived a thick vapour, like a cloud of dust raised by a whirlwind, advancing towards them. When it had come up to them, it suddenly vanished, and the genie appeared; who, without saluting them, went to the merchant with a drawn scimitar, and, taking him by the arm, said, Get thee up, that I may kill thee, as thou didst my son. The merchant and the two old men began to lament and fill the air with their cries.

When the old man who led the hind saw the genie lay hold of the merchant, and about to kill him, he threw himself at the feet of the monster, and kissing them, said to him, Prince of genies, I most humbly request you to suspend your anger, and do me the favour to listen to the history of my life, and of the hind you see ; and if you think it more wonderful and surprising than the adventure of the merchant, I hope you will pardon the unfortunate man one half of his offence. The genie took some time to deliberate on this proposal, but answered at last, Well, then, I agree.

The Story of the First Old Man and the Hind.

THIS hind you see is my wife, whom I married when she was twelve years old, and we lived together for twenty years without having any children.

My desire of having children induced me to adopt the son of a slave. My wife, being jealous, cherished a hatred for both the child and his mother, but concealed her aversion so well that I knew nothing of it till it was too late.

While I was away on a long journey, she applied herself to magic, and by her enchantments she changed the child into a calf, and the mother into a cow, and gave them both into the charge of my farmer.

On my return, I inquired for the mother and child. The slave, said she, is dead; and as for your adopted son, I know not what is become of him, I have not seen him these two months. I was afflicted at the death of the slave; but as my son had only disappeared, I was in hopes he would shortly return. However, eight months passed, and I heard nothing of him. When the festival of the great Bairam [1] was to be celebrated, I sent to my farmer for one of the fattest cows to sacrifice. He accordingly sent me one, and I bound her; but as I was going to sacrifice her, she bellowed piteously, and I could perceive tears streaming from her eyes. This seemed to me very extraordinary,

[1] One of the annual feasts observed by Mohammedans.

and finding myself moved with compassion, I could not find in my heart to give her a blow, but ordered my farmer to get me another.

My wife, who was present, was enraged at my tenderness, and resisting an order which disappointed her malice, she cried out, What are you doing, husband ? Sacrifice that cow ; your farmer has not a finer, nor one fitter for the festival. Out of deference to my wife, I ordered the farmer, less compassionate than myself, to sacrifice her ; but when he flayed her, he found her to be nothing except bones, though to us she seemed very fat. Take her away, said I to him, dispose of her in alms, or any way you please ; and if you have a very fat calf, bring it me in her stead. He returned with a fat calf, which, as soon as it beheld me, made so great an effort to come near me, that he broke his cord, threw himself at my feet, with his head against the ground, as if he meant to excite my compassion, and implore me not to be so cruel as to take his life.

I was more surprised and affected with this action than with the tears of the cow, and, addressing my wife, said, Wife, I will not sacrifice this calf, and pray do not you oppose me. The wicked woman had no regard to my wishes, but urged me until I yielded. I tied the poor creature, and, taking up the fatal knife, was going to plunge it into the calf's throat, when turning his eyes, bathed with tears, in a languishing manner, towards me, he affected me so much that I had not the strength to kill him. I let the knife fall, and told my wife positively that I would have another calf to sacrifice, and pacified her a little by promising that I would sacrifice him against the Bairam of the following year.

The next morning my farmer desired to speak with me alone. He told me that his daughter, who had some skill in magic, desired to see me. When she was admitted, she informed me that while I was on my journey my wife had changed the slave into a cow, and the child into a calf. She could not restore the slave, who, in the shape of a cow, had been sacrificed, but she could give me my adopted son again, and would do so if she might have him for a husband, and also punish my wife as she deserved.

When I had given my consent to these proposals, the damsel then took a vessel full of water, pronounced over it words that I did not understand, and throwing the water over the calf, he in an instant recovered his natural form.

My son, my dear son, cried I, immediately embracing him

'. . . he in an instant recovered his natural form.'

with a transport of joy, this young maid has removed the horrible charm by which you were enchanted, and I doubt not but in acknowledgment you will make your deliverer your wife, as I have promised. He joyfully consented; but, before they married, she changed my wife into a hind; and this is she whom you see here.

Since that time, my son is become a widower, and gone to travel. It being now several years since I heard of him, I am come abroad to inquire after him; and not being willing to trust anybody with my wife, till I should return home, I thought fit to take her everywhere with me. This is the history of myself and this hind: is it not one of the most wonderful and surprising? I admit it is, said the genie, and on that account forgive the merchant one half of his crime.

When the first old man had finished his story, the second, who led the two black dogs, addressed the genie, and said: I am going to tell you what happened to me, and these two black dogs you see by me. But when I have done this, I hope you will pardon the merchant the other half of his offence. I will, replied the genie, provided your story surpass that of the hind. Then the second old man began in this manner.

The Story of the Second Old Man: The Two Black Dogs

GREAT prince of genies, said the old man, you must know that we are three brothers, the two black dogs and myself. Our father, when he died, left each of us one thousand sequins. With that sum, we all became merchants. My brothers resolved to travel, and trade in foreign countries.

At the end of a year they returned in abject poverty, having, in unfortunate enterprises, lost all. I welcomed them home, and having prospered, gave each of them a thousand sequins to start them again as merchants. After a while they came to me to propose that I should join them in a trading voyage. I immediately declined. But after having resisted their solicitation five whole years, they importuned me so much, that at last they overcame my resolution. When, however, the time arrived that we were to buy the goods necessary to the undertaking, I found they had spent all, and had nothing left of the thousand sequins I had given to each of them. I did not, on this account, upbraid them. On the contrary, my stock being now six thousand sequins, I gave each of them a thousand, and keeping as much for myself, I buried the other three thousand in a corner of my house. We purchased goods, and having embarked them on board a vessel, which we freighted betwixt us, we put to sea with a favourable wind. After two months' sail, we arrived happily at port, where we landed, and had a very good market for our goods. I, especially, sold mine so well, that I gained ten to one.

When we were ready to embark on our return, I met on

the seashore a lady, very handsome, but poorly clad. She walked up to me gracefully, kissed my hand, and besought me with the greatest earnestness imaginable to marry her. I

'. . . I buried the other three thousand.'

made some difficulty before agreeing to this proposal; but she urged so many things to persuade me that I ought not to object to her on account of her poverty, and that I should have all the reason in the world to be satisfied with her conduct, that at

28

last I yielded. I ordered proper apparel to be made for her; and after having married her, according to form, I took her on board, and we set sail. I found my wife possessed so many good qualities, that my love to her every day increased. In the meantime my two brothers, who had not managed their affairs as successfully as I had mine, envied my prosperity; and suffered their feelings to carry them so far, that they conspired against my life; and one night, when my wife and I were asleep, threw us both into the sea.

I had scarcely fallen into the water, when she took me up, and carried me to an island. When day appeared, she said to me, You see, husband, that by saving your life, I have not rewarded you ill for your kindness to me. You must know, that I am a fairy, and being upon the seashore, when you were going to embark, I had a mind to try your goodness, and presented myself before you in disguise. You have dealt generously by me, and I am glad of an opportunity of returning my acknowledgment. But I am incensed against your brothers, and nothing will satisfy me but their lives.

I listened to this discourse with admiration. I thanked the fairy, the best way I could, for the great kindness she had done me: but, Madam, said I, as for my brothers, I beg you to pardon them; whatever cause of resentment they have given me, I am not cruel enough to desire their death. I then informed her what I had done for them, but this increased her indignation; and she exclaimed, I must immediately pursue those ungrateful traitors, and take speedy vengeance on them. I will destroy their vessel, and sink them into the bottom of the sea. My good lady, replied I, for Heaven's sake forbear; moderate your anger, consider that they are my brothers, and that we ought to return good for evil.

I pacified her by these words; and as soon as I had concluded, she transported me in a moment from the island to the roof of my own house. I descended, opened the doors, and dug up the three thousand sequins I had formerly secreted. I went afterwards to my shop, which I also opened; and was complimented by the merchants, my neighbours, upon my return. When I went back to my house, I perceived there two black dogs, which came up to me in a very submissive manner. I could not divine the meaning of this circumstance, which greatly astonished me. But the fairy, who immediately appeared, said, Husband, be not surprised to see these dogs, they are your brothers. I was troubled at this declaration, and asked her by what power they were so transformed. I did it, said she, and at the same time sunk their ship. You have lost the goods you had on board, but I will compensate you another way. As to your two brothers, I have condemned them to remain five years in that shape. Their perfidiousness too well deserves such a penance. Having thus spoken and told me where I might hear of her, she disappeared.

The five years being now nearly expired, I am travelling in quest of her. This is my history, O prince of genies! do not you think it very extraordinary? I own it is, replied the genie, and on that account I remit the merchant the other half of the crime which he has committed against me. With these words the genie rose, and disappeared in a cloud of smoke, to the great delight of the merchant and the two old men.

The merchant failed not to make due acknowledgment to his deliverers. They rejoiced to see him out of danger ; and bidding him adieu, each of them proceeded on his way. The merchant returned to his wife and children, and passed the rest of his days with them in peace.

The Story of the Fisherman

THERE was an aged fisherman, who was so poor, that he could scarcely earn as much as would maintain himself, his wife, and three children. He went every day to fish betimes in the morning; and imposed it as a law upon himself, not to cast his nets above four times a day. He went one morning by moonlight, and, coming to the seaside, undressed himself. Three several times did he cast his net, and have a heavy haul. Yet, to his indescribable disappointment and despair, the first proved to be an ass, the second a basket full of stones, and the third a mass of mud and shells.

As day now began to appear he said his prayers, for he was a good Mussulman, and commended himself and his needs to his Creator. Having done this, he cast his nets the fourth time, and drew them as formerly, with great difficulty; but, instead of fish, found nothing in them but a vessel of yellow copper, having the impression of a seal upon it. This turn of fortune rejoiced him : I will sell it, said he, to the founder, and with the money buy a measure of corn. He examined the vessel on all sides, and shook it, to try if its contents made any noise, but heard nothing. This circumstance, with the impression of the seal upon the leaden cover, made him think it enclosed something precious. To try this, he took a knife and opened it. He turned the mouth downward, but nothing came out; which surprised him extremely. He placed it before him, but while

31

he viewed it attentively, there came out a very thick smoke, which obliged him to retire two or three paces back.

The smoke ascended to the clouds, and, extending itself

'. . . he took a knife and opened it.'

along the sea and upon the shore, formed a great mist, which we may well imagine filled the fisherman with astonishment. When the smoke was all out of the vessel, it reunited, and became a solid body, of which was formed a genie twice as high as the greatest of giants. At the sight of such a monster, the fisherman would fain have fled, but was so frightened that he could not move.

The genie regarded the fisherman with a fierce look, and exclaimed in a terrible voice, Prepare to die, for I will surely kill thee. Ah! replied the fisherman, why would you kill me? Did I not just now set you at liberty, and have you already forgotten my kindness? Yes, I remember it, said the genie, but that shall not save thy life: I have only one favour to grant thee. And what is that? asked the fisherman. It is, answered the genie, to give thee thy choice, in what manner thou wouldst have me put thee to death. But wherein have I offended you? demanded the fisherman. Is that your reward for the service I have rendered you? I cannot treat thee otherwise, said the genie: and that thou mayest know the reason, hearken to my story.

I am one of those rebellious spirits that opposed the will of Heaven.

Solomon, the son of David, commanded me to acknowledge his power, and to submit to his commands: I refused, and told him, I would rather expose myself to his resentment, than swear fealty as he required. To punish me, he shut me up in this copper vessel; and that I might not break my prison, he himself stamped upon this leaden cover, his seal with the great name of God engraven upon it. He then gave the vessel to a genie, with orders to throw me into the sea.

During the first hundred years of my imprisonment, I swore that if any one should deliver me before the expiration of that period, I would make him rich. During the second, I made an oath, that I would open all the treasures of the earth to any one that might set me at liberty. In the third, I promised to make my deliverer a potent monarch, to be always near him in spirit, and to grant him every day three requests, of whatsoever nature they might be. At last, being angry, or rather mad, to find myself a prisoner so long, I swore, that if any one should deliver me, I would kill him without mercy, and grant

33

him no other favour but to choose the manner of his death; and therefore, since thou hast delivered me to-day, I give thee that choice.

The fisherman was extremely grieved, not so much for himself, as on account of his three children; and bewailed the misery they must be reduced to by his death. He endeavoured to appease the genie, and said, Alas! be pleased to take pity on me, in consideration of the service I have done you. I have told thee already, replied the genie, it is for that very reason I must kill thee. Do not lose time, interrupted the genie; all thy reasonings shall not divert me from my purpose: make haste, and tell me what kind of death thou preferest?

Necessity is the mother of invention. The fisherman bethought himself of a stratagem. Since I must die then, said he to the genie, I submit to the will of Heaven; but before I choose the manner of my death, I conjure you by the great name which was engraven upon the seal of the prophet Solomon, the son of David, to answer me truly the question I am going to ask you.

The genie, finding himself obliged to a positive answer by this adjuration, trembled; and replied to the fisherman, Ask what thou wilt, but make haste.

I wish to know, asked the fisherman, if you were actually in this vessel. Dare you swear it by the name of the great God? Yes, replied the genie, I do swear, by that great name, that I was. In good faith, answered the fisherman, I cannot believe you; the vessel is not capable of holding one of your feet, and how should it be possible that your whole body could lie in it? Is it possible, replied the genie, that thou dost not believe me after the solemn oath I have taken? Truly not I, said the fisherman; nor will I believe you, unless you go into the vessel again.

Upon which the body of the genie dissolved and changed itself into smoke, extending as before upon the seashore; and at last, being collected, it began to re-enter the vessel, which it continued to do till no part remained out; when immediately the fisherman took the cover of lead, and having speedily replaced it on the vessel, Genie, cried he, now it is your turn to beg my favour ; but I shall throw you into the sea, whence I took you : and then I will build a house upon the shore, where I will reside and give notice to all fishermen who come to throw in their nets, to beware of such a wicked genie as thou art, who hast made an oath to kill him that shalt set thee at liberty.

The genie omitted nothing that he thought likely to prevail with the fisherman : Open the vessel, said he, give me my liberty, and I promise to satisfy thee to thy own content. Thou art a traitor, replied the fisherman ; I should deserve to lose my life, if I were such a fool as to trust thee : thou wilt not fail to treat me in the same manner as a certain Grecian king treated the physician Douban. It is a story I have a mind to tell thee, therefore listen to it.

The Story of the Grecian King & the Physician Douban

THERE was once a king who suffered from leprosy, and his physicians had in vain endeavoured his cure; when a very able physician, named Douban, arrived at his court.

He was an experienced natural philosopher, and fully understood the good and bad qualities of plants and drugs. As soon as he was informed of the king's distemper, and understood that his physicians had given him over, he found means to present himself before him. I know, said he, after the usual ceremonials, that your majesty's physicians have not been able to heal you of the leprosy: but if you will accept my service, I will engage to cure you without potions, or external applications.

The king answered, If you be able to perform what you promise, I will enrich you and your posterity. You may make the trial.

The physician returned to his quarters, made a hollow mace, and in the handle he put drugs; he made also a ball in such a manner as suited his purpose, with which next morning he presented himself before the king, and said to him, Let your majesty take horse, and exercise yourself with this mace, and strike the ball until you find your hands and body perspire. When the medicine I have put up in the handle of the mace is heated with your hand, it will penetrate your whole body; and as soon as you perspire, you may leave off the exercise, for then the medicine will have had its effect. Immediately on your return to your palace, go into the bath, and cause yourself to be well washed and rubbed; then retire to bed, and when you rise to-morrow you will find yourself cured.

The king took the mace, and struck the ball, which was

'. . . made a hollow mace, and in the handle he put drugs.'

returned by his officers who played with him; he played so long that his hands and his whole body were in a sweat, and then the medicine shut up in the handle of the mace operated as the physician had said. Upon this the king left off play, returned to his palace, entered the bath, and observed very exactly what his physician had prescribed to him.

The next morning when he arose, he perceived with equal wonder and joy, that his leprosy was cured, and his body as clean as if it had never been affected. As soon as he was dressed, he came into the hall of audience, where he ascended his throne, and showed himself to his courtiers: who, eager to know the success of the new medicine, came thither betimes, and, when they saw the king perfectly cured, expressed great joy. The physician Douban, entering the hall, bowed himself before the throne, with his face to the ground. The king, perceiving him, made him sit down by his side, presented him to the assembly, and gave him all the commendation he deserved. His majesty did not stop here, but daily showered upon him marks of his esteem.

Now this king had a vizier, who was avaricious, envious, and naturally capable of every kind of mischief. He could not behold without envy the presents that were given to the physician, and he therefore resolved to lessen him in the king's esteem. Sire, said he to the king, are you wise in allowing about your person a man who, for aught you know, may have been sent here by your enemies to attempt your life?

No, no, vizier, interrupted the king; I am certain that this physician, whom you suspect to be a villain and a traitor, is one of the best and most virtuous of men. You know he cured me of my leprosy. If he had had a design upon my life, why did he save me then? He needed only to have left me to my disease. I perceive it to be his virtue that raises your envy; but do not think I will be unjustly prejudiced against him. I will tell you what a vizier said to King Sinbad, his master, to prevent his putting to death the prince, his son. This vizier having represented that the king ought to hesitate to do a thing which was founded on the suggestion of another, related the following story.

The Story of the Husband & the Parrot

A CERTAIN good man had a beautiful wife, whom he loved so dearly, that he could scarcely allow her to be out of his sight. One day, some urgent affairs obliging him to go from home, he went to a place where all sorts of birds were sold, and bought a parrot, which not only spoke well, but could also give an account of everything that was done in its presence. He brought it in a cage to his house, desired his wife to put it in her chamber, and take care of it during his absence, and then departed.

On his return, he questioned the parrot concerning what had passed while he was from home, and the bird told him such things as gave him occasion to upbraid his wife. She concluded some of her slaves had betrayed her, but all of them swore they had been faithful, and agreed that the parrot must have been the tell-tale.

Upon this, the wife began to devise how she might remove her husband's jealousy, and at the same time revenge herself on the parrot. Her husband being gone another journey, she commanded a slave in the night-time to turn a hand-mill under the parrot's cage; she ordered another to sprinkle water, in resemblance of rain, over the cage; and a third to move a looking-glass, backward and forward against a candle, before the parrot. The slaves spent great part of the night in doing what their mistress desired them, and acquitted themselves with much skill.

Next night the husband returned, and examined the parrot again about what had passed during his absence. The bird answered, Good master, the lightning, thunder, and rain so much disturbed me all night, that I cannot tell how much I suffered. The husband, who knew that there had been neither thunder, lightning, nor rain in the night, fancied that the parrot, not having spoken truth in this, might also have lied in the other relation; upon which he took it out of the cage and

'. . . *threw it with so much force to the ground that he killed it.*'

threw it with so much force to the ground that he killed it. Yet afterwards he understood from his neighbours, that the poor parrot had not deceived him in what it had stated of his wife's base conduct, which made him repent he had killed it.

And you, vizier, said the king, because of the hatred you bear to the physician, Douban, who never did you any injury, you would have me cut him off ; but I will beware lest I should repent, as the husband did after killing his parrot.

Sir, replied the vizier, the death of the parrot was but a trifle, and I believe his master did not mourn for him long : but why should your fear of wronging an innocent man, hinder your putting this physician to death ? It is not envy which makes me his enemy. If the accusation be false, I deserve to be punished in the same manner as a certain vizier of whom I will tell you, if you will be pleased to hear me.

THERE was a king who had a son that loved hunting. He allowed him to pursue that diversion often, but gave orders to his grand vizier always to attend him. One hunting-day, the huntsman having roused a deer, the prince, who thought the vizier followed him, pursued the game so far, and with so much earnestness, that he separated himself from the company. Perceiving he had lost his way, he stopped, and endeavoured to return to the vizier; but not knowing the country, he wandered farther.

Whilst he was thus riding about, he met on his way a handsome lady, who wept bitterly because she had fallen from her horse, which had run away. The young prince, taking compassion on her, requested her to get up behind him, which she willingly did.

As they were passing by the ruins of a house, the lady expressed a desire to alight. The prince stopped, and having put her down, dismounted himself, and went near the building, leading his horse after him. But you may judge how much he was surprised, when he heard the pretended lady utter these words: 'Be glad, my children, I bring you a young man for your repast'; and other voices, which answered immediately, 'Where is he, for we are very hungry?'

The prince heard enough to convince him of his danger. He rode off with all possible haste, and having happily found his way, arrived safe at the court of his father, to whom he gave a particular account of the danger he had been in through the vizier's neglect: upon which the king, being incensed against that minister, ordered him to be immediately strangled.

Sir, continued the king's vizier, to return to the physician Douban. He has cured you, you say: but, alas! who can assure you of that? Who knows but the medicine he has given you may in time have pernicious effects?

The king was not able to discover the wicked design of his vizier, nor had he firmness enough to persist in his first opinion. This discourse staggered him. Vizier, said he, thou art in the right; he may be come on purpose to take away my life, which he may easily do by his drugs.

When he had spoken thus, he called for one of his officers, and ordered him to go for the physician; who, knowing nothing of the king's purpose, came to the palace in haste.

Knowest thou, said the king, when he saw him, why I sent for thee? No, sir, answered he; I wait till your majesty be pleased to inform me. I sent for thee, replied the king, to rid myself of thee by taking away thy life.

No man can express the surprise of the physician, when he heard these words. Sir, said he, why would your majesty take my life? What crime have I committed? I am informed, replied the king, that you came to my court only to attempt my life; but to prevent you, I will be sure of yours. Give the blow, said he to the executioner, who was present, and deliver me from a perfidious wretch, who came hither on purpose to assassinate me.

When the physician heard this cruel order, he readily judged that the honours and presents he had received from the king had procured him enemies, and that the weak prince was imposed on. He repented that he had cured him of his leprosy; but it was now too late. Is it thus, asked the physician, that you reward me for curing you? Alas, sir, cried he, prolong my days, and God will prolong yours; do not put me to death, lest God treat you in the same manner.

44

STORY OF THE VIZIER THAT WAS PUNISHED

The king cruelly replied, No, no; I must of necessity cut you off, otherwise you may assassinate with as much art as you cured me. The physician, without bewailing himself for being so ill rewarded by the king, prepared for death. The executioner tied his hands, and was going to draw his scimitar, when the physician addressed himself once more to the king: Sir, said he, since your majesty will not revoke the sentence of death, I beg, at least, that you would give me leave to return to my house, to give orders about my burial, to bid farewell to my family, to give alms, and to bequeath my books to those who are capable of making good use of them. I have one particularly I would present to your majesty; it is a very precious book, and worthy of being laid up carefully in your treasury. What is it, demanded the king, that makes it so valuable? Sir, replied the physician, it possesses many singular and curious properties; of which the chief is, that if your majesty will give yourself the trouble to open it at the sixth leaf, and read the third line of the left page, my head, after being cut off, will answer all the questions you ask it. The king, being curious, deferred his death till next day, and sent him home under a strong guard.

The physician, during that time, put his affairs in order; and a report being spread, that an unheard-of prodigy was to happen after his death, the viziers, emirs, officers of the guard, and, in a word, the whole court, repaired next day to the hall of audience, that they might be witnesses of it.

The physician, Douban, was brought in, and advancing to the foot of the throne, with a book in his hand, he called for a basin, and laid upon it the cover in which the book was wrapped; then presenting the book to the king: Take this, said he, and after my head is cut off, order that it be put into the basin upon that cover; as soon as it is placed there, the blood will stop flowing; then open the book, and my head will answer your questions. But permit me once more to implore your majesty's clemency; I protest to you that I am innocent. Your prayers, answered the king, are in vain; and were it for

45

nothing but to hear your head speak after your death, it is my will you should die. As he said this, he took the book out of the physician's hand, and ordered the executioner to do his duty.

The head was so dexterously cut off that it fell into the basin, and was no sooner laid upon the cover of the book than the blood stopped; then, to the great surprise of the king, and all the spectators, it opened its eyes, and said, Sir, will your majesty be pleased to open the book? The king proceeded to do so; but finding that the leaves adhered to each other, that he might turn them with more ease, he put his finger to his mouth and wetted it. He did this till he came to the sixth leaf, and finding no writing on the place where he was desired to look for it, Physician, said he, there is nothing written. Turn over some more leaves, replied the head. The king went on, putting always his finger to his mouth, until he found himself suddenly taken with an extraordinary fit, his eyesight failed, and he fell down at the foot of the throne in violent convulsions.

When the physician Douban, or rather his head, saw that the poison had taken effect, and that the king had but a few moments to live; Tyrant, it cried, now you see how princes are treated, who, abusing their authority, cut off innocent men: God punishes soon or late their injustice and cruelty. Scarcely had the head spoken these words, when the king fell down dead, and the head itself lost what life it had.

As soon as the fisherman had concluded the history of the Greek king and his physician Douban, he applied it to the genie, whom he still kept shut up in the vessel. If the king, said he, had suffered the physician to live, God would have continued his life also. The case is the same with thee, O genie; but I am obliged, in my turn, to be equally hard-hearted to thee.

Hear me one word more, cried the genie; I promise to do thee no hurt; nay, far from that, I will show thee a way to become exceedingly rich.

The hope of delivering himself from poverty, prevailed with the fisherman. I could listen to thee, said he, were there any

STORY OF THE VIZIER THAT WAS PUNISHED

'. . . he found himself suddenly taken with an extraordinary fit.'

credit to be given to thy word. Swear to me by the great name of God, that you will faithfully perform what you promise, and I will open the vessel; I do not believe you will dare to break such an oath.

The genie swore to him, upon which the fisherman immediately took off the covering of the vessel, and at once the smoke ascended, and the genie having resumed his form, kicked the vessel into the sea.

Be not afraid, fisherman, said the genie; I only did it to see if thou wouldst be alarmed : but to convince thee that I am in earnest, take thy nets and follow me. They passed by the town, and came to the top of a mountain, from whence they descended into a vast plain, which brought them to a lake that lay betwixt four hills.

When they reached the side of the lake, the genie said to the fisherman, Cast in thy nets, and catch fish : the fisherman did not doubt of taking some, because he saw a great number in the water; but he was extremely surprised, when he found they were of four colours, that is to say, white, red, blue, and yellow. He threw in his nets, and brought out one of each colour. Having never seen the like before, he could not but admire them, and judging that he might get a considerable sum for them, he was very joyful. Carry those fish, said the genie to him, and present them to thy sultan; he will give thee more money for them. Thou mayest come every day to fish in this lake; but I give thee warning not to throw in thy nets above once a day, otherwise thou wilt repent. Having spoken thus, he struck his foot upon the ground, which opened, and after it had swallowed him up closed again.

THE STORY OF THE FISHERMAN

THE STORY OF THE VIZIER THAT WAS PUNISHED

The further adventures of the fisherman

THE fisherman being resolved to follow the genie's advice, forbore casting in his nets a second time, and returned to the town very well satisfied. He went immediately to the sultan's palace, to offer his fish.

The sultan was much surprised when he saw the four fish which the fisherman presented. He took them up one after another, and viewed them with attention; and after having admired them a long time, Take those fish, said he to his vizier, and carry them to the cook; I cannot imagine but that they must be as good as they are beautiful; and give the fisherman four hundred pieces of gold.

The fisherman, who had never seen so much money, could scarcely believe his good fortune, but thought the whole must be a dream, until he found it otherwise, by being able to provide necessaries for his family.

As soon as the cook had cleaned the fish, she put them upon the fire in a frying-pan, with oil, and when she thought them fried enough on one side, she turned them upon the other; but, O monstrous prodigy! scarcely were they turned, when the wall of the kitchen divided, and a young lady of wonderful beauty entered from the opening. She was clad in flowered satin, with pendants in her ears, a necklace of large pearls, and bracelets of gold set with rubies, with a rod in her hand. She moved towards the frying-pan, to the great amazement of the cook, who continued fixed by the sight, and striking one of the fish with the end of the rod, said 'Fish, fish, are you in

49

'. . . *a young lady of wonderful beauty entered.*'

duty ? ' The fish having answered nothing, she repeated these words, and then the four fish lifted up their heads, and replied, ' Yes, yes : if you reckon, we reckon ; if you pay your debts, we pay ours ; if you fly, we overcome, and are content.' As soon as they had finished these words, the lady overturned the frying-pan, and returned into the open part of the wall, which closed immediately, and became as it was before.

The cook was greatly frightened at what had happened, and coming a little to herself, went to take up the fish that had fallen on the hearth, but found them blacker than coal, and not fit to be carried to the sultan. Alas ! said she, what will become of me ? If I tell the sultan what I have seen, I am sure he will not believe me, but will be enraged against me.

While she was thus bewailing herself, the grand vizier entered, and asked her if the fish were ready. She told him all that had occurred, which we may easily imagine astonished him ; but without speaking a word of it to the sultan, he invented an excuse that satisfied him, and sending immediately for the fisherman, bid him bring four more such fish, which the fisherman promised to do on the morrow.

Accordingly the fisherman threw in his nets betimes next morning, took four fish like the former, and brought them to the vizier at the hour appointed. The minister took them himself, carried them to the kitchen, and shut himself up with the cook. She cleaned them, and put them on the fire, as she had done the four others the day before, and when they were fried on one side, and she had turned them upon the other, the vizier became a witness of the same events as the cook had narrated to him.

This is too wonderful and extraordinary, said he, to be concealed from the sultan ; I will inform him of this prodigy.

The sultan, being much surprised, sent immediately for the fisherman, and said to him, Friend, cannot you bring me four more such fish ? The fisherman replied, If your majesty will be pleased to allow me until to-morrow, I will do it. He caught four fish, and brought them to the sultan, who was so much rejoiced that he ordered the fisherman four hundred pieces of gold. The sultan had the fish carried into his closet, with all that was necessary for frying them; and having shut himself up with the vizier, the minister put them into the pan, and when they were fried on one side, turned them upon the other; then the wall of the closet opened, but instead of the young lady, there came out a black, in the habit of a slave, and of a gigantic stature, with a great green staff in his hand. He advanced towards the pan, and touching one of the fish with his staff, said with a terrible voice, ' Fish, are you in your duty ? ' At these words, the fish raised up their heads, and answered, ' Yes, yes, we are : if you reckon, we reckon ; if you pay your debts, we pay ours ; if you fly, we overcome, and are content.'

The fish had no sooner finished these words, than the black threw the pan into the middle of the closet, and reduced the fish to a coal. Having done this, he retired fiercely, and entering again into the aperture, it closed, and the wall appeared just as it did before.

After what I have seen, said the sultan to the vizier, it will not be possible for me to be easy : these fish, without doubt, signify something extraordinary. He sent for the fisherman, and on hearing where the fish had been caught, he commanded all his court to take horse, and the fisherman served them for a guide. They all ascended the mountain, and at the foot of it they saw, to their great surprise, a vast plain, that nobody had observed till then, and at last they came to the lake, which they found to be situated betwixt four hills as the fisherman had described. The water was so transparent, that they observed all the fish to be like those which the fisherman had brought to the palace.

The sultan stood upon the bank of the lake, beholding the fish with admiration. On his demanding of his courtiers if it were possible they had never seen this lake, which was within so short a distance of the town, they all answered, that they had never so much as heard of it.

Since you all agree that you never heard of it, and as I am

no less astonished than you are at this novelty, I am resolved
not to return to my palace till I learn how this lake came here,

'. . . the fish raised up their heads, and answered . . .'

and why all the fish in it are of four colours. Having spoken
thus, he ordered his court to encamp; and immediately his

pavilion and the tents of his household were planted upon the banks of the lake.

Resolved to withdraw alone from the camp to discover the secret of the portents that so disturbed his mind, the sultan bade his grand vizier inform the court that illness accounted for his absence until such time as he should return.

The grand vizier endeavoured to divert the sultan from his design; but all to no purpose; the sultan was resolved. He put on a suit fit for walking, and took his scimitar; and as soon as he found that all was quiet in the camp, went out alone. As the sun arose, he saw before him, at a considerable distance, a vast building of black polished marble, covered with fine steel, as smooth as glass. Being highly pleased that he had so speedily met with something worthy of his curiosity, he advanced towards the gate, which was partially open. Though he might immediately have entered, yet he thought it best to knock. This he did again and again, but no one appearing, he was exceedingly surprised.

At last he entered, and when he came within the porch, he cried, Is there no one here to receive a stranger, who comes in for some refreshment as he passes by? But though he spoke very loud, he was not answered. The silence increased his astonishment: he came into a spacious court, and looked on every side for inhabitants, but discovered none.

He then entered several grand halls, which were hung with silk tapestry, the alcoves and sofas being covered with stuffs of Mecca, and the porches with the richest stuffs of India, mixed with gold and silver. He came next into a superb saloon, in the middle of which was a fountain, with a lion of massy gold at each angle.

The castle, on three sides, was encompassed by a garden, with parterres of flowers and shrubberies; and to complete the beauty of the place, an infinite number of birds filled the air with their harmonious notes. The sultan walked from apartment to apartment, where he found everything rich and magnificent. Being tired with walking, he sat down in a verandah, which had a view over the garden, when suddenly he heard the voice of one complaining, in lamentable tones. He listened with attention, and heard these words : ' O fortune ! thou who wouldst not suffer me long to enjoy a happy lot, forbear to persecute me, and by a speedy death put an end to my sorrows.'

The sultan rose up, advanced toward the place whence came

' The sultan drew near, and saluted him.'

the voice, and opening the door of a great hall, pushed aside a curtain. A handsome young man, richly habited, was seated upon a throne. Melancholy was depicted on his countenance. The sultan drew near, and saluted him ; the young man returned his salutation, by an inclination of his head, at the same time, saying, My lord, I should rise to receive you ; but I am hindered by sad necessity, and therefore hope you will not be offended.

55

My lord, replied the sultan, I am much obliged to you for having so good an opinion of me : as to the reason of your not rising, whatever your apology be, I heartily accept it. Being drawn hither by your complaints, I come to offer you my help ; would to God that it lay in my power to ease you or your trouble ! Relate to me the history of your misfortunes ; but inform me first of the meaning of the lake near the palace, where the fish are of four colours ? whose this castle is ? how you came to be here ? and why you are alone ?

Instead of answering these questions, the young man began to weep bitterly. 'How inconstant is fortune ! ' cried he ; ' she takes pleasure to pull down those she has raised. How is it possible that I should grieve, and my eyes be inexhaustible fountains of tears ? ' At these words, lifting up his robe, he showed the sultan that he was a man only from the head to the girdle, and that the other half of his body was black marble.

You may easily imagine that the sultan was much surprised when he saw the deplorable condition of the young man. That which you show me, said he, while it fills me with horror, excites my curiosity, so that I am impatient to hear your history, and I am persuaded that the lake and the fish make some part of it ; therefore I conjure you to relate it. I will not refuse your request, replied the young man, though I cannot comply without renewing my grief. Thereupon he narrated :—

YOU must know, my lord, continued he, that my father, named Mahmoud, was king of this country. This is the kingdom of the Black Isles, which takes its name from the four small neighbouring mountains; for those mountains were formerly isles: the capital was on the spot now occupied by the lake you have seen.

The king, my father, died when he was seventy years of age; I had no sooner succeeded him than I married my cousin. At first nothing could surpass the harmony and pleasure of our union. This lasted five years, at the end of which time I perceived she ceased to delight in my attentions.

One day, after dinner, while she was at the bath, I lay down upon a sofa. Two of her ladies came and sat down, one at my head, and the other at my feet, with fans in their hands to moderate the heat, and to prevent the flies from disturbing me. They thought I was asleep, and spoke in whispers; but as I only closed my eyes, I heard all their conversation.

One of them said to the other, Is not the queen wrong, not to love so amiable a prince? Certainly, replied the other; I do not understand the reason, neither can I perceive why she goes out every night, and leaves him alone. Is it possible that he does not perceive it? Alas, said the first, how should he? she mixes every evening in his liquor the juice of a certain herb, which makes him sleep so sound all night, that she has

57

'*They thought I was asleep, and spoke in whispers.*'

time to go where she pleases, and as day begins to appear she comes and lies down by him again, and wakes him by the smell of something she puts under his nostrils.

You may guess, my lord, how much I was surprised at this conversation. I had, however, self-control enough to dissemble and feign to awake without having heard a word.

The queen returned from the bath; we supped together, and she presented me with a cup full of such water as I was accustomed to drink; but instead of putting it to my mouth, I went to a window that was open, and threw out the water so quickly, that she did not perceive it, and returned.

Soon after, believing that I was asleep, she said, loud enough for me to hear her distinctly, Sleep on, and may you never wake again! So saying, she dressed herself, and went out of the chamber.

No sooner was she gone than I dressed myself in haste, took my scimitar, and followed her so quickly that I soon heard the sound of her feet before me, and then walked softly after her, for fear of being heard. She passed through several gates, which opened upon her pronouncing some magical words, and the last she opened was that of the garden, which she entered. I stopped at this gate, that she might not perceive me, as she passed along a parterre; then looking after her as far as the darkness of the night permitted, I saw her enter a little wood. I went thither by another way, and concealing myself, saw her walking there with a man.

I did not fail to lend the most attentive ear to their discourse, and heard her address herself thus to her gallant: What proof of my devotion is lacking, that you doubt my constancy? Bid me but do so, and before sunrise I will convert this great city, and this superb palace into frightful ruins, inhabited only by wolves, owls, and ravens. Or would you have me transport all the stones of these walls, so solidly built, beyond Mount Caucasus, or the bounds of the habitable world? Speak but the word, and all shall be changed.

As the queen finished these words, she and her lover turned

and passed before me. I had already drawn my scimitar, and her lover being next me, I struck him to the ground. I concluded I had killed him, and therefore retired speedily without making myself known to the queen.

The wound I had given her lover was mortal; but by her enchantments she preserved him in an existence in which he

'. . . I struck him to the ground.'

could not be said to be either dead or alive. As I crossed the garden to return to the palace, I heard the queen loudly lamenting, and judging by her cries how much she was grieved, I was pleased that I had spared her life.

As soon as I had reached my apartment, I went to bed, and being satisfied with having punished the villain who had injured me, fell asleep; and when I awoke next morning, found the queen lying by me.

I cannot tell you whether she slept or not; but I arose, went to my closet, and dressed myself. I afterwards held my council. At my return the queen, clad in mourning, her hair dishevelled, and part of it torn off, presented herself before me, and said: I come to beg your majesty not to be surprised to see me in this condition. My heavy affliction is occasioned by intelligence of three distressing events—the death of the queen my dear mother, that of the king my father, killed in battle, and of one of my brothers, who has fallen down a precipice.

I was not displeased that she used this pretext to conceal the true cause of her grief, and I concluded she had not suspected me of being the author of her lover's death. Madam, said I, so far from blaming, I assure you I heartily commiserate your sorrow. I merely therefore expressed the hope that time and reflection would moderate her grief.

After a whole year's mourning, she begged permission to erect a burying-place for herself, within the bounds of the palace, where she would continue, she told me, to the end of her days: I consented, and she built a stately edifice, and called it the Palace of Tears. When it was finished, she caused her lover to be conveyed thither: she had hitherto prevented his dying, by potions which she had administered to him; and she continued to convey them to him herself every day after he came to the Palace of Tears.

Yet, with all her enchantments, she could not cure him; he was not only unable to walk or support himself, but had also lost the use of his speech, and exhibited no sign of life except in his looks. Every day the queen made him two long visits, a fact of which I was well apprised, but pretended ignorance.

One day, my curiosity inducing me to go to the Palace of Tears, I heard her thus address her lover: I am afflicted to the highest degree to behold you in this condition; I am as sensible as yourself of the tormenting pain you endure; but, dear soul, I am continually speaking to you, and you do not answer me : how long will you remain silent ? O tomb ! hast thou destroyed that excess of affection which he bare me ? Hast thou closed those eyes that evinced so much love, and were all my delight ? No, no, this I cannot think. Tell me rather, by what miracle thou becamest the depositary of the rarest treasure the world ever contained.

I must confess, my lord, I was enraged at these expressions, and apostrophising the tomb in my turn, I cried, O tomb ! why dost not thou swallow up that monster so revolting to human nature, or rather why dost not thou swallow up both the lover and his mistress ?

I had scarcely uttered these words, when the queen rose up like a fury. Miscreant ! said she, thou art the cause of my grief ; do not think I am ignorant of this, I have dissembled too long. At the same time she pronounced words I did not understand ; and afterwards added, ' By virtue of my enchantments, I command thee to become half marble and half man.' Immediately, my lord, I became what you see, a dead man among the living, and a living man among the dead.

After this cruel sorceress, unworthy of the name of queen, had metamorphosed me thus, and brought me into this hall, by another enchantment she destroyed my capital, which was very flourishing and populous ; she annihilated the houses, the public places and markets, and reduced the site of the whole to the lake and desert plain you have seen ; the fishes of four colours in the lake are the four kinds of inhabitants of different religions, which the city contained. The white are the Mussulmans ; the red, the Persians, who worship fire ; the blue, the Christians ; and the yellow, the Jews. The four little hills were the four islands that gave name to this kingdom. But her revenge not being satisfied with the destruction of my dominions, and the metamorphosis of my person, she comes every day, and gives me over my naked shoulders a hundred lashes with a whip until I am covered with blood. When she has finished this part of my punishment, she throws over me a coarse stuff

62

of goat's hair, and over that this robe of brocade, not to honour, but to mock me.

When he came to this part of his narrative, the sultan, filled with righteous anger, and anxious to revenge the sufferings of the unfortunate prince, said to him, Inform me whither this perfidious sorceress retires, and where may be found her vile paramour, who is entombed before his death. My lord, replied the prince, her lover, as I have already told you, is lodged in the Palace of Tears, in a superb tomb constructed in the form of a dome: this palace joins the castle on the side in which the gate is placed. Every day at sunrise the queen goes to visit her paramour, after having executed her bloody vengeance upon me; and you see I am not in a condition to defend myself.

Prince, said the sultan, your condition can never be sufficiently deplored: and it surpasses all that has hitherto been recorded. One thing only is wanting: the revenge to which you are entitled, and I will omit nothing in my power to effect it.

In subsequent conversation they agreed upon the measures they were to take for accomplishing their design for revenge, but deferred the execution of it till the following day.

The young prince, as was his wont, passed the time in continual watchfulness, never having slept since he was enchanted.

The sultan arose with the dawn, and proceeded to the Palace of Tears. He found it lighted up with an infinite number of flambeaux of white wax, and perfumed by a delicious scent issuing from several censers of fine gold of admirable workmanship. As soon as he perceived the bed where the black lay, he drew his scimitar, and without resistance, deprived him of his wretched life, dragged his corpse into the court of the castle, and threw it into a well. After this he went and lay down in the black's bed, placed his scimitar under the covering, and waited to complete his design.

The queen arrived shortly after. She first went into the chamber of her husband, the king of the Black Islands, stripped him, and with unexampled barbarity gave him a hundred stripes.

She then put on again his covering of goat's hair, and his

63

brocade gown over all; she went afterwards to the Palace of Tears, and thus addressed herself to the person whom she conceived to be the black: My sun, my life, will you always be silent? Are you resolved to let me die, without affording me the comfort of hearing again from your own lips that you love me? My soul, speak one word to me at least, I conjure you.

The sultan, as if he had awaked out of a deep sleep, and counterfeiting the pronunciation of the blacks, answered the queen with a grave tone, 'There is no strength or power but in God alone, who is almighty.' At these words the enchantress uttered a loud exclamation of joy. My dear lord, cried she, do not I deceive myself; is it certain that I hear you, and that you speak to me? Unhappy woman, said the sultan, art thou worthy that I should answer thee? Alas! replied the queen, why do you reproach me thus? The cries, returned the sultan, the groans and tears of thy husband, whom thou treatest every day with so much indignity and barbarity, prevent my sleeping night or day. Make haste to set him at liberty, that I be no longer disturbed by his lamentations.

The enchantress went immediately out of the Palace of Tears to fulfil these commands, and by the exercise of her spells soon restored to the young king his natural shape, bidding him, however, on pain of death, to begone from her presence instantly. The young king, yielding to necessity, retired to a remote place, where he patiently awaited the event of the design which the sultan had so happily begun. Meanwhile, the enchantress returned to the Palace of Tears, and supposing that she still spoke to the black, assured him his behest had been obeyed.

The sultan, still counterfeiting the pronunciation of the blacks, said, What you have now done is by no means sufficient for my cure; bethink thee of the town, the islands, and the inhabitants destroyed by thy fatal enchantments. The fish every night at midnight raise their heads out of the lake and cry for vengeance against thee and me. This is the true cause of the delay of my cure. Go speedily, restore things to their former

state, and at thy return I will give thee my hand, and thou
shalt help me to arise.

The enchantress, inspired with hope, lost no time, but betook
herself in all haste to the brink of the lake, where she took a
little water in her hand, and sprinkling it, pronounced some
word over the fish, whereupon the city was immediately restored.
The fish became men, women, and children ; Mahommedans,
Christians, Persians, or Jews ; freemen or slaves, as they were
before : every one having recovered his natural form. The
houses and shops were immediately filled with their inhabitants,
who found all things as they were before the enchantment.
The sultan's numerous retinue, who found themselves encamped
in the largest square, were astonished to see themselves in an
instant in the middle of a large, handsome, well-peopled
city.

To return to the enchantress. As soon as she had effected
this wonderful change, she returned with all expedition to the
Palace of Tears, that she might receive her reward. 'Come
near,' said the sultan, still counterfeiting the pronunciation
of the blacks. She did so. 'You are not near enough,' he
continued ; 'approach nearer.' She obeyed. He then rose
up, and seizing her by the arm so suddenly, that she had not
time to discover him, he with a blow of his scimitar cut her
in two, so that one half fell one way and the other another.
This done, he left the body on the spot, and going out of the
Palace of Tears, went to seek the young king of the Black Isles.
'Prince,' said he, embracing him, 'rejoice ; you have now
nothing to fear ; your cruel enemy is dead.'

The young prince returned thanks to the sultan, and wished
him long life and happiness. You may henceforward, said the
sultan, dwell peaceably in your capital, unless you will accompany me to mine, which is not above four or five hours' journey
distant. Potent monarch, replied the prince, I do indeed believe
that you came hither from your capital in the time you mention,
because mine was enchanted ; but since the enchantment is
taken off, things are changed : it will take you no less than a

year to return : however, this shall not prevent my following you, were it to the utmost corners of the earth.

The sultan was extremely surprised to understand that he was so far from his dominions, and could not imagine how it could be. But, said he, it is no matter ; the trouble of returning to my own country is sufficiently recompensed by the satisfaction of having obliged you, and by acquiring you for a son ; for since you will do me the honour to accompany me, as I have no child, I look upon you as such, and from this moment appoint you my heir and successor.

At length, the sultan and the young prince began their journey, with a hundred camels laden with inestimable riches from the treasury of the young king, followed by fifty handsome gentlemen on horseback, perfectly well mounted and dressed. The inhabitants came out in great crowds, received him with acclamations, and made public rejoicings for several days.

The day after his arrival the sultan gave all his courtiers a complete account of the circumstances, which, contrary to his expectation, had detained him so long. He informed them that he had adopted the king of the Four Black Islands, who was willing to leave a great kingdom, to accompany and live with him ; and, in reward for their loyalty, he made each of them presents according to their rank.

As for the fisherman, as he was the first cause of the deliverance of the young prince, the sultan gave him a plentiful fortune, which made him and his family happy the rest of his days.

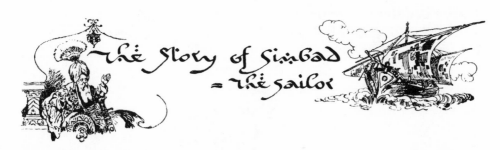

The Story of Sinbad the Sailor

IN the reign of the Caliph Haroun al Raschid there dwelt, in Bagdad, a poor porter named Hindbad, who often had to carry heavy burdens, which he could scarcely support. One very hot day he was labouring along a strange street, and overcome by fatigue he sat down near a great house to rest. The porter complimented himself upon his good fortune in finding such a pleasant place, for while he sat there reached his ears sweet sounds of music, and his senses were also soothed by sweet smells. Wondering who lived in so fine a house, he inquired of one of the servants. What, said the man, do you not know that Sinbad the Sailor, the famous circumnavigator of the world, lives here? Alas, replied Hindbad, what a difference there is between Sinbad's lot and mine. Yet what greater merits does he possess that he should prosper and I starve? Now Sinbad happened to overhear this remark, and anxious to see a man who expressed such strange views he sent for Hindbad. Accordingly Hindbad was led into the great hall, where there was a sumptuous repast spread, and a goodly company assembled. The poor porter felt very uncomfortable, until Sinbad bade him draw near, and seating him at his right hand, served him himself, and gave him excellent wine, of which there was abundance upon the sideboard.

When the repast was over, Sinbad asked him why he complained of his condition. My lord, replied Hindbad, I confess that my fatigue put me out of humour, and occasioned me to utter some indiscreet words, which I beg you to pardon. Do

not think I am so unjust, resumed Sinbad, as to resent such a
complaint. But that you may know that my wealth has not been
acquired without labour, I recite the history of travels for your
benefit; and I think that, when you have heard it, you will

'. . . sat down near a great house to rest.'

acknowledge how wonderful have been my adventures. Sinbad
then related the story of his first voyage as follows :—

When still a very young man I inherited a large fortune from
my father, and at once set about amusing myself. I lived

luxuriously, and soon found that money was decreasing, while nothing was added to replace the expenditure. Quickly seeing the folly of my ways, I invested the remainder of my fortune with some merchants of Bussorah, and joined them in their voyage, which was towards the Indies by way of the Persian Gulf.

In our voyage we touched at several islands, where we sold or exchanged our goods. One day, whilst under sail, we were becalmed near a small island, but little elevated above the

'. . . . but for myself I was still upon the back of the creature.'

level of the water, and resembling a green meadow. The captain ordered his sails to be furled, and permitted such persons as were so inclined to land; of this number I was one.

But while we were enjoying ourselves in eating and drinking, and recovering ourselves from the fatigue of the sea, the island on a sudden trembled, and shook us terribly.

The trembling of the island was perceived on board the ship, and we were called upon to re-embark speedily, or we should all be lost; for what we took for an island proved to be the back of a sea monster. The nimblest got into the sloop, others betook themselves to swimming ; but for myself I was still upon the back of the creature, when he dived into the sea, and I had time only to catch hold of a piece of wood that we had brought out of the ship to make a fire. Meanwhile, the captain, having received those on board who were in the sloop, and taken up some of those that swam, resolved to improve the favourable gale that had just risen, and hoisting his sails pursued his voyage, so that it was impossible for me to recover the ship.

Thus was I exposed to the mercy of the waves. I struggled for my life all the rest of the day and the following night. By this time I found my strength gone, and despaired of saving my life, when happily a wave threw me against an island. I struggled up the steep bank by aid of some roots, and lay down upon the ground half dead, until the sun appeared. Then, though I was very feeble, both from hard labour and want of food, I crept along to find some herbs fit to eat, and had the good luck not only to procure some, but likewise to discover a spring of excellent water, which contributed much to recover me. As I advanced farther into the island, I was not a little surprised and startled to hear a voice and see a man, who asked me who I was. I related to him my adventure, after which, taking me by the hand, he led me into a cave, where there were several other people, no less amazed to see me than I was to see them.

I partook of some provisions which they offered me. I then asked them what they did in such a desert place, to which they answered, that they were grooms belonging to Maha-rájah, sovereign of the island, and that they were about to lead the king's horses back to the palace. They added, that they were to return home on the morrow, and, had I been one day later, I must have perished, because the inhabited part of the island was at a great distance, and it would have been impossible for me to have got thither without a guide.

When the grooms set out I accompanied them, and was duly presented to the Maha-rájah, who was much interested in my adventure, and bade me stay with him as long as I desired.

Being a merchant, I met with men of my own profession, and particularly inquired for those who were strangers, that perchance I might hear news from Bagdad, or find an oppor-

'I . . . was presented to the Maha-râjah.'

tunity to return. For the Maha-râjah's capital is situated on the seacoast, and has a fine harbour, where ships arrive daily from the different quarters of the world. I frequented also the society of the learned Indians, and took delight to hear them converse; but withal, I took care to make my court regularly to the Maha-râjah, and conversed with the governors and petty kings, his tributaries, that were about him. They put a thousand questions respecting my country; and I, being willing to inform myself as to their laws and customs, asked them concerning everything which I thought worth knowing.

There belongs to this king an island named Cassel. They assured me that every night a noise of drums was heard there, whence the mariners fancied that it was the residence of Degial. I determined to visit this wonderful place, and in my way thither saw fishes of a hundred and two hundred cubits long, that occasion more fear than hurt; for they are so timorous, that they will fly upon the rattling of two sticks or boards. I saw likewise other fish that had heads like owls.

As I was one day at the port after my return, the ship in which I had set sail arrived, and the crew began to unload the goods. I saw my own bales with my name upon them, and going up to the captain said, I am that Sinbad whom you thought to be dead, and those bales are mine.

When the captain heard me speak thus, Heavens, he exclaimed, whom can we trust in these times? There is no faith left among men. I saw Sinbad perish with my own eyes, as did also the passengers on board, and yet you tell me you are that Sinbad. What impudence is this? To look on you, one would take you to be a man of probity, and yet you tell a horrible falsehood in order to possess yourself of what does not belong to you. After much discussion, the captain was convinced of the truth of my words, and, having seen me identified by members of the crew, he handed me over my goods, congratulating me upon my escape.

I took out what was most valuable in my bales, and presented them to the Maha-râjah, who, knowing my misfortune, asked me how I came by such rarities. I acquainted him with the circumstance of their recovery. He was pleased at my good luck, accepted my present, and in return gave me one much more considerable. Upon this, I took leave of him, and went aboard the same ship, after I had exchanged my goods for the commodities of that country. We passed by several islands, and at last arrived at Bussorah, from whence I came to this city with the value of one hundred thousand sequins.

Sinbad stopped here, and ordered the musicians to proceed with their concert, which the story had interrupted. The company continued enjoying themselves till the evening, and it was time to retire, when Sinbad sent for a purse of one hundred sequins, and giving it to the porter, said, Take this, Hindbad, return to your home, and come back to-morrow to hear more of my adventures. The porter went away, astonished at the honour done, and the present made him, and arrayed in his best apparel returned to Sinbad's house next day. After he had graciously received and feasted his guest, Sinbad continued his narrative.

Sinbads second Voyage

I DESIGNED, after my first voyage, to spend the rest of my days at Bagdad; but it was not long ere I grew weary of an indolent life, and, therefore, I set out a second time upon a voyage. We embarked on board a good ship, and, after recommending ourselves to God, set sail. We traded from island to island, and exchanged commodities with great profit. One day we landed at an island covered with several sorts of fruit-trees, but we could see neither man nor animal. We went to take a little fresh air in the meadows, along the streams that watered them. Whilst some diverted themselves with gathering flowers, and other fruits, I took my wine and provisions and sat down near a stream betwixt two high trees, which formed a thick shade. I made a good meal, and afterwards fell asleep. I cannot tell how long I slept, but when I awoke the ship was gone.

I was much alarmed, said Sinbad, at finding the ship gone. I got up and looked around me, but could not see one of the merchants who landed with me. I perceived the ship under sail, but at such a distance, that I lost sight of her in a short time. I upbraided myself a hundred times for not being content with the produce of my first voyage, that might have sufficed me all my life. But all this was in vain, and my repentance too late. Not knowing what to do, I climbed up to the top of a lofty tree, whence I looked about on all sides to see if I could discover anything that could give me hopes. When

74

I gazed over the land I beheld something white; and coming down, I took what provision I had left, and went towards it, the distance being so great, that I could not distinguish what it was.

As I approached, I thought it to be a white dome of a prodigious height and extent; and when I came up to it, I touched it, and found it to be very smooth. I went round to see if it was open on any side, but saw it was not, and that there was no climbing up to the top as it was so smooth. It was at least fifty paces round.

By this time the sun was about to set, and all of a sudden the sky became as dark as if it had been covered with a thick cloud. I was much astonished at this sudden darkness, but much more when I found it occasioned by a bird of monstrous size, that came flying toward me. I remembered that I had

'*I climbed up to the top of a lofty tree.*'

often heard mariners speak of a miraculous bird called a roc, and conceived that the great dome which I so much admired must be its egg. In a short time, the bird alighted, and sat over the egg. As I perceived her coming, I crept close to the egg, so

75

that I had before me one of the legs of the bird, which was as big as the trunk of a tree. I tied myself strongly to it with my turban, in hopes that the roc next morning would carry me with her out of this desert island. After having passed the night in this condition, the bird flew away as soon as it was

'. . . tied myself strongly to it with my turban.'

daylight, and carried me so high, that I could not discern the earth; she afterwards descended with so much rapidity that I lost my senses. But when I found myself on the ground, I speedily untied the knot, and had scarcely done so, when the roc, having taken up a serpent of a great length in her bill, flew away.

76

SINBAD'S SECOND VOYAGE

The spot where it left me was encompassed on all sides by mountains, that seemed to reach above the clouds, and so steep that there was no possibility of getting out of the valley. This was a new perplexity; so that when I compared this place with the desert island from which the roc had brought me, I found that I had gained nothing by the change.

As I walked through this valley, I perceived it was strewn with diamonds, some of which were of a surprising size. I took pleasure in looking upon them; but shortly saw at a distance some objects as greatly diminished my satisfaction, and which I could not view without terror, namely, a great number of serpents, so monstrous, that the least of them was capable of swallowing an elephant. They retired in the day-time to their dens, where they hid themselves from the roc, their enemy, and came out only in the night.

I spent the day in walking about in the valley, resting myself at times in such places as I thought most convenient. When night came on, I went into a cave, where I thought I might repose in safety. I secured the entrance, which was low and narrow, with a great stone to preserve me from the serpents; but not so far as to exclude the light. I supped on part of my provisions, but the serpents, which began hissing round me, put me into such extreme fear, that you may easily imagine I did not sleep. When day appeared the serpents retired, and I came out of the cave trembling. I can justly say that I walked upon diamonds without feeling any inclination to touch them. At last I sat down, and notwithstanding my apprehensions, not having closed my eyes during the night, fell asleep, after having eaten a little more of my provision. But I had scarcely shut my eyes, when something that fell by me with a great noise awaked me. This was a large piece of raw meat; and at the same time I saw several others fall down from the rocks in different places.

I had always regarded as fabulous what I had heard sailors and others relate of the valley of diamonds, and of the stratagems employed by merchants to obtain jewels from thence; but now

I found that they had stated nothing but the truth. For as a fact, the merchants come to the neighbourhood of this valley, when the eagles have young ones, and throwing great joints of meat into the valley, the diamonds, upon whose points they fall, stick to them; the eagles, which are stronger in this country than anywhere else, pounce with great force upon those pieces of meat, and carry them to their nests on the precipices of the rocks to feed their young; the merchants at this time run to their nests, disturb and drive off the eagles by their shouts, and take away the diamonds that stick to the meat.

The happy idea struck me that here was a means of escape from my living tomb; so I collected a number of the largest diamonds, with which I filled my wallet, which I tied to my girdle. Then I fastened one of the joints of meat to the middle of my back by means of my turban cloth, and lay down with my face to the ground.

I had scarcely placed myself in this posture when the eagles came. Each of them seized a piece of meat, and one of the strongest having taken me up, with the piece of meat to which I was fastened, carried me to his nest on the top of the mountain. The merchants began their shouting to frighten the eagles; and when they had obliged them to quit their prey, one of them came to the nest where I was. He was much alarmed when he saw me; but recovering himself, instead of inquiring how I came thither, began to quarrel with me, and asked why I stole his goods. You will treat me, replied I, with more civility, when you know me better. Do not be uneasy; I have diamonds enough for you and myself, more than all the other merchants together. Whatever they have they owe to chance, but I selected for myself in the bottom of the valley those which you see in this bag. I had scarcely done speaking, when the other merchants came crowding about us, much astonished to see me; but they were much more surprised when I told them my story. Yet they did not so much admire my stratagem to effect my deliverance, as my courage in putting it into execution.

They conducted me to their encampment, and there, having

opened my bag, they were surprised at the largeness of my diamonds, and confessed that in all the courts which they had visited they had never seen any of such size and perfection. I prayed the merchant, who owned the nest to which I had been carried (for every merchant had his own), to take as many for his share as he pleased. He contented himself with one, and that too the least of them ; and when I pressed him to take more, without fear of doing me any injury, No, said he, I am very well satisfied with this which is valuable enough to save me the trouble of making any more voyages, and will raise as great a fortune as I desire.

I spent the night with the merchants, to whom I related my story a second time, for the satisfaction of those who had not heard it. I could not moderate my joy when I found myself delivered from the danger I have mentioned. I thought myself in a dream, and could scarcely believe myself out of danger. When at length I reached home I gave large presents to the poor, and lived luxuriously upon my hard-earned wealth.

Then Sinbad ended the account of his second voyage, and, having given Hindbad another hundred sequins, asked him to come on the next day to hear his further adventures.

Sinbad's Third Voyage

I SOON wearied of the idle, luxurious life I led, and therefore I undertook another voyage. Overtaken by a dreadful tempest in the main ocean, we were driven upon an island which, the captain told us, was inhabited by hairy savages, who would speedily attack us; and, though they were but dwarfs, yet our misfortune was such, that we must make no resistance, for they were more in number than the locusts; and if we happened to kill one of them, they would all fall upon us and destroy us.

It was not long before the captain's words were proved, for an innumerable multitude of frightful savages, about two feet high, covered all over with red hair, came swimming towards us, and encompassed our ship. We advanced into the island on which we were, and came to a palace, elegantly built, and very lofty, with a gate of ebony of two leaves, which we forced open. We entered the court, where we saw before us a large apartment, with a porch, having on one side a heap of human bones, and on the other a vast number of roasting spits. Our fears were not diminished when the gate of the apartment opened with a loud crash, and there came out the horrible figure of a black man, as tall as a lofty palm-tree. He had but one eye, and that in the middle of his forehead, where it looked as red as a burning coal. His foreteeth were very long and sharp, and stood out of his mouth, which was as deep as that of a horse. His upper lip hung down upon his breast. His ears resembled those of an elephant, and covered his shoulders; and his nails

80

THE STORY OF SINBAD THE SAILOR

THE STORY OF PRINCE AHMED AND THE FAIRY PERIE BANOU

. . . turned me round as a butcher would do a sheep's head.'

were as long and crooked as the talons of the greatest birds. At the sight of so frightful a giant, we became insensible, and lay like dead men. When he had considered us well, he advanced towards us, and laying his hand upon me, took me up by the nape of my neck, and turned me round as a butcher would do a sheep's head. After having examined me, and perceiving me to be so lean that I had nothing but skin and bone, he let me go. He took up all the rest one by one, and viewed them in the same manner. The captain being the fattest, he held him with one hand, as I would do a sparrow, and thrust a spit through him; he then kindled a great fire, roasted, and ate him in his apartment for his supper. Having finished his repast, he returned to his porch, where he lay and fell asleep, snoring louder than thunder.

We all sat numbed by fear, but the next day, after the giant had gone out, we devised a means of vengeance. And so, when he had again made a supper off one of our number, and lay down to sleep, we prepared to execute the daring design. Therefore nine of us and myself, when we heard him snore, each armed with a spit, the points of which we had made red hot, approached the monster and thrust the spits into his eye at the same time, so that he was blind. The giant made wild efforts to seize us, but finding that we had hidden he went out roaring in his agony.

We lost no time in fleeing from the palace, and soon reached the shore, where we contrived to construct some rafts upon which to sail away in case of need. But, knowing the danger that such a voyage would entail, we waited in the hope that the giant might be dead, since he had ceased to howl. Day had scarcely dawned, however, when we saw our enemy coming towards us, led by two others, nearly as big as himself, and accompanied by a host of others.

We immediately took to our rafts; whereupon the giants, enraged at being thus baulked, took up great stones, and, running to the shore, entered the water up to the middle, and threw so exactly that they sunk all the rafts but that I was upon; and all my companions, except the two with me, were drowned.

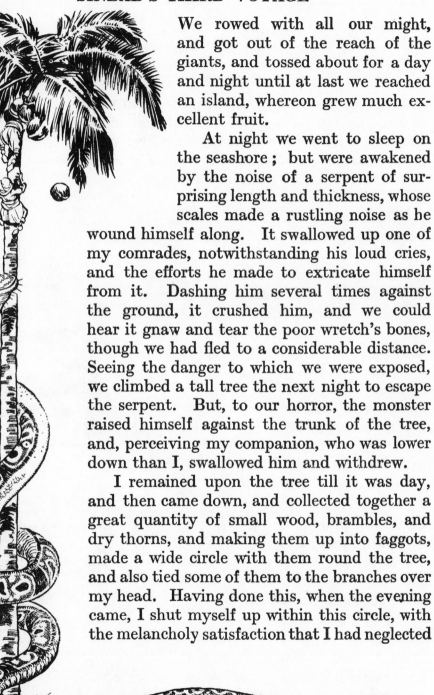

We rowed with all our might, and got out of the reach of the giants, and tossed about for a day and night until at last we reached an island, whereon grew much excellent fruit.

At night we went to sleep on the seashore; but were awakened by the noise of a serpent of surprising length and thickness, whose scales made a rustling noise as he wound himself along. It swallowed up one of my comrades, notwithstanding his loud cries, and the efforts he made to extricate himself from it. Dashing him several times against the ground, it crushed him, and we could hear it gnaw and tear the poor wretch's bones, though we had fled to a considerable distance. Seeing the danger to which we were exposed, we climbed a tall tree the next night to escape the serpent. But, to our horror, the monster raised himself against the trunk of the tree, and, perceiving my companion, who was lower down than I, swallowed him and withdrew.

I remained upon the tree till it was day, and then came down, and collected together a great quantity of small wood, brambles, and dry thorns, and making them up into faggots, made a wide circle with them round the tree, and also tied some of them to the branches over my head. Having done this, when the evening came, I shut myself up within this circle, with the melancholy satisfaction that I had neglected

'. . . we climbed a tall tree the next night to escape the serpent.'

nothing which could preserve me from the cruel destiny with which I was threatened. The serpent failed not to come at the usual hour, and went round the tree, seeking for an opportunity to devour me, but was prevented by the rampart I had made; so that he lay till day, like a cat watching in vain for a mouse that has fortunately reached a place of safety. When day appeared he retired, but I dared not to leave my fort until the sun arose.

As I ran towards the sea, determined no longer to prolong my miserable existence, I perceived a ship at a considerable distance. I called as loud as I could, and taking the linen from my turban, displayed it, that they might observe me. This had the desired effect; the crew perceived me, and the captain sent his boat for me. As soon as I came on board, the merchants and seamen flocked about me, to know how I came into that desert island; and after I had related to them all that had befallen me, the oldest among them said to me, They had several times heard of the giants that dwelt in that island, that they were cannibals, and

'I called as loud as I could.'

ate men raw as well as roasted; and as to the serpents, they

added, that there were abundance in the island, that hid
themselves by day, and came abroad by night. After having
testified their joy at my escaping so many dangers, they
brought me the best of their provisions; and the captain, as
being the man who had deserted me upon my second voyage,
seeing that I was in rags, was so generous as to give me one of
his own suits. I soon made myself known to him, whereupon
he exclaimed, God be praised. I rejoice that fortune has recti-
fied my fault. There are your goods, which I always took care
to preserve. I took them from him, thanked him warmly for
his honesty, and contrived to deal so well on the voyage that I
arrived at Bussorah with another vast fortune. From Bussorah
I returned to Bagdad, where I gave a great deal to the poor,
and bought another considerable estate in addition to what I
had already.

Having thus finished the account of his third voyage, Sinbad
sent Hindbad on his way, after he had given him another hundred
sequins, and invited him to dinner the next day to hear the
continuation of his adventures.

Sinbads Fourth Voyage

IT was not long before I again started on a journey. This time I travelled through Persia and arrived at a port, where I took ship. We had not been long at sea when a great storm overtook us, which was so violent that the sails were split into a thousand pieces, and the ship was stranded; several of the merchants and seamen were drowned, and the cargo was lost.

I had the good fortune, with several of the merchants and mariners, to get upon some planks, and we were carried by the current to an island which lay before us. There we found fruit and spring water, which preserved our lives; and we lay down almost where we had landed and slept.

Next morning, as soon as the sun was up, we walked from the shore, and advancing into the island saw some houses, which we approached. As soon as we drew near, we were encompassed by a great number of negroes, who seized us, shared us among them, and carried us to their respective habitations.

I and five of my comrades were carried to one place; here they made us sit down, and gave us a certain herb, which they made signs to us to eat. My comrades not taking notice that the blacks ate none of it themselves, thought only of satisfying their hunger, and ate with greediness. But I, suspecting some trick, would not so much as taste it, which happened well for me; for in a little time after, I perceived my companions had lost their senses, and that when they spoke to me, they knew not what they said.

86

The negroes fed us afterwards with rice, prepared with oil of cocoa-nuts; and my comrades, who had lost their reason, ate of it greedily. I also partook of it, but very sparingly. They gave

'*I and five of my comrades . . .*'

us that herb at first on purpose to deprive us of our senses, that we might not be aware of the sad destiny prepared for us; and they supplied us with rice to fatten us; for, being cannibals, their design was to eat us as soon as we grew fat. This accordingly happened, for they devoured my comrades, who were not

'*. . . called to me as loud as he could to return.*'

sensible of their condition; but my senses being entire, you may easily guess that instead of growing fat, as the rest did, I grew leaner every day. The fear of death under which I laboured

87

turned all my food into poison. I fell into a languishing distemper, which proved my safety; for the negroes, having killed and eaten my companions, seeing me to be withered, lean, and sick, deferred my death.

Meanwhile I had much liberty, so that scarcely any notice was taken of what I did, and this gave me an opportunity one day to get at a distance from the houses and to make my escape. An old man, who saw me, and suspected my design, called to me as loud as he could to return; but instead of obeying him, I redoubled my speed, and quickly got out of sight. I travelled as fast as I could, and chose those places which seemed most deserted, living for seven days on the fruit I gathered.

On the eighth day I came near the sea, and saw some white people like myself, gathering pepper, of which there was great plenty in that place. As soon as they saw me they came to meet me, and asked me in Arabic, who I was, and whence I came. I was overjoyed to hear them speak in my own language, and satisfied their curiosity by giving them an account of my shipwreck, and how I fell into the hands of the negroes. Those negroes, replied they, eat men, and by what miracle did you escape their cruelty? I related to them the circumstances I have just mentioned, at which they were wonderfully surprised.

I stayed with them till they had gathered their quantity of pepper, and then sailed with them to the island from whence they had come. They presented me to their king, who was a good prince. He listened to my story, bade me welcome, and soon had conceived a great friendship for me, which fact made me a person of importance in the capital.

None of these people ride with either saddle or bridle, and so, wishing to honour the king, I went to a workman, and gave him a model for making the stock of a saddle. When that was done, I covered it myself with velvet and leather, and embroidered it with gold. I afterwards went to a smith, who made me a bit, according to the pattern I showed him, and also some stirrups. When I had all the trappings completed, I presented them to the king, and put them upon one of his horses. His majesty mounted immediately, and was so pleased with them, that he testified his satisfaction by large presents, and said: I wish you to marry and think no more of your own land, but stay here as long as you live. I durst not resist the prince's will, and he gave me one of the ladies of his court, noble, beautiful, and

'None of these people ride with either saddle or bridle.'

rich. The ceremonies of marriage being over, I went and dwelt with my wife, and for some time we lived together in perfect harmony. I was not, however, satisfied with my banishment, therefore designed to make my escape upon the first opportunity, and to return to Bagdad, which my present settlement, howsoever advantageous, could not make me forget.

At this time the wife of one of my neighbours, with whom

I had contracted a very strict friendship, fell sick, and died. I went to see and comfort him in his affliction, and finding him absorbed in sorrow, I said to him as soon as I saw him, God preserve you and grant you a long life. Alas! replied he, your good wishes are vain, for I must be buried this day with my wife. This is a law which our ancestors established in this

'... he gave me one of the ladies of his court.'

island, and it is always observed inviolably. The living husband is interred with the dead wife, and the living wife with the dead husband. Nothing can save me; every one must submit to this law.

While he was giving me an account of this barbarous custom, the very relation of which chilled my blood, his kindred, friends, and neighbours, came in a body to assist at the funeral. They dressed the body of the woman in her richest apparel, and all

90

her jewels, as if it had been her wedding-day; then they placed her on an open coffin, and began their march to the place of burial. The husband walked at the head of the company, and followed the corpse. They proceeded to a high mountain, and when they had reached the place of their destination, they took up a large stone, which covered the mouth of a deep pit, and let down the corpse with all its apparel and jewels. Then the husband, embracing his kindred and friends, suffered himself

I pursued it.'

to be put into another open coffin without resistance, with a pot of water, and seven small loaves, and was let down in the same manner. The mountain was of considerable length, and extended along the seashore, and the pit was very deep. The ceremony being over, the aperture was again covered with the stone, and the company returned.

Not long after this I was destined to share a like fate, for my wife, of whose health I took particular care, fell sick, and died. In spite of every effort on my part, the law of the land had to be fulfilled; and so, accompanied by the king and the chief nobles, who had come to honour me at the grave, I was lowered into the tomb with my wife's body and the usual supply of bread and water. I had come to the end of my provisions, and was expecting death, when I heard a puffing noise as of something breathing. I moved towards the place whence the sound came, and heard a skurrying of feet as the creature ran away. I pursued it, and at last perceived what seemed to be a star in the distance. The speck of light grew larger as I approached, and I soon found that it was a hole in the side of the mountain, above the seashore. I cast myself upon the sand overcome with joy, and as I raised my eyes to heaven, I perceived a ship at no great distance. I waved my turban linen, which attracted the attention of those on board; whereupon they sent a boat which carried me safely on board. I told the captain that I was a shipwrecked merchant, and he believed my story, and without asking any questions took me with him.

After a long voyage, during which we called at several ports, whereat I made much money, I arrived happily at Bagdad with infinite riches, of which it is needless to trouble you with the detail. Out of gratitude to God for His mercies, I contributed liberally towards the support of several mosques, and the subsistence of the poor, gave myself up to the society of my kindred and friends, enjoying myself with them in festivities and amusements.

Sinbad then presented another hundred sequins to the porter, and bade him honour him with his presence again next day.

Sinbads fifth Voyage

THE pleasures I enjoyed had again charms enough to make me forget all the troubles and calamities I had undergone, but could not cure me of my inclination to make new voyages. I therefore bought goods, departed with them for the best seaport; and there, that I might not be obliged to depend upon a captain, but have a ship at my own command, I remained till one was built on purpose, at my own charge. When the ship was ready, I went on board with my goods; but not having enough to load her, I agreed to take with me several merchants of different nations with their merchandise.

We sailed with the first fair wind, and after a long navigation, the first place we touched at was a desert island, where we found an egg of a roc, equal in size to that I formerly mentioned. There was a young roc in it just ready to be hatched, and its bill had begun to appear.

The merchants who landed with me broke the egg with hatchets, and pulled out the young roc piecemeal, and roasted it. I had earnestly entreated them not to meddle with the egg, but they would not listen to me.

Scarcely had they finished their repast, when there appeared in the air at a considerable distance from us two great clouds. The captain whom I had hired to navigate my ship, knowing by experience what they meant, said they were the male and female roc that belonged to the young one, and pressed us to re-embark with all speed, to prevent the misfortune which he saw would otherwise befall us. We hastened on board, and set sail with all possible expedition.

In the meantime, the two rocs approached with a frightful noise, which they redoubled when they saw the egg broken and their young one gone. They flew back in the direction they had come, and disappeared for some time, while we made all the

'*The merchants . . . broke the egg with hatchets.*'

sail we could to endeavour to prevent that which unhappily befell us.

They soon returned, and we observed that each of them carried between its talons stones of a monstrous size. When they came directly over my ship, they hovered, and one of them let fall a stone, but by the dexterity of the steersman it missed us, and falling into the sea, divided the water so that we could almost see the bottom. The other roc, to our misfortune, threw his massive burden so exactly upon the middle of the ship as to split it into a thousand pieces. The mariners and passengers were all crushed to death, or sunk. I myself was of the number of the latter; but as I came up again, I fortunately caught hold of a piece of the wreck, and swimming sometimes with one hand, and sometimes with the other, but always holding fast my board, the wind and the tide favouring me, I came to an island, whose shore was very steep. I overcame that difficulty, however, and got ashore.

I sat down upon the grass, to recover myself from my fatigue, after which I went into the island to explore it. It seemed to be a delicious garden. I found trees everywhere, some of them bearing green, and others ripe fruits, and streams of fresh pure water running in pleasant meanders. I ate of the fruits, which I found excellent; and drank of the water, which was very sweet and good.

When night closed in, I lay down upon the grass in a convenient spot, but could not sleep an hour at a time, my mind being apprehensive of danger. I spent the best part of the night in alarm, and reproached myself for my imprudence in not remaining at home, rather than undertaking this last voyage. These reflections carried me so far, that I began to form a design against my life; but daylight dispersed these melancholy thoughts. I got up, and walked among the trees, but not without some fears.

As I advanced into the island, I saw an old man who appeared very weak and infirm. He was sitting on the bank of a stream, and at first I took him to be one who had been shipwrecked like myself. I went towards him and saluted him, but he only slightly bowed his head. I asked him why he sat so still, but instead of answering me, he made a sign for me to take him upon my back, and carry him over the brook, signifying that it was to gather fruit.

I believed him really to stand in need of my assistance, took him upon my back, and having carried him over, bade him get down, and for that end stooped, that he might get off with ease; but instead of doing so the old man, who to me appeared quite decrepit, clasped his legs nimbly about my neck, so tightly that I swooned.

'I saw an old man who appeared very weak and infirm.'

Notwithstanding my fainting, the ill-natured old fellow kept fast about my neck, but opened his legs a little to give me time to recover my breath. When I had done so, he thrust one of his feet against my stomach, and struck me so rudely on the side

96

with the other, that he forced me to rise up against my will. Having arisen, he made me walk under the trees, and forced me now and then to stop, to gather and eat fruit such as we found. He never left me all day, and when I lay down to rest at night, laid himself down with me, holding always fast about my neck.

'. . . *crushed his head to pieces.*'

Every morning he pushed me to make me awake, and afterwards obliged me to get up and walk, and pressed me with his feet. You may judge then, gentlemen, what trouble I was in, to be loaded with such a burden of which I could not get rid.

One day I found in my way several dry calabashes that had fallen from a tree. I took a large one, and after cleaning it, pressed into it some juice of grapes, which abounded in the island; having filled the calabash, I put it by in a convenient place, and going thither again some days after, I tasted it, and found the wine so good that it soon made me forget my sorrow, gave me new vigour, and so exhilarated my spirits that I began to sing and dance as I walked along.

The old man perceiving the effect which this liquor had upon me, and that I carried him with more ease than before, made me a sign to give him some of it. I handed him the calabash, and the liquor pleasing his palate, he drank it all off, and was soon so intoxicated that his grip released. Seizing this opportunity, I threw him upon the ground, where he lay without motion; I then took up a great stone, and crushed his head to pieces.

I was extremely glad to be thus freed for ever from this troublesome fellow. I now walked towards the beach, where I met the crew of a ship that had cast anchor to take in water. They were surprised to see me, but more so at hearing the particulars of my adventures. You fell, said they, into the hands of the Old Man of the Sea, and are the first who ever escaped strangling by his malicious tricks. He never quitted those he had once made himself master of, till he had destroyed them, and he has made this island notorious by the number of men he has slain; so that the merchants and mariners who landed upon it, durst not advance into the island but in numbers at a time. After saying this, they carried me with them to the ship. The captain received me with great kindness when they told him what had befallen me. He put out again to sea, and after some days' sail, we arrived at the harbour of a great city, the houses of which were built with hewn stone.

One of the merchants who had taken me into his friendship invited me to go along with him, and gave me a large bag, and having recommended me to some people of the town, who used to gather cocoa-nuts, desired them to take me with them. Go, said he, follow them, and act as you see them do, but do not separate from them, otherwise you may endanger your life. Having thus spoken, he gave me provisions for the journey, and I went with them.

'. . . the apes threw cocoa-nuts at us so fast . . .'

We came to a thick forest of cocoa palms, very lofty, with trunks so smooth that it was not possible to climb to the branches that bore the fruit. When we entered the forest we saw a great number of apes of several sizes, who fled as soon as they perceived us, and climbed up to the top of the trees with surprising swiftness.

The merchants with whom I was gathered stones and threw them at the apes on the trees. I did the same, and the apes out of revenge threw cocoa-nuts at us so fast, and with such gestures, as sufficiently testified their anger and resentment. We gathered up the cocoa-nuts, and from time to time threw stones to provoke the apes; so that by this stratagem we filled our bags with cocoa-nuts. I soon sold mine, and returned several times to the forest, so that I made a considerable sum.

The vessel in which I had come sailed with some merchants, who loaded her with cocoa-nuts. I expected the arrival of another, which anchored soon after for the like loading. I embarked in her all the cocoa-nuts I had, and when she was ready to sail, took leave of the merchant who had been so kind to me; but he could not embark with me, because he had not finished his business at the port. We sailed towards the islands, where pepper grows in great plenty. From thence we went to the Isle of Comari, where the best species of wood of aloes grows, and whose inhabitants have made it an inviolable law to themselves to drink no wine. I exchanged my cocoa-nuts in those islands for pepper and wood of aloes, and went with other merchants pearl-fishing. I hired divers, who brought me up some that were very large and pure. I embarked in a vessel that happily arrived at Bussorah; from thence I returned to Bagdad, where I made vast sums of my pepper, wood of aloes, and pearls. I gave the tenth of my gains in alms, as I had done upon my return from my other voyages, and endeavoured to dissipate my fatigues by amusements of different kinds.

When he had thus finished his story Sinbad presented Hindbad with a hundred sequins, as before, and entreated him to present himself at the usual hour the next day.

Sinbad's sixth Voyage

THE roving spirit being in me, I could not stay long idle; and so, after a year's rest, I made ready for my sixth voyage, in spite of the entreaties of my friends and kinsfolk. This time I travelled through Persia and the Indies before taking ship, and at last embarked, at a distant port, in a vessel that was bound for a long voyage. We had sailed far when one day the captain quitted his post in great grief, and casting away his turban, cried, in a voice of agony, 'A rapid current carries the ship along with it, and we shall all perish in less than a quarter of an hour. Pray to God to deliver us from this peril; we cannot escape if He does not take pity on us.' At these words he ordered the sails to be lowered; but all the ropes broke, and the ship was carried by the current to the foot of an inaccessible mountain, where she struck and went to pieces, yet in such a manner that we saved our lives, our provisions, and the best of our goods.

This being over, the captain said to us, God has done what pleased Him. Each of us may dig his grave, and bid the world adieu; for we are all in so fatal a place that none shipwrecked here ever returned to their homes. His discourse afflicted us sensibly, and we embraced each other, bewailing our deplorable lot.

The mountain at the foot of which we were wrecked formed part of the coast of a very large island. It is also incredible what a quantity of goods and riches we found cast ashore. All these objects served only to augment our despair. In all other places, rivers run from their channels into the sea, but here a

'. . . we shall all perish.'

river of fresh water runs out of the sea into a dark cavern, whose entrance is very high and spacious. What is most remarkable in this place is, that the stones of the mountain are of crystal,

102

rubies, or other precious stones. Trees also grow here, most of which are wood of aloes, equal in goodness to those of Comari.

To finish the description of this place, which may well be called a gulf, since nothing ever returns from it, it is not possible for ships to get off when once they approach within a certain distance. If they be driven thither by a wind from the sea, the wind and the current impel them; and if they come into it when a land-wind blows, which might seem to favour their getting out again, the height of the mountain stops the wind, and occasions a calm, so that the force of the current carries them ashore: and what completes the misfortune is, that there is no possibility of ascending the mountain, or of escaping by sea.

We were, indeed, in a sorry plight; and the number of wrecks and skeletons which were upon the coast confirmed the captain's statement that our chance of escape was very small, and although the spot was fair enough to see, we mourned our lot, and awaited death with such patience as we could command.

At last our provisions began to run short, and one by one the members of the company died, until I was left alone out of the whole number. Those who died first, continued Sinbad, were interred by the survivors, and I paid the last duty to all my companions: nor are you to wonder at this; for besides that I husbanded the provisions that fell to my share better than they, I had some of my own, which I did not share with my comrades; yet when I buried the last, I had so little remaining, that I thought I could not long survive: I dug a grave, resolving to lie down in it, because there was no one left to inter me. I must confess to you at the same time, that while I was thus employed, I could not but reproach myself as the cause of my own ruin, and repented that I had ever undertaken this last voyage. Nor did I stop at reflections only, but had wellnigh hastened my own death, and began to tear my hands with my teeth.

But it pleased God once more to take compassion on me, and put it in my mind to go to the bank of the river which ran into the great cavern. Considering its probable course with great attention, I said to myself: This river, which runs thus underground, must somewhere have an issue. If I make a raft, and leave myself to the current, it will convey me to some inhabited country, or I shall perish. If I be drowned, I lose nothing, but only change one kind of death for another; and if I get out of this fatal place, I shall not only avoid the sad fate of my comrades, but perhaps find some new occasion of enriching myself. Who knows but fortune waits, upon my getting off this dangerous shelf, to compensate my shipwreck with usury.

'I made a very solid raft.'

I immediately went to work upon large pieces of timber and cables, for I had choice of them, and tied them together so strongly, that I soon made a very solid raft. When I had finished, I loaded it with some bulses of rubies, emeralds, ambergris, rock-crystal, and bales of rich stuffs, and leaving it to the course of the river, resigned myself to the will of God, comforting myself in the reflection that in any case it little mattered how death came, whether in the form of drowning or starvation.

As soon as I entered the cavern, I lost all light, and the stream carried me I knew not whither. Thus I floated some days in perfect darkness, and once found the arch so low that it very nearly touched my head, which made me cautious afterwards to avoid the like danger. All this while I ate nothing but what was just necessary to support nature; yet, notwithstanding my frugality, all my provisions were spent, and I lost consciousness. I cannot tell how long I remained insensible; but when I revived, I was surprised to find myself in an extensive plain on the brink of a river, where my raft was tied, amidst a great number of negroes. I got up as soon as I saw them, and saluted them. They spoke to me, but I did not understand their language. I was so transported with joy that I cried aloud in Arabic, expressing my gratitude to God.

One of the blacks, who understood Arabic, hearing me speak thus, came towards me, and said, Brother, pray tell us your history, for it must be extraordinary; how did you venture yourself upon this river, and whence did you come? I begged of them first to give me something to eat, and assured them I would then satisfy their curiosity. They gave me several sorts of food, and when I had satisfied my hunger I related all that had befallen me, which they listened to with attentive surprise, and, having brought a horse they conducted me to their king, that he might hear so remarkable a story.

We marched till we came to the capital of Serendib, for it was in that island I had landed. The blacks presented me to their king; I approached his throne, and saluted him as I used to do the Kings of the Indies; that is to say, I prostrated myself at his feet. The prince ordered me to rise, received me with an obliging air, and made me sit down near him. He first asked me my name, and I answered, People call me Sinbad the voyager, because of the many voyages I have undertaken, and I am a citizen of Bagdad. I then narrated all my adventures without reserve, and observing that he looked on my jewels with pleasure, and viewed the most remarkable among them one after another, I fell prostrate at his feet, and took the liberty to say to him, Sir, not only my person is at your majesty's service, but the cargo of the raft, and I would beg of you to dispose of it as

105

your own. He answered me with a smile, Sinbad, instead of taking from you, I intend to add presents worthy of your acceptance. All the answer I returned was a prayer for the prosperity of that nobly-minded prince and commendations of his generosity and bounty. He charged one of his officers to take care of me, and ordered people to serve me at his own expense. The officer was very faithful in the execution of his commission, and caused all the goods to be carried to the lodgings provided for me.

The Isle of Serendib is situated just under the equinoctial line; so that the days and nights there are always of twelve hours each, and the island is eighty parasangs in length, and as many in breadth.

The capital stands at the end of a fine valley, in the middle of the island, encompassed by mountains the highest in the world. They are seen three days' sail off at sea. Rubies and several sorts of minerals abound, and the rocks are for the most part composed of a metalline stone made use of to cut and polish other precious stones. All kinds of rare plants and trees grow there, especially cedars and cocoa-nut. There is also a pearl-fishery in the mouth of its principal river; and in some of its valleys are found diamonds.

Having spent some time in the capital, and visited all the places of interest around, among which is the place where Adam dwelt after his banishment from Paradise, I prayed the king to allow me to return to my own country, and he granted me permission in the most obliging and most honourable manner. He forced a rich present upon me; and when I went to take my leave of him, he gave me one much more considerable, and at the same time charged me with a letter for the Commander of the Faithful, our sovereign, saying to me, I pray you give this present from me, and this letter to the caliph, and assure him of my friendship.

The letter from the King of Serendib was written on the skin of a certain animal of great value, because of its being so scarce, and of a yellowish colour. The characters of this letter were of azure, and the contents as follows :—

'. . . a female of exceeding beauty.'

' The King of the Indies, before whom march one hundred elephants, who lives in a palace that shines with one hundred thousand rubies, and who has in his treasury twenty thousand crowns enriched with diamonds, to Caliph Haroun al Raschid.

' Though the present we send you be inconsiderable, receive it however as a brother and a friend, in consideration of the hearty friendship which we bear for you, and of which we are willing to give you proof. We desire the same part in your friendship, considering that we believe it to be our merit, being of the same dignity with yourself. We conjure you this in quality of a brother. Adieu.'

The present consisted firstly of one single ruby made into a cup, about half a foot high, an inch thick, and filled with round pearls of half a drachm each. Secondly, the skin of a serpent, whose scales were as large as an ordinary piece of gold, and had the virtue to preserve from sickness those who lay upon it. Thirdly, fifty thousand drachms of the best wood of aloes, with thirty grains of camphire as big as pistachios. And, fourthly, a female of exceeding beauty, whose apparel was all covered over with jewels.

The ship set sail, and after a very successful navigation we landed at Bussorah, and from thence I went to Bagdad, where I immediately went to deliver the king's letter to the caliph. And after I had presented myself, the caliph listened with attention to my description of the Indies, which showed that the king had in no way exaggerated his wealth. And I likewise described the manners and customs of the people, which also interested the Commander of the Faithful.

Having spoken thus, Sinbad notified that the account of his sixth voyage was at an end, and presented Hindbad with another hundred sequins, urging him to return next day to hear the history of his seventh and last voyage.

Sinbads Seventh & Last Voyage

AFTER my sixth voyage I had made up my mind to stay at home. I absolutely laid aside all thoughts of travelling; for, besides that my age now required rest, I was resolved no more to expose myself to such risks as I had encountered; so that I thought of nothing but to pass the rest of my days in tranquillity. But one day a messenger came from the caliph summoning me to the palace, and when I came into the presence chamber the caliph said, Sinbad, I stand in need of your service; you must carry my answer and present to the King of Serendib. It is but just I should return his civility.

I tried to escape from this new trial, and narrated all my adventures to the caliph. As soon as I had finished, I confess, said he, that the things you tell me are very extraordinary, yet you must for my sake undertake this voyage which I propose to you. You will only have to go to the Isle of Serendib, and deliver the commission which I give you. After that you are at liberty to return. But you must go; for you know it would not comport with my dignity, to be indebted to the king of that island. Perceiving that the caliph insisted upon my compliance, I submitted, and told him that I was willing to obey. He was very well pleased, and ordered me one thousand sequins for the expenses of my journey. I therefore prepared for my departure in a few days; and as soon as the caliph's letter and present were delivered to me, I went to Bussorah, where I embarked, and had a very happy voyage. Having arrived at the

Isle of Serendib, I was at once led, with great ceremony, to the palace, where the king, seeing me, exclaimed, Sinbad, you are welcome; I have many times thought of you since you departed; I bless the day on which we see one another once more. I made my compliment to him, and after having thanked him for his kindness, delivered the caliph's letter and present, which he received with all imaginable satisfaction.

The caliph's present was a complete suit of cloth of gold, valued at one thousand sequins; fifty robes of rich stuff; a hundred of white cloth, the finest of Cairo, Suez, and Alexandria; a vessel of agate broader than deep, an inch thick, and half a foot wide, the bottom of which represented in bas-relief a man with one knee on the ground, who held a bow and an arrow ready to discharge at a lion. He sent him also a rich tablet, which, according to tradition, belonged to the great Solomon.

The caliph's letter was as follows :—

' Greeting, in the name of the sovereign guide of the right way, from the dependant on God, Haroun al Raschid, whom God hath set in the place of vicegerent to His Prophet, after his ancestors of happy memory, to the potent and esteemed Rajah of Serendib.

' We received your letter with joy, and send you this from our imperial residence, the garden of superior wits. We hope, when you look upon it, you will perceive our good intention and be pleased with it. Adieu.'

The King of Serendib was highly gratified that the caliph answered his friendship. A little time after this audience, I, with great difficulty, obtained permission to return, and with a very handsome present I embarked to return to Bagdad, but had not the good fortune to arrive there so speedily as I had hoped. God ordered it otherwise.

Three or four days after my departure, we were attacked by corsairs, who easily seized upon our ship, and took those of the crew who did not fall in the fight into a far country, and sold us as slaves.

110

SINBAD'S SEVENTH AND LAST VOYAGE

I, being one of the number, fell into the hands of a rich merchant, who, as soon as he bought me, carried me to his house, treated me well, and clad me handsomely for a slave. Some days after, not knowing who I was, he asked me if I understood any trade. I answered that I was no mechanic, but a merchant, and that the corsairs, who sold me, had robbed me of all I possessed. But tell me, replied he, can you shoot with a bow ? I answered that the bow was one of my exercises in my youth. He gave me a bow and arrows, and, taking me behind him upon an elephant, carried me to a thick forest some leagues from the town. We penetrated a great way into the wood, and when he thought fit to stop, he bade me alight ; then showing me a great tree, Climb up that, said he, and shoot at the elephants as you see them pass by, for there is a prodigious number of them in this forest ; and if any of them fall, come and give me notice. Having spoken thus, he left me victuals, and returned to the town, and I continued upon the tree all night.

I saw no elephant during that time, but next morning, as soon as the sun was up, I perceived a great number. I shot several arrows among them, and at last one of the elephants fell, when the rest retired immediately, and left me at liberty to go and acquaint my patron with my booty. When I had informed him, he gave me a good meal, commended my dexterity, and caressed me highly. We went afterwards together to the forest, where we dug a hole for the elephant, my patron designing to return when it was rotten and take his teeth to trade with.

I continued this employment for two months, and killed an elephant every day, getting sometimes upon one tree and sometimes upon another. One morning, as I looked for the elephants, I perceived with extreme amazement that, instead of passing by me across the forest as usual, they stopped, and came to me with a horrible noise, in such number that the plain was covered and shook under them. They encompassed the tree in which I was concealed, with their trunks extended, and all fixed their eyes upon me. At this alarming spectacle I continued immovable,

111

and was so much terrified that my bow and arrows fell out of my hand.

My fears were not without cause; for after the elephants had stared upon me some time, one of the largest of them put his trunk round the foot of the tree, plucked it up, and threw it on the ground. I fell with the tree, and the elephant, taking me up with his trunk, laid me on his back, and, followed by all the others, carried me to a hill, where he deposited me and withdrew with the herd. Imagine my surprise when I got up and saw that the hill was covered with elephants' bones and teeth. I at once guessed that this was the burial-ground of the elephants, and admired the instinct of the animals; for I doubted not but that they carried me thither on purpose to tell me that I should forbear to persecute them, since I did it only for their teeth. I did not stay on the hill, but turned towards the city, and, after having travelled a day and a night, I came to my patron. I met no elephant in my way, which made me think they had retired farther into the forest, to leave me at liberty to come back to the hill without any obstacle.

My master was overjoyed to see me. Ah, poor Sinbad, exclaimed he, I was in great trouble to know what was become of you. I have been at the forest, where I found a tree newly pulled up, and a bow and arrows on the ground, and after having sought for you in vain, I despaired of ever seeing you more. Pray tell me what befell you, and by what good chance thou art still alive. I satisfied his curiosity, and going both of us next morning to the hill, he found to his great joy that what I had told him was true. We loaded the elephant which had carried us with as many teeth as he could bear; and when I told him what I had found he hastened to reach the hill, and we carried away as much ivory as we could. After we reached home, he said, Sinbad, not only are we made rich, but you have also saved many lives, for hitherto a large number of slaves perished in the task of obtaining ivory. Consider yourself no longer a slave, and ask whatever

112

'*The elephant . . plucked it up.*'

you will from me, for you are evidently chosen by God for some great work.

To this obliging declaration I replied, Your giving me my liberty is enough to discharge what you owe me, and I desire no other reward for the service I had the good fortune to do to you but leave to return to my own country. Very well, said he, the monsoon will in a little time bring ships for ivory. I will then send you home, and give you wherewith to bear your charges. I thanked him again for my liberty and his good intentions towards me. I stayed with him expecting the monsoon, and during that time we made so many journeys to the hill that we filled all our warehouses with ivory. The other merchants who traded in it did the same, for it could not be long concealed from them.

The ships arrived at last, and my patron, himself having made choice of the ship wherein I was to embark, loaded half of it with ivory on my account, laid in provisions in abundance for my passage, and besides obliged me to accept a present of some curiosities of the country of great value, for which I returned him a thousand thanks, and then departed, after a sad leave-taking.

We stopped at some islands to take in fresh provisions. Our vessel being come to a port on the mainland in the Indies, we touched there, and not being willing to venture by sea to Bussorah, I landed my proportion of the ivory, resolving to proceed on my journey by land. I made vast sums of my ivory, bought several rarities, which I intended for presents, and when my equipage was ready, set out in company with a large caravan of merchants. I was a long time on the way, and suffered much, but endured all with patience, when I considered that I had nothing to fear from the seas, from pirates, from serpents, or from the other perils to which I had been exposed.

All these fatigues ended at last, and I arrived safe at Bagdad. I went immediately to wait upon the caliph, and gave him an account of my embassy. That prince said he had been uneasy,

114

as I was so long in returning, but that he always hoped God would preserve me. When I told him the adventure of the elephants he seemed much surprised, and would never have given any credit to it had he not known my veracity. He deemed this story, and the other relations I had given him, to be so curious that he ordered one of his secretaries to write them in characters of gold and lay them up in his treasury. I retired well

'. . . ordered one of his secretaries to write them.'

satisfied with the honours I received and the presents which he gave me, and ever since I have devoted myself wholly to my family, kindred, and friends.

Sinbad here finished the relation of his seventh and last voyage, and then addressing himself to Hindbad, Well, friend, said he, did you ever hear of any person that suffered so much as I have done, or of any mortal that has gone through so many vicissitudes ? Is it not reasonable that, after all this, I should enjoy a quiet and pleasant life ? Hindbad drew near and kissed his hand in token of his respect, and said how insignificant were his own troubles compared with those he had heard related. Sinbad gave him another hundred sequins, and told him that every day there would be a place laid for him at his table, and that he could always rely upon the friendship of Sinbad the Sailor.

The Story of Prince Ahmed & the Fairy Perie Banou

THERE was once a sultan of India who had three sons and one niece, the ornaments of his court. The eldest of the princes was called Houssain, the second Ali, the youngest Ahmed, and the princess his niece Nouronnihar. The Princess Nouronnihar having lost her father while she was still very young, had been brought up by the sultan. And now that she was grown to womanhood, the sultan thought of marrying her to some prince worthy of the alliance. She was very beautiful, and when the sultan's idea became known the princes informed him, singly, that they loved her and would fain marry her. This discovery pained the sultan, because he knew that there would be jealousy among his sons. He therefore sent for each separately and spoke with him, urging him to abide permanently by the lady's choice, but none of them would yield without a struggle. As he found them obstinate, he sent for them all together, and said, My children, since I have not been able to dissuade you from aspiring to marry the princess your cousin; and as I have no inclination to use my authority, to give her to one in preference to his brothers, I trust I have thought of an expedient which will please you all, and preserve harmony among you, if you will but hear me, and follow my advice. I think it would not be amiss if you were to travel separately into different countries, so that you might not meet each other: and as you know I am very curious, and delight in everything that is rare and singular, I

117

promise my niece in marriage to him who shall bring me the most extraordinary rarity.

The three princes, each hoping that fortune would be favourable to him, consented to this proposal. The sultan gave them money; and early the next morning they started from the city, disguised as merchants. They departed by the same gate,

'He therefore sent for each separately.'

each attended by a trusty servant, and for one day they journeyed together. Then they halted at a khan, and having agreed to meet in one year's time at the same place, they said farewell, and early the next morning started on their several journeys.

Prince Houssain, the eldest brother, who had heard wonders of the extent, power, riches, and splendour of the kingdom of

Bisnagar, bent his course towards the Indian coast; and after three months' travelling, sometimes over deserts and barren mountains, and sometimes through populous and fertile countries, arrived at Bisnagar, the capital of the kingdom of that name, and the residence of its Maha-râjah. He lodged at a khan appointed for foreign merchants; and having learnt that there were four principal divisions where merchants of all sorts kept their shops, in the midst of which stood the Maha-râjah's palace, surrounded by three courts, and each gate distant two leagues from the other, he went to one of these quarters the next day.

It was large, divided into several streets, all vaulted and shaded from the sun, but yet very light. The shops were all of the same size and proportion; and all who dealt in the same sort of goods, as well as all the artists of the same profession, lived in one street.

Prince Houssain marvelled at the variety and richness of the articles exposed for sale. And as he wandered from street to street he wondered still more; for on all sides he saw the products of every country in the world. Silks, porcelain, and precious stones in abundance, indicated the enormous wealth of the people. Another object which Prince Houssain particularly admired was the great number of flower-sellers who crowded the streets; for the Indians are such great lovers of flowers that not one will stir without a nosegay in his hand, or a garland on his head; and the merchants keep them in pots in their shops, so that the air of the whole quarter is perfectly perfumed.

Prince Houssain had finished his inspection, when a merchant, perceiving him passing with weary steps, asked him to sit down in his shop. Before long a crier came past, carrying a piece of carpet for which he asked forty purses of gold. It was only about six feet square, and the prince was astonished at the price. Surely, said he, there must be something very extraordinary about this carpet, which I cannot see, for it looks poor enough.

You have guessed right, sir, replied the crier, and will own it when you learn, that whoever sits on this piece of carpeting

119

'. . . *carrying a piece of carpet.*'

may be transported in an instant whithersoever he desires to be, without being stopped by any obstacle.

The prince was overjoyed, for he had found a rarity which would secure the hand of the princess. If, said he, the carpet has this virtue, I will gladly buy it.

Sir, replied the crier, I have told you the truth; and it will be an easy matter to convince you. I will spread the carpeting; and when we have both sat down, and you have formed the wish to be transported into your apartment at the khan, if we are not conveyed thither, it shall be no bargain.

On this assurance of the crier, the prince accepted the conditions, and concluded the bargain: then having obtained the master's leave, they went into his back shop, where they both sat down on the carpeting; and as soon as the prince had formed his wish to be transported into his apartment at the khan, he in an instant found himself and the crier there: as he wanted not a more convincing proof of the virtue of the carpeting, he counted to the crier forty purses of gold, and gave him twenty pieces for himself.

In this manner Prince Houssain became the possessor of the carpeting, and was overjoyed at having so speedily found something worth bringing to his father. He could at will have transported himself to the khan where he had parted from his brothers; but, knowing that they would not have returned, he decided to tarry in the city and study the manners and customs of the people. He gained much satisfaction and information from visiting the different buildings and witnessing the various ceremonies which took place. He thus became the spectator of a solemn festival attended by a multitude of Hindus. This great assembly encamped in variously coloured tents on a plain of vast extent, as far as the eye could reach, formed an imposing sight. And he also presented himself at the Court of the Maha-râjah by whose wealth he was greatly impressed. All these things made his stay at Bisnagar very pleasant; but he desired to be nearer to the Princess Nouronnihar whom he most ardently loved, and he considered that he could rely upon claiming her as his **bride**. Therefore, although he might have remained in the city much longer, he paid his reckoning at the khan, spread the carpet upon the floor of his room, and he and his attendant were instantly transported to the meeting-place from which he had set out.

Prince Ali, the second brother, joined a caravan; and in four months arrived at Shiraz, which was then the capital of the empire of Persia; and having in the way contracted a friendship with some merchants, passed for a jeweller, and lodged in the same khan with them.

On the morning after his arrival Prince Ali started to inspect the valuable articles which were exposed for sale in the quarter where the jewellers lodged. He was astonished by all the wealth which he saw; and he wandered from street to street lost in admiration. But what surprised him most was a crier who walked to and fro carrying an ivory tube in his hand, for which he asked forty purses of gold. Prince Ali thought the man mad, but he was anxious to find out why the tube was so expensive. Sir, said the crier, when the prince addressed him, this tube is furnished with a glass; by looking through it, you will see whatever object you wish to behold.

The crier presented the tube for his inspection; and he, wishing to see his father, looked through it and beheld the sultan in perfect health, sitting on his throne, in his council chamber. Next he wished to see the Princess Nouronnihar, and immediately he saw her sitting laughing among her companions.

Prince Ali wanted no other proof to persuade him that this tube was the most valuable article, not only in the city of Shiraz, but in all the world; and believed, that if he should neglect to purchase it, he should never meet with an equally wonderful curiosity. He said to the crier, I will purchase this tube from you for the forty purses. He then took him to the khan where he lodged, told him out the money, and received the tube.

Prince Ali was overjoyed at his purchase; and persuaded himself, that as his brothers would not be able to meet with anything so rare and admirable, the Princess Nouronnihar must

'Prince Ali wanted no other proof . . .'

be the recompense of his fatigue and travels. While he was waiting for the caravan to start on its return journey, he visited the court of Persia and saw all the wonders in the neighbourhood of the city. When all was ready, he joined his friends, and arrived, happily without any accident or trouble, at the meeting-place, where he found Prince Houssain, and both waited for Prince Ahmed.

Prince Ahmed took the road of Samarcand, and the day after his arrival, as he went through the city, he saw a crier who had an artificial apple in his hand for which he demanded thirty-five purses of gold. Let me see that apple, said the prince, and tell me what virtue or extraordinary property it possesses, to be valued at so high a rate. Sir, replied the crier, giving it into his hand, if you look at the mere outside of this apple, it is not very remarkable ; but if you consider its properties, and the great use and benefit it is of to mankind, you will say it is invaluable, and that he who possesses it is master of a great treasure. It cures all sick persons of the most mortal diseases ; and this merely by the patient's smelling it.

If one may believe you, replied Prince Ahmed, the virtues of this apple are wonderful, and it is indeed valuable ; but what proof have you of what you say ? Sir, replied the crier, the truth is known to the whole city of Samarcand.

While the crier was detailing to Prince Ahmed the virtues of the artificial apple, many persons came about them, and confirmed what he declared ; and one amongst the rest said he had a friend dangerously ill, whose life was despaired of, which was a favourable opportunity to show the experiment. Upon which Prince Ahmed told the crier he would give him forty purses for the apple if it cured the sick person by smelling it.

The crier said to Prince Ahmed, Come, sir, let us go and make the experiment, and the apple shall be yours. The experiment succeeded ; and the prince, after he had counted out to the crier forty purses, and had received the apple from him, waited with the greatest impatience for the departure of a caravan for the Indies. In the meantime he saw all that was curious at and about Samarcand; and when a caravan set out, he joined it, and arrived safely at the appointed place, where the Princes Houssain and Ali waited for him.

When Prince Ahmed joined his brothers, they embraced

'Let me see that apple, said the Prince.'

with tenderness, and expressed much joy at meeting again. Then Prince Houssain said: Brothers, let us postpone the narrative of our travels, and let us at once show each other what we have brought as a curiosity that we may do ourselves justice beforehand, and judge to which of us our father may give the preference. To set the example, I will tell you, that

125

the rarity which I have brought from the kingdom of Bisnagar is the carpeting on which I sit, which looks but ordinary, and makes no show; but it possesses wonderful virtues. Whoever sits on it, and desires to be transported to any place, is immediately carried thither. I made the experiment myself, before I paid the forty purses, which I most readily gave for it. I expect now that you should tell me whether what you have brought is to be compared with this carpet.

Prince Ali spoke next, and said: I must own that your carpet is very wonderful; yet I am as well satisfied with my purchase as you can possibly be with yours. Here is an ivory tube which also cost me forty purses; it looks ordinary enough, yet on looking through it you can behold whatever you desire to see, no matter how far distant it may be. Take it, brother, and try for yourself.

Houssain took the ivory tube from Prince Ali, with an intention to see the Princess Nouronnihar, when Ali and Prince Ahmed, who kept their eyes fixed upon him, were extremely surprised to see his countenance change in such a manner, as expressed extraordinary alarm and affliction. And he cried out, Alas! princes, to what purpose have we undertaken such long and fatiguing journeys, with but the hope of being recompensed by the possession of the charming Nouronnihar, when in a few moments that lovely princess will breathe her last. I saw her in her bed, surrounded by her women all in tears, who seem to expect her death. Take the tube, behold yourselves the miserable state she is in, and mingle your tears with mine.

Prince Ali took the tube out of Houssain's hand, and after he had seen the same object, with sensible grief presented it to Ahmed, who took it, to behold the melancholy sight which so much concerned them all.

When Prince Ahmed had taken the tube out of Ali's hands, and saw that the Princess Nouronnihar's end was so near, he addressed himself to his two brothers, and said, Brothers, the Princess Nouronnihar is indeed at death's door; but provided we lose no time, we may preserve her life. He then took the artificial apple out of his bosom and resumed, This apple cost me as much as the carpet or tube, and has healing properties. If a sick person smells to it, though in the last agonies, it will restore him to perfect health immediately. I have made the experiment, and can show you its wonderful effect on the person of the Princess Nouronnihar, if we hasten to assist her.

We cannot make more despatch, said Prince Houssain, than by transporting ourselves instantly into her chamber by means of my carpet. Come, lose no time ; sit down ; it is large enough to hold us all.

The Princes Ali and Ahmed sat down by Houssain, and as their interest was the same, they all framed the same wish, and were transported instantaneously into the Princess Nouronnihar's chamber.

The presence of three princes, who were so little expected, alarmed the princess's women, who could not comprehend by what enchantment three men should be among them ; for they did not know them at first.

Prince Ahmed no sooner saw himself in Nouronnihar's chamber, and perceived the princess dying, than he rose off the carpet, and went to the bedside, and put the apple to her nostrils. The princess instantly opened her eyes, and asked to be dressed, with the same freedom and recollection as if she had awaked out of a sound sleep. Her women presently informed her that she was obliged to the three princes, her cousins, and particularly to Prince Ahmed, for the sudden recovery of her health. She immediately expressed her joy at seeing them, and thanked them all together, but afterwards Prince Ahmed in particular. As she desired to dress, the princes hastened to express the pleasure they felt at her recovery ; after which they retired.

While the princess was dressing, the princes went to throw themselves at their father's feet ; but when they came to him, they found he had been previously informed of their unexpected arrival, and by what means the princess had been so suddenly cured. The sultan received and embraced them with the greatest joy, both for their return, and the wonderful recovery of the princess his niece, who had been given over by the physicians. After the usual compliments, each of the princes presented the rarity which he had brought : Prince Houssain his carpet, Prince Ali his ivory tube, and Prince Ahmed the artificial apple ; and after each had commended his present, as he put it into the sultan's hands, they begged of him to pronounce their fate, and declare to which of them he would give the Princess Nouronnihar, according to his promise.

The Sultan of the Indies having heard all that the princes had to say, remained some time silent, considering what answer he should make. At last he said to them in terms full of wisdom, I would declare for one of you, my children, if I could do it with justice ; but consider whether I can ? It is true, Ahmed, the princess is beholden to your artificial apple for her cure ; but let me ask you, whether you could have been of such service to her if you had not known by Ali's tube the danger she was in, and if Houssain's carpet had not brought you to her so soon ? Your tube, Ali, informed you and your brothers that you were likely to lose the princess, and so far she is greatly obliged to you. You must also grant that the knowledge of her illness would have been of no service without the artificial apple and the carpet. And as for you, Houssain, the princess would be very ungrateful if she did not show her sense of the value of your carpet, which was so necessary a means towards effecting her cure. But consider, it would have been of little use, if you had not been acquainted with her illness by Ali's tube, or if Ahmed had not applied his artificial apple. Therefore, as neither the carpet, the ivory tube, nor the artificial apple has the least preference to the other articles, I cannot grant the princess to any one of you ; and the only fruit you have reaped from your travels is the glory of having equally contributed to restore her to health. As this is the case, you see that I must have recourse to other means to determine the choice I ought to make ; and as there is time enough between this and night, I will do it to-day. Go and procure each of you a bow and arrow, repair to the plain where the horses are exercised ; I will soon join you, and will give the Princess Nouronnihar to him who shoots the farthest.

The three princes had no objection to the decision of the sultan. When they were dismissed his presence, each provided himself with a bow and arrow, and they went to the plain appointed, followed by a great concourse of people.

The sultan did not make them wait long for him ; as soon as he arrived, Prince Houssain, as the eldest, took his bow and arrow, and shot first. Prince Ali shot next, and much beyond him ; and Prince Ahmed last of all ; but it so happened, that nobody could see where his arrow fell ; and notwithstanding all the search made by himself and all the spectators, it was not to be found. Though it was believed that he had shot the farthest, still, as his arrow could not be found, the sultan determined in favour of Prince Ali, and gave orders for preparations to be made for the solemnisation of the nuptials, which were celebrated a few days after with great magnificence.

Prince Houssain would not honour the feast with his presence ; he could not bear to see the Princess Nouronnihar wed Prince Ali, who, he said, did not deserve her better nor love her more than himself. In short, his grief was so extreme, that he left the court, and renounced all right of succession to the crown, to turn dervise, and put himself under the discipline of a famous sheikh, who had gained great reputation for his exemplary life.

Prince Ahmed, urged by the same motive, did not assist at Prince Ali and the Princess Nouronnihar's nuptials, any more than his brother Houssain ; yet he did not renounce the world as he had done. But as he could not imagine what could have become of his arrow, he resolved to search for it, that he might not have anything to reproach himself with. With this intent he went to the place where the Princes Houssain's and Ali's were gathered up, and proceeding straight forwards from thence looked carefully on both sides as he advanced. He went so far, that at last he began to think his labour was in vain ; yet he could not help proceeding till he came to some steep craggy rocks, which completely barred the way.

To his great astonishment he perceived an arrow, which he recognised as his own, at the foot of the rocks. Certainly, said he to himself, neither I, nor any man living, could shoot an arrow

'His grief was so extreme, that he left the court.'

so far. Perhaps fortune, to make amends for depriving me of what I thought the greatest happiness of my life, may have reserved a greater blessing for my comfort.

130

PRINCE AHMED AND THE FAIRY PERIE BANOU

There were many cavities, into one of which the prince entered, and looking about, beheld an iron door, which he feared was fastened; but pushing against it, it opened, and disclosed an easy descent, which he walked down with his arrow in his hand. At first he thought he was going into a dark place, but presently a light quite different from that which he had quitted succeeded; and entering into a spacious square, he beheld a

'Come near, Prince Ahmed; you are welcome.'

magnificent palace. At the same instant, a lady of majestic air and of remarkable beauty, advanced, attended by a troop of ladies, all magnificently dressed.

As soon as Ahmed perceived the lady, he hastened to pay his respects; and the lady, seeing him, said, Come near, Prince Ahmed; you are welcome.

Prince Ahmed was surprised at hearing himself addressed by name, but he bowed low, and followed into the great hall. Here she seated herself upon a sofa, and requested the prince to sit

131

beside her. Then she said : You are surprised that I know you,
yet you cannot be ignorant, as the Koran informs you that the
world is inhabited by genies as well as men : I am the daughter
of one of the most powerful and distinguished of these genies,
and my name is Perie Banou. I am no stranger to your loves or
your travels, since it was I myself who exposed to sale the
artificial apple, which you bought at Samarcand ; the carpet
which Prince Houssain purchased at Bisnagar ; and the tube
which Prince Ali brought from Shiraz. This is sufficient to let
you know that I am not unacquainted with everything that
relates to you. You seemed to me worthy of a more happy
fate than that of possessing the Princess Nouronnihar ; and
that you might attain to it, I carried your arrow to the place
where you found it. It is in your power to avail yourself of the
favourable opportunity which presents itself to make you happy.

Ahmed made no answer to this declaration, but knelt to kiss
the hem of her garment ; but she would not allow him, and
presented her hand, which he kissed a thousand times, and kept
fast locked in his. Well, Prince Ahmed, said she, will you pledge
your faith to me, as I do mine to you ? Yes, madam, replied
the prince in an ecstasy of joy, what can I do more fortunate
for myself, or with greater pleasure ? Then, answered the fairy,
You are my husband, and I am your wife. Our fairy marriages
are contracted with no other ceremonies, and yet are more in-
dissoluble than those among men, with all their formalities. The
fairy Perie Banou then conducted Prince Ahmed round the
palace, where he saw much that delighted him, and showed the
wealth of the palace. At last she led him to a rich apartment
in which the marriage feast was spread. The fairy had ordered
a sumptuous repast to be prepared ; and the prince marvelled
at the variety and delicacy of the dishes, many of which were
quite strange to him. While they ate there was music ; and
after dessert a large number of fairies and genies appeared and
danced before them. Day after day new amusements were
provided, each more entrancing than the last. For the fairy's
intention was not only to give the prince convincing proofs of the

sincerity of her love, but to let him see that, at his father's court, he could meet with nothing comparable to the happiness he enjoyed with her, and to attach him entirely to herself. In this attempt she entirely succeeded.

At the end of six months, Prince Ahmed, who loved and honoured the sultan his father, felt a great desire to know how he was. He mentioned his wish to the fairy, who, lest this should be an excuse to leave her, begged him to abandon the idea of visiting the capital.

My queen, replied the prince, since you do not consent that I shall go, I will deny myself the pleasure, and there is nothing to which I would not submit to please you.

These words greatly pleased the fairy; but the prince grieved lest his father should think him dead.

As the prince had supposed, the Sultan of the Indies, in the midst of the rejoicings on account of the nuptials of Prince Ali and the Princess Nouronnihar, was sensibly afflicted at the absence of his other two sons. It was not long before he was informed of the resolution Houssain had taken to forsake the world, and the place he had chosen for his retreat. He made the most diligent search after Ahmed, and despatched couriers to all the provinces of his dominions, with orders to the governors to stop him, and oblige him to return to court; but all the pains he took had not the desired success, and his affliction, instead of diminishing, increased. He consulted the Grand Vizier, saying: Vizier, thou knowest I always loved Ahmed the most of all my sons. My grief is so heavy that I shall sink under it, if thou hast not compassion on me; I conjure thee to assist and advise me. The Grand Vizier, considering how to give his sovereign some ease, recollected a sorceress, of whom he had heard wonders, and proposed to send for and consult her. The sultan consented, and she was introduced into his presence.

The sultan said to the sorceress, By thy art and skill canst thou tell me what is become of Prince Ahmed? If he be alive, where he is? And if I may hope ever to see him again? To this the sorceress replied, It is impossible, sir, for me to answer immediately the questions, but if you allow me till to-morrow, I will endeavour to satisfy you. The sultan granted her the time, and promised to reward her richly.

The sorceress returned the next day, and said : Sir, I have only been able to discover that Prince Ahmed is alive ; but where he is I cannot discover.

The Sultan of the Indies was obliged to remain satisfied with this answer, which left him in the same uneasiness as before as to the prince's situation.

Meanwhile Prince Ahmed had never again asked the fairy, Perie Banou, to allow him to visit his father, but he often spoke to her of the sultan ; and she perceived the desire that was in his mind. One day she said to him, Prince, since I am now convinced of the fidelity of your love, I grant you the permission you sought, on condition that you will first swear to me that your absence shall not be long. Let me give you some advice : Do not inform your father of our marriage, neither of my quality, nor the place of our residence. Beg of him to be satisfied with knowing that you are happy, and that the sole end of your visit is to make him easy respecting your fate.

Prince Ahmed was greatly pleased at this ; and accompanied by twenty horsemen, he set out on a charger, which was most richly caparisoned, and as beautiful a creature as any in the Sultan of the Indies' stables. It was no great distance to his father's capital ; and, when Prince Ahmed arrived, the people received him with acclamations, and followed him in crowds to the palace. The sultan embraced him with great joy, complaining at the same time, with a fatherly tenderness, of the affliction his long absence had occasioned.

Sir, replied Prince Ahmed, when my arrow so mysteriously disappeared, I wanted to find it ; and returning alone, I commenced my search. I sought all about the place where Houssain's and Ali's arrows were found, and where I imagined mine must have fallen, but all my labour was in vain. I proceeded along the plain in a straight line for a league, and found nothing. I was about to give up my search, when I found myself drawn

'. . . he set out on a charger.'

forward against my will; and after having gone four leagues, to that part of the plain where it is bounded by rocks, I perceived an arrow. I ran to the spot, took it up, and knew it to be the same which I had shot. Then I knew that your decision was faulty, and that some power was working for my good. But as to this mystery I beg you will not be offended if I remain silent, and that you will be satisfied to know from my own mouth that I am happy, and content with my fate. Nevertheless, I was grieved lest you should suffer in uncertainty, and I beg you to allow me to come here occasionally to visit you.

Son, I wish to penetrate no farther into your secrets. Your presence has restored to me the joy I have not felt for a long time, and you shall always be welcome when you can come.

Prince Ahmed stayed three days at his father's court, and on the fourth returned to the fairy, Perie Banou, who received him with great joy.

A month after Prince Ahmed's return from visiting his father, the fairy said: Do not you remember the promise you made to your father? I think you should not be longer in renewing your visits. Pay him one to-morrow; and after that, go and visit once a month, without speaking to me, or waiting for my permission. I readily consent to such an arrangement.

Prince Ahmed went the next morning with the same attendants as before, but much more magnificently mounted, equipped, and dressed, and was received by the sultan with the same joy and satisfaction. For several months he constantly paid him visits, and always with a richer and more brilliant equipage.

At last the sultan's favourites, who judged of Prince Ahmed's power by the splendour of his appearance, strove to make him jealous of his son. They represented that it was but common prudence to discover where the prince had retired, and how he could afford to live so magnificently, since he had no revenue assigned for his expenses; that he seemed to come to court only to insult him; and that it was to be feared he might court the people's favour and dethrone him. And they brought many cunning arguments to bear, in support of their words, adding:

136

PRINCE AHMED AND THE FAIRY PERIE BANOU

It is dangerous to have so powerful a neighbour; for he must live near at hand, since neither horses nor men bear marks of travel.

When the favourites had concluded these insinuations, the sultan said, I do not believe my son Ahmed is so wicked as you would persuade me he is; however, I am obliged to you for your advice, and do not doubt that it proceeds from good intention and loyalty to my person.

The Sultan of the Indies said this, that his favourites might not know the impression their observations had made on his mind. He was, however, so much alarmed by them, that he resolved to have Prince Ahmed watched. For this end he sent for the sorceress, who was introduced by a private door into his closet. My son Ahmed, said the sultan, comes to my court every month; but I cannot learn from him where he resides, and do not wish to force his secret from him. He is at this time with me, and usually departs without taking leave of me, or any of my court. You must watch him, so as to find out where he retires to, and bring me information. The sorceress left the sultan, and knowing the place where Prince Ahmed had found his arrow, went immediately thither, and concealed herself near the rocks, so as not to be seen.

The next morning Prince Ahmed set out by daybreak, without taking leave either of the sultan or any of his court, according to custom. The sorceress watched him until suddenly he disappeared among the rocks. The steepness of the rocks formed an insurmountable barrier to men, whether on horseback or on foot, so that the sorceress judged that the prince retired cither into some cavern, or some subterraneous place, the abode of genies or fairies. When she thought the prince and his attendants must have far advanced into whatever concealment they inhabited, she came out of her hiding-place and explored the hollow way where she had lost sight of them, but could find no trace of them. The sorceress, who saw it was in vain for her to search any farther, returned to the sultan. Though I have failed this time, she said, I hope ere long to succeed.

137

The sultan was pleased, and said, Do as you think fit. And to encourage her, he presented her with a diamond of great value, telling her it was only an earnest of the ample recompense she should receive when she should have performed this important service. A day or two before the prince's next visit the sorceress went to the foot of the rock where she had lost sight of him and his attendants, and waited there to execute the project she had formed.

As Prince Ahmed started upon his journey, he saw her lying on the ground, groaning and bewailing the fact that she was far from aid. The prince pitied her, turned his horse, and said: Good woman, you are not so far from help as you imagine. I will assist you, and convey you where you shall have all possible care taken of you, and where you will find a speedy cure. Rise, and let one of my people take you behind him.

At these words the sorceress, who pretended sickness only to explore where the prince resided, made many efforts to rise, pretending that the violence of her illness prevented her. Then two of the prince's attendants alighted, and helped her arise. They placed her on to a horse behind one of their companions. The prince turned back to the iron gate, and when he had entered the outer court, he sent to ask Perie Banou to see him. The fairy came with all imaginable haste, and the prince said to her, My princess, I desire you would have compassion on this good woman. I found her in the condition you see her, and promised her the assistance she requires. I recommend her to your care, and am persuaded that you will not abandon her.

The fairy, who had her eyes fixed on the pretended sick woman all the time the prince was speaking, ordered two of her women to take her from the men who supported her, conduct her into an apartment of the palace, and take as much care of her as they would of herself.

Whilst the two women were executing the fairy's commands, she went up to Prince Ahmed, and whispering in his ear, said, Prince, this woman is not so sick as she pretends to be ; and I am much mistaken if she is not sent hither on purpose to occasion

138

you great trouble. But do not be concerned; I will deliver you out of all the snares that shall be laid for you. Go and pursue your journey.

This address of the fairy's did not in the least alarm Prince Ahmed. My princess, said he, as I do not remember I ever did, or designed to do, anybody injury, I cannot believe any one can have a thought of injuring me; but if they have, I shall not forbear doing good whenever I have an opportunity. So saying, he took leave of the fairy, and set forward again for his father's capital, where he soon arrived, and was received as usual by the sultan, who constrained himself as much as possible, to disguise the anxiety arising from the suspicions suggested by his favourites.

In the meantime, the two women to whom Perie Banou had given her orders conveyed the sorceress into an elegant apartment, richly furnished. When they had put her into bed, one of the women went out, and returned soon with a china cup in her hand, full of a certain liquor, which she presented to the sorceress, while the other helped her to sit up. Drink this, said the attendant; it is the water of the fountain of lions, and a sovereign remedy against fevers. You will find the effect of it in less than an hour's time.

The attendants then left her, and returned at the end of an hour, when they found the sorceress seated on the sofa. When she saw them open the door of the apartment, she cried out, O the admirable potion! it has wrought its cure, and I have waited with impatience to desire you to conduct me to your charitable mistress, as I would not lose time, but prosecute my journey.

The two women conducted her through several apartments, all more superb than that wherein she had lain, into a large hall, the most richly and magnificently furnished in all the palace.

Perie Banou was seated in this hall, upon a throne of massive gold, enriched with diamonds, rubies, and pearls of an extraordinary size, and attended on each hand by a great number of beautiful fairies, all richly dressed. At the sight of so much splendour, the sorceress was not only dazzled, but so struck, that after she had prostrated herself before the throne, she could not open her lips to thank the fairy, as she had proposed. However, Perie Banou saved her the trouble, and said, Good woman, I am glad that you are able to pursue your journey. I will not detain you; but perhaps you may like to see my palace : follow my women, and they will show it you.

The old sorceress, who had not power or courage to say a word, prostrated herself once more, with her head on the carpet that covered the foot of the throne, took her leave, and was conducted by the two fairies through the same apartments which were shown to Prince Ahmed at his first arrival. Afterwards they conducted her to the iron gate through which she had entered, and let her depart, wishing her a good journey.

After the sorceress had gone a little way, she turned to observe the door, that she might know it again, but all in vain; for it was invisible to her and all other women. Except in this circumstance, she was very well satisfied with her success, and posted away to the sultan. When she came to the capital, she went by many byways to the private door of the palace, and was at once admitted to the sultan.

The sorceress related to the sultan how she had succeeded in entering the fairy's palace, and told him all the wonders she had seen there. When she had finished her narrative, the sorceress said : I shudder when I consider the misfortunes which may happen to you, for who can say that the fairy may not inspire him with the unnatural design of dethroning your majesty, and seizing the crown of the Indies ? This is what your majesty ought to consider as of the utmost importance.

The Sultan of the Indies had been consulting with his favourites, when he was told of the sorceress's arrival. He now ordered her to follow him to them. He acquainted them with what he had learnt might happen. Then one of the favourites said : In order to prevent this, now that the prince is in your power, you ought to put him under arrest; I will not say take away his life, but make him a close prisoner. This advice all the other favourites unanimously applauded.

The sorceress asked the sultan leave to speak, which being granted, she said : If you arrest the prince, you must also detain his retinue. But they are all genies, and will disappear, by the property they possess of rendering themselves invisible, and transport themselves instantly to the fairy, and give her an account of the insult offered her husband. And can it be supposed she will let it go unrevenged ? Could you not find other means which would answer the same purpose, and yet be of advantage to you ? Make demands upon his filial love ; and if he fail, then you have cause of complaint against him. For example, request the prince to procure you a tent, which can be carried in a man's hand, but so large as to shelter your whole army. If the prince brings such a tent, you may make other demands of the same nature, so that at last he may sink under the difficulties and the impossibility of executing them.

When the sorceress had finished her speech, the sultan asked his favourites if they had anything better to propose ; and finding them all silent, determined to follow her advice.

The next day when the prince came into his father's presence, the sultan said, Son, you are fortunate to have wed a fairy so rich and so worthy of your love. And since I hear that she is powerful, I would ask you to beg of her to do me a great service. You know to what great expense I am put every time I take the field to provide tents for my army. I am persuaded you could easily procure from the fairy a pavilion that might be carried in a man's hand, and which would extend over my whole army, and I am sure you will do this for me.

Prince Ahmed was in the greatest embarrassment what answer to make. At last he replied : I know not how this mystery has been revealed to you ; I cannot deny but your information is correct. I have married the fairy you speak of. I love her, and am persuaded she loves me in return. But I can say nothing as to the influence I have over her. However, the demand of a father is a command upon every child. And though it is with the greatest reluctance, I will not fail to ask my wife the favour you desire, but cannot promise you to obtain it ; and if I should not have the honour to come again to pay you my respects, it will be a sign that I have not been able to succeed in my request.

Son, replied the Sultan of the Indies, I should be sorry that what I ask should oblige you to deprive me of the gratification of seeing you as usual. I find you do not know the power a husband has over a wife ; and yours would show that her love to you was very slight, if, with the power she possesses as a fairy, she should refuse so trifling a request as that I have begged you to make.

All these representations could not satisfy Prince Ahmed ; and so great was his vexation that he left the court two days sooner than he used to do.

When he returned, the fairy, to whom he always before had appeared with a gay countenance, asked him the cause of the alteration she perceived in his looks. Yielding to her insistence, Ahmed confessed that the sultan had discovered the secret of his abode, and knew that he was married to her, though he was ignorant of the means by which he had gained his information. Here the fairy reminded him of the woman he had helped, and added : But, surely, there must be something more than this to make you so downcast—tell me, I pray ? Prince Ahmed replied : My father doubts my allegiance to him, and demands that I should ask you for a pavilion which may be carried in a man's hand, and which will cover his whole army.

Prince, replied the fairy, smiling, what the sultan requests is a trifle ; upon occasion I can do him more important service. Therefore be persuaded that far from thinking myself importuned, I shall always take real pleasure in performing whatever you can desire. Perie Banou then sent for her treasurer, to whom she said, Noor-Jehaun, bring me the largest pavilion in my treasury. Noor-Jehaun returned presently with a pavilion, which could not only be held, but concealed, in the palm of the hand, and presented it to her mistress, who gave it Prince Ahmed to look at.

142

PRINCE AHMED AND THE FAIRY PERIE BANOU

. . . gave it Prince Ahmed to look at.'

When Prince Ahmed saw the pavilion, which the fairy called the largest in her treasury, he fancied she had a mind to banter him, and his surprise soon appeared in his countenance, which Perie Banou perceived, and laughed. What! prince, cried she, do you think I jest with you ? You will see that I am in earnest. Noor-Jehaun, said she to her treasurer, go and set it up, that he may judge whether the sultan will think it large enough.

The treasurer went out immediately with it from the palace, and set it up. The prince found it large enough to shelter two armies as numerous as that of his father. You see, said the fairy, that the pavilion is larger than your father may have occasion for ; but you are to observe that it has one property, that it becomes larger or smaller, according to the extent of the army it has to cover, without applying any hands to it.

The treasurer took down the tent again, reduced it to its first size, brought it and put it into the prince's hands. He took it, and without staying longer than till the next day, mounted his horse, and went with the usual attendants to the sultan his father.

The sultan was in great surprise at the prince's speedy return. He took the tent ; but after he had admired its smallness, his amazement was so great that he could not recover himself when he had it set up in the great plain before mentioned, and found it large enough to shelter an army twice as large as he could bring into the field.

The sultan expressed great obligation to the prince for so noble a present, desiring him to return his thanks to the fairy ; and to show what a value he set upon it, ordered it to be carefully laid up in his treasury. But within himself he felt greater jealousy than ever of his son ; therefore, more intent upon his ruin, he went to consult the sorceress again, who advised him to engage the prince to bring him some of the water of the fountain of lions.

In the evening, when the sultan was surrounded as usual by all his court, and the prince came to pay his respects among the rest, he addressed himself to him in these words : Son, I have

THE STORY OF ALI BABA AND THE FORTY ROBBERS

THE STORY OF ALADDIN; OR, THE WONDERFUL LAMP

already expressed to you how much I am obliged for the present of the tent you have procured me, which I esteem the most valuable thing in my treasury: but you must do one thing more, which will be no less agreeable to me. I am informed that the fairy your spouse makes use of a certain water, called the water of the fountain of lions, which cures all sorts of fevers, even the most dangerous; and as I am perfectly well persuaded my health is dear to you, I do not doubt but you will ask her for a bottle of that water, and bring it me as a sovereign remedy, which I may use as I have occasion. Do me this important service, and complete the duty of a good son towards a tender father.

Prince Ahmed, who believed that the sultan his father would have been satisfied with so singular and useful a tent as that which he had brought, and that he would not have imposed any new task upon him which might hazard the fairy's displeasure, was thunderstruck at this new request. After a long silence, he said, I beg of your majesty to be assured, that there is nothing I would not undertake to procure which may contribute to the prolonging of your life, but I could wish it might not be by the means of my wife. For this reason I dare not promise to bring the water. All I can do is, to assure you I will request it of her; but it will be with as great reluctance as I asked for the tent.

The next morning Prince Ahmed returned to the fairy Perie Banou, and related to her sincerely and faithfully all that had passed at his father's court. He added: But, my princess, I only tell you this as a plain account of what passed between me and my father. I leave you to your own pleasure, whether you will gratify or reject this new desire. It shall be as you please.

No, no, replied the fairy, I will satisfy him, and whatever advice the sorceress may give him (for I see that he hearkens to her counsel), he shall find no fault with you or me. There is much wickedness in this demand, as you will understand by what I am going to tell you. The fountain of lions is situated in the middle of a court of a great castle, the entrance into which is guarded by four fierce lions, two of which sleep alternately, while the other two are awake. But let not that frighten you. I will supply you with means to pass by them without danger.

The fairy Perie Banou was at work with her needle; and as she had by her several clues of thread, she took up one, and presenting it to Prince Ahmed, said, First take this clue of thread; I will tell you presently the use of it. In the second place you must have two horses; one you must ride yourself, and the other you must lead, which must be loaded with a sheep cut into four quarters, that must be killed to-day. In the third place, you must be provided with a bottle, which I will give you, to bring the water in. Set out early to-morrow morning, and when you have passed the iron gate, throw before you the clue of thread, which will roll till it reaches the gates of the castle. Follow it, and when it stops, as the gates will be open, you will see the four lions. The two that are awake will, by their roaring, wake the other two. Be not alarmed, but throw each of them a quarter of the sheep, and then clap spurs to your horse, and ride to the fountain. Fill your bottle without alighting, and return with the same expedition. The lions will be so busy eating they will let you pass unmolested.

Prince Ahmed set out the next morning at the time appointed him by the fairy, and followed her directions punctually. When he arrived at the gates of the castle, he distributed the quarters of the sheep among the four lions, and passing through the midst of them with intrepidity, got to the fountain, filled his bottle, and returned safely. When he had got a little distance from the castle gates, he turned about; and perceiving two of the lions coming after him, drew his sabre, and prepared himself for defence. But as he went forwards, he saw one of them turn out of the road at some distance, and showed by his head and tail that he did not come to do him any harm, but only to go before him, and that the other stayed behind to follow. He therefore put his sword again into its scabbard. Guarded in this manner, he arrived at the capital of the Indies; but the lions never left him till they had conducted him to the gates of the sultan's palace; after which they returned the way they had come, though not without alarming the populace, who fled or hid themselves to avoid them, notwithstanding they walked gently and showed no signs of fierceness.

A number of officers came to attend the prince while he dismounted, and conduct him to the sultan's apartment, who was at that time conversing with his favourites. He approached the throne, laid the bottle at the sultan's feet, kissed the carpet which covered the footstool, and rising, said, I have brought you, sir, the salutary water which your majesty so much desired; but at the same time wish you such health as never to have occasion to make use of it.

After the prince had concluded, the sultan placed him on his right hand, and said, Son, I am much obliged to you for this valuable present; but I have one thing more to ask of you, after which I shall expect nothing more from your obedience, nor from your interest with your wife. This request is, to bring me a man not above a foot and a half high, whose beard is thirty feet long, who carries upon his shoulders a bar of iron of five hundredweight, which he uses as a quarter-staff, and who can speak.

The next day the prince returned to Perie Banou, to whom he related his father's new demand, which, he said, he looked upon to be a thing more impossible than the two first: for, added he, I cannot imagine there is or can be such a man in the world.

Do not alarm yourself, prince, replied the fairy; you ran a risk in fetching the water of the fountain of lions for your father: but there is no danger in finding this man. It is my brother Schaibar, who is far from being like me, though we both had the same father. He is of so violent a nature, that nothing can prevent his giving bloody marks of his resentment for a slight offence; yet, on the other hand, is so liberal as to oblige any one in whatever they desire. I will send for him; but prepare yourself not to be alarmed at his extraordinary figure. What! my queen, replied Prince Ahmed, do you say Schaibar is your brother ?   Let him be ever so ugly or deformed, I shall love and honour him as my nearest relation.

The fairy ordered a gold chafing-dish to be set with a fire in it under the porch of her palace.   She took some incense, and threw it into the fire, when there arose a thick cloud of smoke.

Some moments after, the fairy said to Prince Ahmed, Prince, there comes my brother, do you see him ?   The prince immediately perceived Schaibar, who looked at the prince with fierce eyes, and asked Perie Banou who that man was ?   To which she replied, He is my husband, brother ; his name is Ahmed ; he is a son of the Sultan of the Indies ; on his account I have taken the liberty now to call for you.

At these words, Schaibar, looking at Prince Ahmed with a favourable eye, which however diminished neither his fierceness nor savage look, said, It is enough for me that he is your husband to engage me to do for him whatever he desires.   The sultan his father, replied Perie Banou, is curious to see you, and I desire he may be your guide to the sultan's court.   He needs but lead the way, I will follow him, replied Schaibar.

The next morning Schaibar set out with Prince Ahmed to the sultan.   When they arrived at the gates of the capital, the people, as soon as they saw Schaibar, ran and hid themselves in their shops and houses, shutting their doors, while others, taking to their heels, communicated their fear to all they met, who stayed not to look behind them ; insomuch, that Schaibar and Prince Ahmed, as they went along, found all the streets and squares desolate, till they came to the palace, where the porters, instead of preventing Schaibar from entering, ran away too ; so that the prince and he advanced without any obstacle to the council hall, where the sultan was seated on his throne, giving audience.

Schaibar went fiercely up to the throne, without waiting to be presented, and accosted the sultan in these words : You have asked for me.   What would you have with me ?

The sultan turned away his head to avoid the sight of so terrible an object. Schaibar was so much provoked at this rude reception, that he instantly lifted up his iron bar, and let it fall on his head, killing him, before Prince Ahmed could intercede in his behalf.

'. . . and let it fall on his head, killing him.'

Schaibar then smote all the favourites who had given the sultan bad advice; he spared the grand vizier, who was a just man. When this terrible execution was over, Schaibar came out of the council hall into the courtyard with the iron bar upon

149

his shoulder, and looking at the grand vizier, said, I know there is here a certain sorceress, who is a greater enemy of the prince my brother-in-law than all those base favourites I have chastised ; let her be brought to me immediately. The grand vizier instantly sent for her, and as soon as she was brought, Schaibar knocked her down with his iron bar, and killed her.

After this he said, I will treat the whole city in the same manner, if they do not immediately acknowledge Prince Ahmed my brother-in-law as Sultan of the Indies. Then all who were present made the air ring with the repeated acclamations of Long life to Sultan Ahmed ! Schaibar caused him to be clothed in the royal vestments, installed him on the throne, and after he had made all swear homage and fidelity, returned to his sister Perie Banou, whom he brought with great pomp, and made her to be owned Sultana of the Indies.

Prince Ali and Princess Nouronnihar were given a considerable province, with its capital, where they spent the rest of their lives. Afterwards he went as officer to Houssain to acquaint him with the change, and make him an offer of any province he might choose ; but that prince thought himself so happy in his solitude that he desired the officer to return his brother thanks for the kindness he designed him, assuring him of his submission ; but that the only favour he desired was to be indulged with leave to retire to the place he had chosen for his retreat.

The Story of Ali Baba & the Forty Robbers

IN a town in Persia, there lived two brothers, one named Cassim, the other Ali Baba. Their father left them scarcely anything; but Cassim married a wealthy wife and prospered in life, becoming a famous merchant. Ali Baba, on the other hand, married a woman as poor as himself, and lived by cutting wood, and bringing it upon three asses into the town to sell.

One day, when Ali Baba was in the forest, he saw at a distance a great cloud of dust, which seemed to be approaching. He observed it very attentively, and distinguished a body of horse.

Fearing that they might be robbers, he left his asses and climbed into a tree, from which place of concealment he could watch all that passed in safety.

The troop consisted of forty men, all well mounted, who, when they arrived, dismounted and tied up their horses and fed them. They then removed their saddle-bags, which seemed heavy, and followed the captain, who approached a rock that stood near Ali Baba's hiding-place. When he was come to it, he said, in a loud voice: Open, Sesame! As soon as the captain had uttered these words, a door opened in the rock; and after he had made all his troop enter before him, he followed them, when the door shut again of itself.

Although the robbers remained some time in the rock, Ali Baba did not dare to move until after they had filed out again, and were out of sight. Then, when he thought that all was safe,

151

he descended, and going up to the door, said : Open, Sesame !
as the captain had done, and instantly the door flew open.

Ali Baba, who expected a dark, dismal cavern, was surprised
to see it well lighted and spacious, receiving light from an opening
at the top of the rock. He saw all sorts of provisions, rich bales
of silk, brocades, and valuable carpeting, piled upon one another ;
gold and silver ingots in great heaps, and money in bags. The
sight of all these riches made him suppose that this cave must
have been occupied for ages by robbers, who had succeeded one
another.

Ali Baba loaded his asses with gold coin, and then covering
the bags with sticks he returned home. Having secured the door
of his house, he emptied out the gold before his wife, who was
dazzled by its brightness, and told her all, urging upon her the
necessity of keeping the secret.

The wife rejoiced at their good fortune, and would count all
the gold, piece by piece. Wife, said Ali Baba, you do not know
what you undertake when you pretend to count the money ;
you will never have done. I will dig a hole, and bury it ; there
is no time to be lost. You are right, husband, replied she ; but
let us know, as nigh as possible, how much we have. I will borrow
a small measure and measure it while you dig the hole.

Away the wife ran to her brother-in-law Cassim, who lived
just by, and addressing herself to his wife, desired her to lend
her a measure for a little while. The sister-in-law did so, but
as she knew Ali Baba's poverty, she was curious to know what
sort of grain his wife wanted to measure, and artfully putting
some suet at the bottom of the measure, brought it to her with
an excuse that she was sorry that she had made her stay so long,
but that she could not find it sooner.

Ali Baba's wife went home and continued to fill the measure
from the heap of gold and empty it till she had done : when she
was very well satisfied to find the number of measures amounted
to as many as they did, and went to tell her husband, who had
almost finished digging the hole. While Ali Baba was burying
the gold, his wife, to show her exactness and diligence to her

sister-in-law, carried the measure back again, but without taking notice that a piece of gold had stuck to the bottom. Sister, said she, giving it to her again, you see that I have not kept your measure long; I am obliged to you for it, and return it with thanks.

As soon as Ali Baba's wife was gone, Cassim's looked at the bottom of the measure, and was in inexpressible surprise to find a piece of gold stuck to it. Envy immediately possessed her breast. What! said she, has Ali Baba gold so plentiful as to measure it? When Cassim came home, his wife said to him, I know you think yourself rich, but you are much mistaken; Ali Baba is infinitely richer than you. He does not count his money, but measures it. Cassim desired her to explain the riddle, which she did, by telling him the stratagem she had used to make the discovery, and showed him the piece of money, which was so old that they could not tell in what prince's reign it was coined.

Cassim was also envious when he heard this, and slept so badly, that he rose early and went to his brother.

Ali Baba, said he, you pretend to be miserably poor, and yet you measure gold. My wife found this at the bottom of the measure you borrowed yesterday.

Ali Baba perceived that Cassim and his wife, through his own wife's folly, knew what they had so much reason to conceal; but what was done could not be recalled; therefore, without showing the least surprise or trouble, he confessed all, and offered him part of his treasure to keep the secret. I expect as much, replied Cassim haughtily; but I must know exactly where this treasure is, and how I may visit it myself when I choose; otherwise I will go and inform against you, and then you will not only get no more, but will lose all you have, and I shall have a share for my information.

Ali Baba told him all he desired, and even the very words he was to use to gain admission into the cave.

Cassim rose the next morning, long before the sun, and set out for the forest with ten mules bearing great chests, which he designed to fill. He was not long before he reached the rock, and found out the place by the tree and other marks which his brother had given him. When he reached the entrance of the cavern, he pronounced the words, Open, Sesame! The door immediately opened, and when he was in, closed upon him. He quickly entered, and laid as many bags of gold as he could carry at the door of the cavern, but his thoughts were so full of the great riches he should possess, that he could not think of the necessary word to make it open, but instead of Sesame, said, Open, Barley! and was much amazed to find that the door remained fast shut. He named several sorts of grain, but still the door would not open.

Cassim had never expected such an incident, and was so alarmed at the danger he was in, that the more he endeavoured to remember the word Sesame, the more his memory was confounded, and he had as much forgotten it as if he had never heard it mentioned. He threw down the bags he had loaded himself with, and walked distractedly up and down the cave, without having the least regard to the riches that were round him.

About noon the robbers chanced to visit their cave, and at some distance from it saw Cassim's mules straggling about the rock, with great chests on their backs. Alarmed at this novelty, they galloped full speed to the cave. Cassim, who heard the noise of the horses' feet from the middle of the cave, never doubted of the arrival of the robbers, and resolved to make one effort to escape from them. To this end he rushed to the door, and no sooner saw it open, than he ran out and threw the leader down, but could not escape the other robbers, who with their sabres soon deprived him of life.

The first care of the robbers after this was to examine the cave. They found all the bags which Cassim had brought to the door, to be ready to load his mules, and carried them again to their places, without missing what Ali Baba had taken away before. Then holding a council, they agreed to cut Cassim's body into four quarters, to hang two on one side and two on the other, within the door of the cave, to terrify any person who should attempt the same thing. This done, they mounted their horses, went to beat the roads again, and to attack the caravans they might meet.

In the meantime, Cassim's wife was very uneasy when night came, and her husband was not returned. She ran to Ali Baba

'He threw down the bags . . .'

in alarm, and said, I believe, brother-in-law, that you know Cassim, your brother, is gone to the forest, and upon what account; it is now night, and he is not returned; I am afraid some misfortune has happened to him. Ali Baba told her that she need not frighten herself, for that certainly Cassim would

155

not think it proper to come into the town till the night should be pretty far advanced.

Cassim's wife passed a miserable night, and bitterly repented of her curiosity. As soon as daylight appeared, she went to Ali Baba, weeping profusely.

Ali Baba departed immediately with his three asses to seek

. . struck with horror at the dismal sight of his brother's quarters.'

for Cassim, begging of her first to moderate her affliction. He went to the forest, and when he came near the rock, having seen neither his brother nor the mules in his way, was seriously alarmed at finding some blood spilt near the door, which he took for an ill omen; but when he had pronounced the word, and the door had opened, he was struck with horror at the dismal sight of his brother's quarters. He loaded one of his asses with them,

156

and covered them over with wood. The other two asses he loaded with bags of gold, covering them with wood also as before; and then bidding the door shut, came away; but was so cautious as to stop some time at the end of the forest, that he might not go into the town before night. When he came home, he drove the two asses loaded with gold into his little yard, and left the care of unloading them to his wife, while he led the other to his sister-in-law's house.

Ali Baba knocked at the door, which was opened by Morgiana, an intelligent slave, whose tact was to be relied upon. When he came into the court, he unloaded the ass, and taking Morgiana aside, said to her, Mention what I say to no one; your master's body is contained in these two bundles, and our business is, to bury him as if he had died a natural death. I can trust you to manage this for me.

Ali Baba consoled the widow as best he could, and having deposited the body in the house returned home.

Morgiana went out at the same time to an apothecary, and asked for a sort of lozenge very efficacious in the most dangerous disorders. The apothecary inquired who was ill. She replied with a sigh, My good master Cassim himself: he can neither eat nor speak. After these words Morgiana carried the lozenges home with her, and the next morning went at the same apothecary's again, and with tears in her eyes, asked for an essence which they used to give to sick people only when at the last extremity. Alas! said she, I am afraid that this remedy will have no better effect than the lozenges; and that I shall lose my good master.

On the other hand, as Ali Baba and his wife were often seen to go between Cassim's and their own house all that day, and to seem melancholy, nobody was surprised in the evening to hear the lamentable shrieks and cries of Cassim's wife and Morgiana, who gave out everywhere that her master was dead. The next morning Morgiana betook herself early to the stall of a cobbler named Mustapha, and bidding him good morrow, put a piece of gold into his hand, saying: Baba Mustapha, you must take your sewing tackle, and come with me; but I must tell you, I shall blindfold you when you come to such a place.

Baba Mustapha hesitated a little at these words. Oh! oh! replied he, you would have me do something against my conscience, or against my honour? God forbid! said Morgiana,

'. . . betook herself early to the stall of a cobbler.'

putting another piece of gold into his hand, that I should ask anything that is contrary to your honour; only come along with me, and fear nothing.

Baba Mustapha went with Morgiana, who, after she had bound his eyes with a handkerchief, conveyed him to her deceased master's house, and never unloosed his eyes till he had entered the room, where she had put the corpse together. Baba Mustapha, said she, you must make haste and sew these quarters together; and when you have done, I will give you another piece of gold.

After Baba Mustapha had finished his task, she once more blindfolded him, gave him the third piece of gold as she had promised, and recommending secrecy to him, conducted him back again to the place where she first bound his eyes, pulled off the bandage, and let him go home, but watched him that he returned towards his stall, till he was quite out of sight, for fear he should have the curiosity to return and dodge her; she then went home.

The ceremony of washing and dressing the body was hastily performed by Morgiana and Ali Baba, after which it was sewn up ready to be placed in the mausoleum. While Ali Baba and other members of the household followed the body, the women of the neighbourhood came, according to custom, and joined their mourning with that of the widow, so that the whole quarter was filled with the sound of their weeping. Thus was Cassim's horrible death successfully concealed.

'We are certainly discovered, said the captain.'

Three or four days after the funeral, Ali Baba removed his goods openly to the widow's house; but the money he had taken from the robbers he conveyed thither by night. When at length the robbers came again to their retreat in the forest, great was their surprise to find Cassim's body taken away, with some of their bags of gold. We are certainly discovered, said the captain, and if we do not find and kill the man who knows our secret, we shall gradually lose all the riches.

The robbers unanimously approved of the captain's speech.

The only way in which this can be discovered, said the captain, is by spying in the town. And, lest any treachery may

'To further impress the cobbler, he gave him a piece of gold.'

be practised, I suggest that whoever undertakes the task shall pay dearly if he fails—even with his life.

One of the robbers immediately started up, and said, I submit to this condition, and think it an honour to expose my life to serve the troop.

The robber's courage was highly commended by the captain and his comrades, and when he had disguised himself so that nobody would know him, he went into the town and walked up and down, till accidentally he came to Baba Mustapha's stall.

Baba Mustapha was seated, with an awl beside him, on the bench, just going to work. The robber saluted him, and perceiving that he was old, said, Honest man, you begin to work very early : is it possible that one of your age can see so well ? I question, even if it were somewhat lighter, whether you could see to stitch.

Why, replied Baba Mustapha, I sewed a dead body together in a place where I had not so much light as I have now.

A dead body ! cried the robber, with affected amazement. It is so, replied Baba Mustapha ; but I will tell you no more. Indeed, answered the robber, I do not want to learn your secret, but I would fain see the house in which this strange thing was done. To further impress the cobbler, he gave him a piece of gold.

If I were disposed to do you that favour, replied Baba Mustapha, I assure you I cannot, for I was led both to and from the house blindfolded.

Well, replied the robber, you may, however, remember a little of the way that you were led blindfolded. Come, let me bind your eyes at the same place. We will walk together ; and as everybody ought to be paid for their trouble, there is another piece of gold for you ; gratify me in what I ask you.

The two pieces of gold were too great a temptation to Baba Mustapha, who said : I am not sure that I remember the way exactly ; but since you desire, I will try what I can do. At these words Baba Mustapha rose up, and led the robber to the place where Morgiana had bound his eyes. It was here, said Baba Mustapha, I was blindfolded ; and I turned as you see me. The robber, who had his handkerchief ready, tied it over his eyes, walked by him till he stopped, partly leading, and partly guided by him. I think, said Baba Mustapha, I went no farther, and he had now stopped directly at Cassim's house, where Ali Baba then lived. The thief before he pulled off the band, marked the door with a piece of chalk, which he had ready in his hand ; and then asked him if he knew whose house that was, to which Baba Mustapha replied, that, as he did not live in that neighbourhood, he could not tell.

The robber, finding he could discover no more from Baba

'*The thief marked the door with a piece of chalk.*'

Mustapha, thanked him for the trouble he had taken, and left him to go back to his stall, while he returned to the forest, persuaded that he should be very well received.

A little after the robber and Baba Mustapha had parted, Morgiana went out of Ali Baba's house upon some errand, and upon her return, seeing the mark the robber had made, stopped to observe it. What can be the meaning of this mark? said she to herself; somebody intends my master no good: however, with whatever intention it was done, it is advisable to guard against the worst. Accordingly, she fetched a piece of chalk, and marked two or three doors on each side in the same manner, without saying a word to her master or mistress.

When the robber reached the camp, he reported the success of his expedition; and it was at once decided that they should very quietly enter the city and watch for an opportunity of slaying their enemy. To the utter confusion of the guide, several of the neighbouring doors were found to be marked in a similar manner. Come, said the captain, this will not do; we must return, and you must die. They returned to the camp, and the false guide was promptly slain.

Then another volunteer came forward, and he in like manner was led by Baba Mustapha to the spot. He more cautiously marked the door with red chalk, in a place not likely to be seen. But the quick eye of Morgiana detected this likewise, and she repeated her previous action, with equal effectiveness, for when the robbers came they could not distinguish the house. Then the captain, in great anger, led his men back to the forest, when the second offender was immediately put to death.

The captain, dissatisfied by this waste of time and loss of men, decided to undertake the task himself. And so having been led to the spot by Baba Mustapha, he walked up and down before the house until it was impressed upon his mind. He then returned to the forest; and when he came into the cave, where the troop waited for him, said: Now, comrades, nothing can prevent our full revenge. He then told them his contrivance; and as they approved of it, ordered them to go into the villages about, and buy nineteen mules, with thirty-eight large leather jars, one full of oil, and the others empty.

In two days all preparations were made, and the nineteen mules were loaded with thirty-seven robbers in jars, and the jar of oil, the captain, as their driver, set out with them, and reached the town by the dusk of the evening, as he had intended. He led them through the streets till he came to Ali Baba's, at whose door he designed to have knocked; but was prevented, as Ali Baba was sitting there after supper to take a little fresh air. He stopped his mules, and said: I have brought some oil a great way, to sell at to-morrow's market; and it is now so late that I do not know where to lodge. Will you allow me to pass the night with you, and I shall be very much obliged by your hospitality.

'. . . walked up and down until it was impressed upon his mind.'

Ali Baba, not recognising the robber, bade him welcome, and gave directions for his entertainment, and after they had eaten he retired to rest.

The captain, pretending that he wished to see how his jars stood, slipped into the garden, and passing from one to the other he raised the lids of the jars and spoke: As soon as I throw some stones out of my window, do not fail to come out, and I will immediately join you. After this he retired to his chamber; and to avoid any suspicion, put the light out soon after, and laid himself down in his clothes, that he might be the more ready to rise.

While Morgiana was preparing the food for breakfast, the lamp went out, and there was no more oil in the house, nor any candles. What to do she did not know, for the broth must be made. Abdalla seeing her very uneasy, said : Do not fret, but go into the yard, and take some oil out of one of the jars.

Morgiana thanked Abdalla for his advice, took the oil-pot, and went into the yard ; when as she came nigh the first jar, the robber within said softly : Is it time ?

Morgiana naturally was much surprised at finding a man in a jar instead of the oil she wanted, but she at once made up her mind that no time was to be lost, if a great danger was to be averted, so she passed from jar to jar, answering at each : Not yet, but presently.

At last she came to the oil-jar, and made what haste she could to fill her oil-pot, and returned into her kitchen ; where, as soon as she had lighted her lamp, she took a great kettle, went again to the oil-jar, filled the kettle, set it on a large wood-fire, and as soon as it boiled went and poured enough into every jar to stifle and destroy the robber within.

When this action, worthy of the courage of Morgiana, was executed without any noise, as she had projected, she returned to the kitchen with the empty kettle ; and having put out the great fire she had made to boil the oil, and leaving just enough to make the broth, put out the lamp also, and remained silent ; resolving not to go to rest till she had observed what might follow through a window of the kitchen, which opened into the yard.

She had not waited long before the captain gave his signal, by throwing the stones. Receiving no response, he repeated it several times, until becoming alarmed he descended into the yard and discovered that all the gang were dead ; and by the oil he missed out of the last jar he guessed the means and manner of their death. Enraged to despair at having failed in his design, he forced the lock of a door that led from the yard to the garden, and climbing over the walls, made his escape.

Morgiana then went to bed, feeling happy at the success of her design.

Ali Baba rose before day, and followed by his slave, went to the baths, entirely ignorant of the important event which had happened at home. When he returned from the baths, the sun was risen; he was very much surprised to see the oil-jars, and that the merchant was not gone with the mules. He asked Morgiana, who opened the door, the reason of it. My good master, answered she, God preserve you and all your family; you will be better informed of what you wish to know when you have seen what I have to show you, if you will but give yourself the trouble to follow me.

Ali Baba followed her, when she requested him to look into the first jar and see if there was any oil. Ali Baba did so, and seeing a man, started back in alarm, and cried out. Do not be afraid, said Morgiana, the man you see there can neither do you nor anybody else any harm. He is dead. Ah, Morgiana! said Ali Baba, what is it you show me? Explain yourself. I will, replied Morgiana; moderate your astonishment, and do not excite the curiosity of your neighbours; for it is of great importance to keep this affair secret. Look into all the other jars.

Ali Baba examined all the other jars, one after another: and when he came to that which had the oil in, found it prodigiously sunk, and stood for some time motionless, sometimes looking at the jars, and sometimes at Morgiana, without saying a word, so great was his surprise. At last, when he had recovered himself, he said, And what is become of the merchant?

Merchant! answered she, he is as much one as I am; I will tell you who he is, and what is become of him. She then told the whole story from beginning to end; from the marking of the house to the destruction of the robbers.

Ali Baba was overcome by this account, and he cried: You have saved my life, and in return I give you your liberty—but this shall not be all.

Ali Baba and his slave Abdalla then dug a long deep trench at the farther end of the garden, in which the robbers were buried. Afterwards the jars and weapons were hidden, and by degrees Ali Baba managed to sell the mules for which he had no use.

Meanwhile the captain, who had returned to the forest, found

' Ali Baba did so . . .'

life very miserable; the cavern became too frightful to be endured. But, resolved to be revenged upon Ali Baba, he laid new plans, and having taken a shop which happened to be opposite Cassim's, where Ali Baba's son now lived, he transported many rich stuffs thither. And, disguised as a silk mercer, he set up in business, under the name of Cogia Houssain.

Having by chance discovered whose son his opposite neigh-

167

bour was, he often made him presents and invited him to dinner, and did everything to win his good opinion.

Ali Baba's son, who did not like to be indebted to any man, told his father that he desired to ask him to dinner in return, and requested him to do so. Ali Baba readily complied with his wishes, and it was arranged that on the following day he should bring Cogia Houssain with him to dinner.

At the appointed time Ali Baba's son conducted Cogia Houssain to his father's house. And strange to say, when the robber found himself at the door, he would have liked to withdraw, though he had now gained access to the very man he wanted to kill. But at that moment Ali Baba came forward to receive him and thank him for his goodness to his son. And now, said Ali Baba, you will do me the honour of dining with me. Sir, replied Cogia Houssain, I would gladly, but that I have vowed to abstain from salt, and I scarcely like to sit at your table under such conditions. Trouble not yourself about that, answered Ali Baba. I will go and bid the cook put no salt in the food.

When Ali Baba went to the kitchen to give this order, Morgiana was much surprised, and desired to see this strange man. Therefore she helped Abdalla to carry up the dishes, and directly she saw Cogia Houssain, she recognised him as the captain of the robbers.

Morgiana at once decided to rescue Ali Baba from this fresh danger, and resolved upon a very daring expedient, by which to frustrate the robber's designs; for she guessed that he intended no good. In order to carry out her plan she went to her room and put on the garments of a dancer, hid her face under a mask, and fastened a handsome girdle round her waist from which hung a dagger. Then she said to Abdalla: Fetch your tabor, that we may divert our master and his guest.

Ali Baba bade her dance, and she commenced to move gracefully about, while Abdalla played on his tabor. Cogia Houssain watched, but feared that he would have no opportunity of executing his fell purpose.

168

ALI BABA AND THE FORTY ROBBERS

'She commenced to move gracefully about.'

169

After Morgiana had danced for some time, she seized the dagger in her right hand and danced wildly, pretending to stab herself the while. As she swept round, she buried the dagger deep in Cogia Houssain's breast and killed him.

Ali Baba and his son, shocked at this action, cried out aloud: Unhappy wretch! what have you done to ruin me and my family? It was to preserve, not to ruin you, answered Morgiana; for see here, continued she, opening the pretended Cogia Houssain's garment, and showing the dagger, what an enemy you had entertained! Look well at him, and you will find him to be both the fictitious oil-merchant and the captain of the gang of forty robbers. Remember, too, that he would eat no salt with you; and what would you have more to persuade you of his wicked design?

Ali Baba, who immediately felt the new obligation he had to Morgiana for saving his life a second time, embraced her: Morgiana, said he, I gave you your liberty, and then promised you that my gratitude should not stop there, but that I would soon give you higher proofs of its sincerity, which I now do by making you my daughter-in-law. Then addressing himself to his son, he said: I believe, son, that you will not refuse Morgiana for your wife. You see that Cogia Houssain sought your friendship with a treacherous design to take away my life; and, if he had succeeded, there is no doubt that he would have sacrificed you also to his revenge. Consider, that by marrying Morgiana you marry the preserver of my family and your own.

The son, far from showing any dislike, readily consented to the marriage; and a few days afterwards, Ali Baba celebrated the nuptials of his son and Morgiana with great solemnity, a sumptuous feast, and the usual dancing and spectacles.

Ali Baba, fearing that the other two robbers might be alive still, did not visit the cave for a whole year. Finding, however, that they did not seek to disturb him he went to the cave, and, having pronounced the words, Open, Sesame, entered and saw that no one had been there recently. He then knew that he alone in the world knew the secret of the cave; and he rejoiced to think of his good fortune. When he returned to the city he took as much gold as his horse could carry from his inexhaustible storehouse.

Afterwards Ali Baba took his son to the cave, taught him the secret, which they handed down to their posterity, who, using their good fortune with moderation, lived in great honour and splendour.

The Story of Aladdin; or, the Wonderful Lamp

ONCE there lived a tailor, by name Mustapha, in one of the wealthy cities of China, who was so poor that he could hardly maintain himself and his family, which consisted only of a wife and son.

His son, who was called Aladdin, was a good-for-nothing, and caused his father much trouble, for he used to go out early in the morning, and stay out all day, playing in the streets with idle children of his own age.

When he was old enough to learn a trade, his father took him into his own shop, and taught him how to use his needle, but to no purpose; for as soon as his back turned, Aladdin was gone for that day. Mustapha chastised him, but Aladdin was incorrigible, and his father was so much troubled about him that he became ill, and died in a few months.

Aladdin, no longer restrained by the fear of his father, gave himself entirely over to his idle habits, and was never out of the streets. This course he followed till he was fifteen years old, without giving his mind to any useful pursuit. As he was one day playing in the street, with his vagabond associates, a stranger passing by stood and watched him closely. The stranger was a sorcerer, known as the African magician, and had been but two days in the city.

The African magician, perceiving that Aladdin was a boy well suited for his purpose, made inquiries about him; and, after

172

he had learned his history, called him aside, and said: Child, was not your father called Mustapha the tailor? Yes, sir, answered the boy, but he has been dead a long time.

At these words the African magician threw his arms about Aladdin's neck, and kissing him with tears in his eyes, said, I am your uncle; your worthy father was my own brother. You are so like him that I knew you at first sight. Then he gave Aladdin a handful of small coins, saying, Go, my son, to your mother, give my love to her, and tell her that I will visit her to-morrow, that I may see where my good brother lived so long, and ended his days.

Aladdin ran to his mother, overjoyed at his uncle's gift. Mother, said he, have I an uncle? No, child, replied his mother, you have no uncle by your father's side, or mine. I am just now come, said Aladdin, from a man who says he is my uncle, my father's brother.

'The stranger was a sorcerer.'

He cried and kissed me when I told

173

my father was dead, and gave me money; also bade me give you his love and say that he will come to see you, that he may be shown the house wherein my father lived and died. Indeed, child, replied the mother, your father had a brother, but he has been dead a long time, and I never heard of another.

The next day Aladdin's uncle found him playing in another part of the town, and embracing him as before, put two pieces of gold into his hand, and said to him, Carry this, child, to your mother. Tell her that I will come and see her to-night, and bid her get us something for supper; but first show me the house where you live.

Aladdin showed the magician the house, and carried the two pieces of gold to his mother, and when he had told her of his uncle's intention, she went out and bought provisions, and borrowed various utensils of her neighbours. She spent the whole day in preparing the supper; and at night, when it was ready, said to her son, Perhaps your uncle will not find the way to our house; go and bring him with you if you meet him.

Aladdin was ready to start, when the magician came in loaded with wine, and all sorts of fruits, for dessert. After the African magician had given what he brought into Aladdin's hands, he saluted his mother, and desired her to show him the place where his brother Mustapha used to sit on the sofa; and when she had so done, he bowed his head down, and kissed it, crying out repeatedly with tears in his eyes, My poor brother! how unhappy am I not to have come soon enough to give you one last embrace. Aladdin's mother desired him to sit down in the same place, but he declined. No, said he, I shall not do that; but let me sit opposite to it, that although I may not see the master of a family so dear to me, I may at least have the pleasure of beholding the place where he used to sit.

When the magician had sat down, he began to enter into discourse with Aladdin's mother: My good sister, said he, do not be surprised at your never having seen me all the time you have been married to my brother Mustapha, of happy memory. I have been forty years absent from this country; and during

ALADDIN ; OR, THE WONDERFUL LAMP

that time have travelled into the Indies, Persia, Arabia, Syria, and Egypt, and afterwards crossed over into Africa, where I

'The magician came in loaded with wine and fruits.'

settled. Being desirous to see my native land once more, and to embrace my brother, I made the necessary preparations, and set out. It was a long and painful journey, but my greatest grief was the news of my brother's death. But it is a comfort for me to find, as it were, my brother in a son, who has his most remarkable features.

The African magician perceiving that the widow began to weep at the remembrance of her husband, changed the conversation, and turning towards her son, asked him his name, and what business he followed.

At this question the youth hung down his head, and was not a little abashed when his mother answered, Aladdin is an idle fellow. His father when alive, strove to teach him his trade, but could not succeed. Since his death he does nothing but idles away his time in the streets, as you saw him, without considering he is no longer a child ; and if you do not make him ashamed of it, I despair of his ever coming to any good. For my part, I am resolved one of these days to turn him out of doors, and let him provide for himself.

After these words, Aladdin's mother burst into tears ; and the magician said, This is not well, nephew ; you must think of helping yourself, and getting your livelihood. There are many sorts of trades : if you have any choice, I will endeavour to help you. Or if you have no mind to learn any handicraft, I will take a shop for you, furnish it with all sorts of fine stuffs and linens ; and with the money you make of them lay in fresh goods, and then you will live in an honourable way. Tell me freely what you think of my proposal ; you shall always find me ready to keep my word.

This plan greatly pleased Aladdin, who hated work. He told the magician he had a greater inclination to that business than to any other, and that he should be much obliged to him for his kindness. Very well, said the African magician, I will carry you with me to-morrow, clothe you as handsomely as the best merchants in the city, and afterwards we will open a shop.

The widow, who never till then could believe that the magician was her husband's brother, no longer doubted after his promises of kindness to her son. She thanked him for his good intentions ; and after having exhorted Aladdin to render himself worthy

176

THE STORY OF ALI COGIA, A MERCHANT OF BAGDAD

THE STORY OF ABOU HASSAN; OR, THE SLEEPER AWAKENED

ALADDIN; OR, THE WONDERFUL LAMP

'. . . took Aladdin . . . to a merchant, who sold all sorts of clothes.'

of his uncle's favour by good behaviour, served up supper, and afterwards the magician took his leave, and retired.

He came again the next day, as he had promised, and took Aladdin with him to a merchant, who sold all sorts of clothes, and a variety of fine stuffs. He bade Aladdin choose those he preferred, and paid for them immediately.

Aladdin was much delighted by his new dress, and thanked his uncle warmly. Then the magician replied : As you are soon to be a merchant, it is proper you should frequent these shops, and be acquainted with them. He then showed him the largest and finest mosques, carried him to the khans, and afterwards to the sultan's palace, where he had free access ; and at last brought him to his own khan, where meeting with some merchants he had become acquainted with since his arrival, he introduced his pretended nephew to them.

This entertainment lasted till night, when Aladdin would have taken leave of his uncle to go home ; the magician would not let him go by himself, but conducted him to his mother, who, as soon as she saw him so well dressed, was transported with joy, and bestowed a thousand blessings upon the magician.

Early the next morning the magician took Aladdin out, saying that he would show him the country road, and that on the following day he would purchase the shop. He then led him out at one of the gates of the city, to some magnificent palaces, to each of which belonged beautiful gardens, into which anybody might enter. At every building he came to, he asked Aladdin if he did not think it fine ; and the youth was ready to answer when any one presented itself, crying out, Here is a finer house, uncle, than any we have seen yet. By this artifice, the cunning magician led Aladdin some way into the country ; and as he meant to carry him farther to execute his design, he took an opportunity to sit down in one of the gardens on the brink of a fountain of clear water, which discharged itself by a lion's mouth of bronze into a basin, pretending to be tired : Come, nephew, said he, you must be weary as well as I ; let us rest ourselves, and we shall be better able to pursue our walk.

ALADDIN ; OR, THE WONDERFUL LAMP

The magician then pulled from his girdle a handkerchief with cakes and fruit, which he had provided, and laid them on the edge of the basin. While they were partaking of this short repast the magician spoke gravely to his nephew, urging him to give up his evil companions and to seek the company of wise men from whose society he would benefit. When he had finished his advice they resumed their walk through the gardens. The African magician drew Aladdin beyond the gardens, and crossed the country, till they reached the mountains.

At last they arrived between two mountains of moderate height, and equal size, divided by a narrow valley, which was the place where the magician intended to execute the design that had brought him from Africa to China. We will go no farther now, said he. I will show you here some extraordinary things, which you will thank me to have seen : but while I strike a light, gather up all the loose dry sticks you can see, to kindle a fire.

Aladdin collected a great heap ; the magician set them on fire ; and when they were in a blaze, threw in some incense, and pronounced several magical words which Aladdin did not understand.

At the same time the earth trembling, opened just before the magician, and uncovered a stone, with a brass ring fixed in the middle. Aladdin was so frightened, that he would have run away, but the magician caught hold of him, abused him, and gave him such a box on the ear, that he knocked him down. Aladdin got up trembling, and with tears in his eyes, said, What have I done, uncle, to be treated in this severe manner ? I supply the place of your father, replied the magician, and you ought to make no reply. But, child, added he, softening, do not be afraid ; for I shall not ask anything of you, but that you obey me punctually, if you would reap the advantages which I intend you. Know then, that under this stone there is hidden a treasure, destined to be yours, and which will make you richer than the greatest monarch in the world. No person but yourself is permitted to lift this stone, or enter the cave ; so you must

179

'. . . *the magician set them on fire.*'

punctually execute what I may command, for it is a matter of great consequence both to you and me.

Aladdin, amazed at all he saw and heard, forgot what was past, and rising, said, Well, uncle, what is to be done ? Command me, I am ready to obey. I am overjoyed, child, said the magician, embracing him. Take hold of the ring, and lift up that stone. Indeed, uncle, replied Aladdin, I am not strong enough ; you must help me. Then we shall be able to do nothing, replied the magician. Take hold of the ring, pronounce the names of your father and grandfather, then lift it up, and you will find it will come easily. Aladdin did as the magician bade him, raised the stone with ease, and laid it on one side.

When the stone was pulled up, there appeared a little door, and steps to go down lower. Descend into the cave, said the magician, and you will find three great halls, in each of which you will see four large brass cisterns placed on each side, full of gold and silver ; but take care you do not meddle with them. Before you enter the first hall, be sure to tuck up your robe, wrap it about you, and then pass through the second into the third without stopping. Above all things, have a care that you do not touch the walls, so much as with your clothes ; for if you do, you will die instantly. At the end of the third hall, you will find a door which opens into a garden planted with fine trees loaded with fruit ; walk across the garden to five steps that will bring you upon a terrace, where you will see a lighted lamp in a niche before you. Take the lamp down, and extinguish it. When you have thrown away the wick, and poured out the liquor, put it in your girdle and bring it to me. Do not be afraid that the liquor will spoil your clothes, for it is not oil ; and the lamp will be dry as soon as it is thrown out.

After these words, the magician drew a ring off his finger, and put it on one of Aladdin's, telling him that it was a talisman. Then he added, Go down boldly, and we shall both be rich all our lives.

Aladdin descended, and found the three halls just as the African magician had described. He went through them with all the precaution the fear of death could inspire, crossed the garden without stopping, took down the lamp from the niche, emptied it, and put it in his girdle. As he came down from the terrace, he stopped in the garden to observe the trees, which were loaded with extraordinary fruit, of different colours on each tree. Some bore fruit entirely white, and some clear and transparent as crystal; some pale red, and others deeper; some green, blue, and purple, and others yellow: in short, there was fruit of all colours. The white were pearls; the clear and transparent, diamonds; the deep red, rubies; the paler, ballas rubies; the green, emeralds; the blue, turquoises; the purple, amethysts; and the yellow, sapphires. Aladdin was ignorant of their worth, and would have preferred figs and grapes, or any other fruits. But thinking them pretty, he collected as many of each sort as he could carry, and filled his purses and the flaps of his robe.

Aladdin having thus loaded himself with riches he knew not the value of, returned through the three halls with the same precaution, and soon arrived at the mouth of the cave, where the magician expected him with the utmost impatience. As soon as Aladdin saw him, he

'. . . took down the lamp from the niche.'

cried out, Pray, uncle, lend me your hand to help me out.

182

ALADDIN; OR, THE WONDERFUL LAMP

Give me the lamp first, replied the magician; it will be troublesome to you. Indeed, uncle, answered Aladdin, I cannot now; but I will as soon as I am up. The African magician was resolved to have the lamp before he would help him up; and Aladdin, who had encumbered himself so much with his fruit that he could not well get at it, refused to give it to him till he was out of the cave. The magician, provoked at this obstinate refusal, flew into a passion, threw a little of his incense into the fire, and pronounced two magical words. Immediately the stone moved into its place, with the earth over it in the same manner as it lay at the arrival of the magician and Aladdin.

This action plainly showed that the magician was not his uncle, but some adventurer who sought to possess the lamp, of which he had read in the magic books. And, moreover, it was but recently that he had learned where the wonderful lamp was concealed. He had also discovered that he must receive the lamp from another's hand, so he chanced to select Aladdin, whose life he reckoned as nought.

When the magician saw that all his hopes were frustrated, he returned the same day to Africa; but kept away from the town, lest Aladdin's absence should be noticed and questions asked. When Aladdin found himself shut in, he cried, and called out to his uncle, to tell him he was ready to give him the lamp; but in vain, since his cries could not be heard. He descended to the bottom of the steps, with a design to get into the garden, but the door, which was opened before by enchantment, was now shut by the same means. He then redoubled his cries and tears, sat down on the steps, without any hopes of ever seeing light again, and in a melancholy certainty of passing from the present darkness into that of a speedy death. Clasping his hands with an entire resignation to the will of God, he said, 'There is no strength or power but in the great and high God,' and in joining his hands he rubbed the ring which the magician had put on his finger. Immediately a genie of frightful aspect rose out of the earth, his head reaching the roof of the vault, and said to him,

What wouldst thou have ?   I am ready to obey thee as thy slave, and the slave of all who may possess the ring on thy finger ; I, and the other slaves of that ring.

At another time, Aladdin would have been so frightened at the sight of so extraordinary a figure that he would not have been able to speak ; but the danger he was in made him answer without hesitation, Deliver me from this place.   He had no sooner spoken these words, than he found himself on the very spot where the magician had caused the earth to open.   Aladdin was greatly astonished ; and, returning God thanks to find himself once more in the world, he made the best of his way home.   When he got within his mother's door, the joy to see her and his weakness for want of sustenance for three days made him faint, and he remained for a long time as dead.   As soon as he recovered, he related to his mother all that had happened, and she was very bitter in her execrations of the magician.   Aladdin then retired to rest, and slept till late the next morning ; when the first thing he said to his mother was, that he wanted something to eat. Alas ! child, said she, I have not a bit of bread to give you; but I have a little cotton, which I have spun, I will go and sell it, buy bread, and something for our dinner.   Mother, replied Aladdin, keep your cotton for another time, and give me the lamp I brought home with me yesterday ; I will go and sell it, and the money I shall get for it will serve both for breakfast and dinner, and perhaps supper too.

Aladdin's mother took the lamp, and said to her son, Here it is, but it is very dirty; if it was a little cleaner I believe it would bring something more.   She took some fine sand and water to clean it ; but had no sooner begun to rub it, than in an instant a hideous genie of gigantic size appeared before her, and said in a voice like thunder, What wouldst thou have ?   I am ready to obey thee as thy slave, and the slave of all those who have that lamp in their hands; I, and the other slaves of the lamp.

Aladdin's mother, terrified at the sight of the genie, fainted; when Aladdin, who had seen such a phantom in the cavern, snatched the lamp out of his mother's hand, and said to the genie boldly, I am hungry, bring me something to eat. The

'. . . and said to the genie boldly, I am hungry.'

genie disappeared immediately, and in an instant returned with a large silver tray, holding twelve covered dishes of the same metal, which contained the most delicious viands; six large white bread cakes on two plates, two flagons of wine, and two silver cups. All these he placed upon a carpet, and disappeared: this was done before Aladdin's mother recovered from her swoon.

Aladdin fetched some water, and sprinkled it in her face, to restore her; and it was not long before she came to herself. Mother, said Aladdin, do not be alarmed: here is what will put you in heart, and at the same time satisfy my extreme hunger.

His mother was much surprised to see the repast spread. Child, said she, to whom are we obliged for this great plenty and liberality? Has the sultan been made acquainted with our poverty, and had compassion on us? It is no matter, mother, said Aladdin, let us sit down and eat; for you have as much need of a good breakfast as myself; when we have done, I will tell you. Accordingly both mother and son sat down, and ate with the better relish as the table was so well furnished. But all the time Aladdin's mother could not forbear looking at and admiring the tray and dishes, though she could not judge whether they were silver or any other metal, and the novelty more than the value attracted her attention.

When Aladdin's mother had taken away and set by what was left, she went and sat down by her son on the sofa, saying: I expect now that you should satisfy my impatience, and tell me exactly what passed between the genie and you while I was in a swoon; which he readily complied with.

She was in as great amazement at what her son told her, as at the appearance of the genie; and said to him: But, son, what have we to do with genii? How came that vile genie to address himself to me, and not to you, to whom he had appeared before in the cave? Mother, answered Aladdin, the genie you saw is not the one who appeared to me, though he resembles him in size; no, they had quite different persons and habits: they belong to different masters. If you remember, he that I first saw called himself the slave of the ring on my finger; and this you saw, called himself the slave of the lamp you had in your hand: but

186

I believe you did not hear him, for I think you fainted as soon as he began to speak.

What! cried the mother, was your lamp then the occasion of the genie's addressing himself rather to me than to you? Ah! my son, take it out of my sight, and put it where you please. I had rather you would sell it, than run the hazard of being frightened to death again by touching it: and if you would take my advice, you would part also with the ring, and not have anything to do with genii, who, as our prophet has told us, are only devils.

With your leave, mother, replied Aladdin, I shall now take care how I sell a lamp which may be so serviceable both to you and me. That false and wicked magician would not have undertaken so tedious a journey, if he had not known the value of this wonderful lamp. And since chance hath given it to us, let us make a profitable use of it, without making any great show, and exciting the envy and jealousy of our neighbours. However, since the genii frighten you so much, I will take it out of your sight, and put it where I may find it when I want it. The ring I cannot resolve to part with; for without that you had never seen me again; and though I am alive now, perhaps, if it was gone, I might not be so some moments hence; therefore I hope you will give me leave to keep it, and to wear it always on my finger. She replied, that he might do what he pleased: for her part, she would have nothing to do with genii, and never say anything more about them.

By the next night they had eaten all the provisions the genie had brought: and the next day Aladdin, who could not bear the thoughts of hunger, putting one of the silver dishes under his vest, went out early to sell it, and addressing himself to a Jew whom he met in the streets, took him aside, and pulling out the plate, asked him if he would buy it. The cunning Jew took the dish, examined it, and as soon as he found that it was good silver, asked Aladdin at how much he valued it. Aladdin, who knew not its value, and never had been used to such traffic, told him he would trust to his judgment and honour. The Jew was somewhat confounded at this plain dealing; and doubting whether Aladdin understood the material or the full value of what he offered to sell, took a piece of gold out of his purse and

'The cunning Jew took the dish.'

gave it him, though it was but the sixtieth part of the worth of the plate. Aladdin, taking the money very eagerly, retired with so much haste, that the Jew, not content with the exorbitancy of his profit, was vexed he had not penetrated into his ignorance, and was going to run after him, to endeavour to get some change out of the piece of gold ; but he ran so fast, and had got so far, that it would have been impossible for him to overtake him.

Before Aladdin went home, he called at a baker's, bought some cakes of bread, changed his money, and on his return gave the rest to his mother, who went and purchased provisions enough to last them some time. After this manner they lived, till Aladdin had sold the twelve dishes singly, as necessity pressed, to the Jew, for the same money ; who, after the first time, durst not offer him less, for fear of losing so good a bargain. When he had sold the last dish, he had recourse to the tray, which weighed ten times as much as the dishes, and would have carried it to his old purchaser, but that it was too large and cumbersome ; therefore he was obliged to bring him home with him to his mother's, where, after the Jew had examined the weight of the tray, he laid down ten pieces of gold, with which Aladdin was very well satisfied.

When all the money was spent, Aladdin had recourse again to the lamp. He took it in his hand and rubbed it, when the genie immediately appeared, and repeated the same words that he had used before. I am hungry, said Aladdin, bring me something to eat. The genie disappeared, and presently returned with a tray, the same number of covered dishes as before, set them down, and vanished.

As soon as Aladdin found that their provisions were expended, he took one of the dishes, and went to look for his Jew chapman ; but passing by a goldsmith's shop, the goldsmith perceiving him, called to him, and said, My lad, I imagine that you carry something which you sell to that Jew with whom I see you speak ; but perhaps you do not know that he is the greatest rogue even among the Jews. I will give you the full worth of it ; or I will direct you to other merchants who will not cheat you.

The hopes of getting more money for his plate induced Aladdin to pull it from under his vest and show it to the goldsmith, who at first sight seeing that it was made of the finest silver, asked him if he had sold such as that to the Jew, when

Aladdin told him that he had sold him twelve such, for a piece of gold each. What a villain! cried the goldsmith; but, added he, my son, what is past cannot be recalled. By showing you the value of this plate, which is of the finest silver we use in our shops, I will let you see how much the Jew has cheated you.

The goldsmith took a pair of scales, weighed the dish, and after he had mentioned how much an ounce of fine silver cost, assured him that his plate would fetch by weight sixty pieces of gold, which he offered to pay down immediately.

Aladdin thanked him for his fair dealing, and sold him all his dishes and the tray, and had as much for them as the weight came to.

Though Aladdin and his mother had an inexhaustible treasure in their lamp, and might have had whatever they wished for, yet they lived with the same frugality as before, and it may easily be supposed that the money for which Aladdin had sold the dishes and tray was sufficient to maintain them for some time.

During this interval, Aladdin frequented the shops of the principal merchants, where they sold cloth of gold and silver, linens, silk stuffs, and jewellery, and oftentimes joining in their conversation, acquired a knowledge of the world. By his acquaintance among the jewellers, he came to know that the fruits which he had gathered when he took the lamp were, instead of coloured glass, stones of inestimable value; but he had the prudence not to mention this to any one, not even to his mother.

One day as Aladdin was walking about the town, he heard an order proclaimed, commanding the people to shut up their shops and houses, and keep within doors, while the Princess Buddir al Buddoor, the sultan's daughter, went to the baths and returned.

This proclamation inspired Aladdin with curiosity to see the princess's face. To achieve this he placed himself behind the door of the bath, which was so situated that he could not fail of seeing her face. Aladdin had not waited long before the princess came. She was attended by a great crowd of ladies and slaves, who walked on each side, and behind her. When she came

190

'The princess was most beautiful.'

within three or four paces of the door of the baths, she took off her veil, and gave Aladdin an opportunity of a full view.

The princess was the most beautiful brunette in the world : her eyes were large and sparkling ; her looks sweet and modest ; her nose faultless ; her mouth small ; her lips vermilion ; and her figure perfect. It is not, therefore, surprising that Aladdin was dazzled and enchanted.

After the princess had passed by, and entered the baths, Aladdin left his hiding-place and went home. His mother perceived that he was much more thoughtful and melancholy than usual ; and asked what had happened to make him so, or if he was ill. For some time he remained silent, but at length he told her all, saying in conclusion, I love the princess, and am resolved to ask her in marriage of the sultan.

Aladdin's mother listened with surprise to what her son told her ; but when he talked of asking the princess in marriage, she said : Child, what are you thinking of ? You must be mad to talk thus. I assure you, mother, replied Aladdin, that I am in my right senses. I foresaw that you would reproach me with folly and extravagance, but I must tell you once more that I am resolved to demand the princess of the sultan in marriage, and your remonstrances shall not prevent me. As for a present worthy of the sultan's acceptance, those pieces of glass which I brought with me from the subterranean storehouse are in reality jewels of inestimable value, and fit for the greatest monarchs. I know the worth of them by frequenting the shops ; and you may take my word that none of the jewellers have stones to be compared to those we have, either for size or beauty, and yet they value theirs at an excessive price. So I am persuaded that they will be received very favourably by the sultan. You have a large porcelain dish fit to hold them ; fetch it, and let us see how they will look when we have arranged them according to their different colours.

Aladdin's mother brought the china dish, when he took the jewels out of the two purses in which he had kept them, and placed them in order according to his fancy. But the brightness

ALADDIN ; OR, THE WONDERFUL LAMP

and lustre they emitted in the day-time, and the variety of the colours, so dazzled their eyes that they were astonished beyond measure. The sight of all these precious stones, of which she knew not the value, only partially removed her anxiety; but, fearing that Aladdin might do something rash, she promised to

'. . . so dazzled their eyes . . .'

go to the palace the next morning. Aladdin rose before day-break, awakened his mother, pressing her to get herself dressed to go to the sultan's palace, and to get admittance, if possible, before the grand vizier and the great officers of state went in to take their seats in the divan, where the sultan held his court.

Aladdin's mother took the china dish, in which they had put

193

the jewels the day before, wrapped in two napkins, and set forwards for the sultan's palace. When she came to the gates, the grand vizier, and the most distinguished lords of the court, were just gone in; but, notwithstanding the crowd of people, she got into the divan, a spacious hall, the entrance into which was very magnificent. She placed herself just before the sultan, grand vizier, and the great lords, who sat in council on his right and left hand. Several causes were called, according to their order, pleaded and adjudged, until the time the divan generally broke up, when the sultan rising, returned to his apartment, attended by the grand vizier.

Aladdin's mother, seeing the sultan retire, and all the people depart, judged rightly that he would not sit again that day, and resolved to go home. Aladdin was greatly disappointed when he heard of her failure, but she soothed him by saying, I will go again to-morrow; perhaps the sultan may not be so busy.

The next morning she repaired to the sultan's palace with the present, as early as the day before, but when she came there she found the gates of the divan shut, and understood that the council sat but every other day, therefore she must come again the next. She went six times afterwards on the days appointed, placed herself always directly before the sultan, but with as little success as the first morning.

On the sixth day, however, after the divan was broken up, when the sultan returned to his own apartment, he said to his grand vizier, I have for some time observed a certain woman, who attends constantly every day that I give audience, with something wrapped up in a napkin; she always stands up from the beginning to the breaking up of the audience, and affects to place herself just before me. If she comes to our next audience, do not fail to call her, that I may hear what she has to say. The grand vizier made answer by lowering his hand, and then lifting it up above his head, signifying his willingness to lose it if he failed.

The next audience-day Aladdin's mother went to the divan, and placed herself in front of the sultan as usual. The grand

'*The grand vizier.*'

vizier immediately called the chief of the mace-bearers, and pointing to her, bade him tell her to come before the sultan. The widow promptly followed him ; and when she reached the throne she bowed her head to the ground, and waited for the sultan's command to rise. The sultan immediately said to her, Good woman, I have observed you to stand a long time, from the beginning to the rising of the divan ; what business brings you here ?

After these words, Aladdin's mother prostrated herself a second time, and said, Monarch of monarchs, I beg of you to pardon the boldness of my request, and to assure me first of your pardon and forgiveness. Well, replied the sultan, I will forgive you, be it what it may, and no hurt shall come to you : speak boldly.

When Aladdin's mother had taken all these precautions, she told him faithfully the errand on which she had come, and made many apologies and explanations in extenuation of her son's love for the princess.

The sultan hearkened to this discourse without showing the least anger ; but before he gave her any answer, asked her what she had brought tied up in the napkin. She took the china dish, which she had set down at the foot of the throne, untied it, and presented it to the sultan.

The sultan's amazement and surprise were inexpressible when he saw so many large, beautiful, and valuable jewels collected in the dish. He remained for some time motionless with admiration. Then he received the present from Aladdin's mother's hand, crying out in a transport of joy, How rich, how beautiful ! After he had admired and handled all the jewels, one after another, he turned to his grand vizier, and showing him the dish, said, Behold, admire, wonder and confess that your eyes never beheld jewels so rich and beautiful before ! The vizier was charmed. Well, continued the sultan, what sayest thou to such a present ? Is it not worthy of the princess my daughter ? And ought I not to bestow her on one who values her at so great price ? I cannot but own, replied the grand vizier, that the present is worthy of the princess ; but I beg of your majesty to grant me three months before you come to a

'The sultan's amazement was inexpressible.'

final resolution. I hope, before that time, my son, whom you have regarded favourably, will be able to make a nobler present than Aladdin, who is an entire stranger to your majesty.

197

The sultan readily granted this request, and said to the widow: Good woman, go home, and tell your son that I agree to the proposal you have made me; but I cannot marry the princess my daughter for the next three months; but at the expiration of that time come again.

Aladdin's mother returned home much more gratified than she had expected, since she had met with a favourable answer, and told her son that she was to attend at the court in three months to hear the sultan's decision.

Aladdin thought himself the most happy of men at hearing this news, and thanked his mother for the pains she had taken in the affair, the good success of which was of so great import-ance to his peace. When two of the three months were passed, his mother one evening went into the town, and found the shops dressed with foliage, silks, and carpeting, and every one rejoicing. The streets were crowded with officers in habits of ceremony, mounted on horses richly caparisoned, each attended by a great many footmen. Aladdin's mother asked what was the meaning of all this preparation of public festivity. Whence came you, good woman, said one, that you don't know that the grand vizier's son is to marry the Princess Buddir al Buddoor, the sultan's daughter, to-night? She will presently return from the baths; and these officers whom you see are to assist at the cavalcade to the palace, where the ceremony is to be solemnized.

The widow hastened home to inform Aladdin: Child, cried she, you are undone! the sultan's fine promises will come to nothing. This night the grand vizier's son is to marry the princess.

At this account Aladdin was thunderstruck, but with a sudden hope he bethought himself of the lamp, vowing to stop the marriage. He therefore went to his chamber, took the lamp, and rubbed it, when immediately the genie appeared, and said to him, What wouldst thou have? Hear me, said Aladdin; thou hast hitherto served me well; but now I entrust to thee a matter of great importance. The sultan's daughter who was to have been mine, is to-night to wed the son of the

ALADDIN; OR, THE WONDERFUL LAMP

'*Remove the bridegroom.*'

grand vizier. It shall not be. Bring them both to me ere the marriage takes place. Master, replied the genie, I will obey you.

Aladdin supped with his mother as usual; he then retired to his own chamber again, and waited for the genie to execute his orders.

At the sultan's palace the greatest rejoicings prevailed at the wedding festivities, which were kept up until midnight. The bride and bridegroom retired to their apartments. They had scarcely entered the room when the genie seized them, and bore them straight to Aladdin's chamber, much to the terror of both, as they could not see by what means they were transported. Remove the bridegroom, said Aladdin, and keep him in close custody until dawn to-morrow, when you shall return with him. Aladdin then tried to soothe the princess's fears by explaining how ill he had been treated; but he did not succeed over well as the princess knew nothing of the matter.

At dawn the genie appeared with the vizier's son, who had been kept in a house all night, near at hand, merely by being breathed upon by the genie. He was left motionless and entranced at the chamber door. At a word from Aladdin the slave of the lamp took the couple and bore them back to the palace.

The genie had only just deposited them in safety when the sultan tapped at the door to wish them good morning. The grand vizier's son, who was almost perished with cold, by standing in his thin undergarment all night, no sooner heard the knocking at the door than he ran into the robing-chamber, where he had undressed himself the night before.

The sultan, having opened the door, went to the bedside, kissed the princess on the forehead, but was extremely surprised to see her so melancholy. She only cast at him a sorrowful look, expressive of great affliction. He suspected that there was something extraordinary in this silence, and thereupon went immediately to the sultana's apartment, told her in what a state he had found the princess, and how she had received him. Sir, said the sultana, I will go and see her; she will not receive me in the same manner.

The princess was quite as reserved when her mother came; but when the sultana pressed her to speak she said, with a deep

'*The sultan, having opened the door, went to the bed-side.*'

sigh and many tears, I am very unhappy. She then narrated all that had taken place. Daughter, replied the sultana, you must keep all this to yourself, for no one would believe that you were sane if you told this strange tale. The sultana then

201

questioned the vizier's son; but he, being proud of the alliance
he had made, denied everything, and so the celebrations of the
marriage went forward that day with equal splendour.

That night Aladdin again summoned the genie, and had
the princess and the vizier's son brought to him as before. And
on the following morning they were conveyed back to the palace,
just in time to receive the visit of the sultan. The princess
answered his inquiries with tears, and at last told him everything
that had happened. The sultan consulted with the grand vizier;
and, learning that his son had suffered even worse than the
princess, he ordered the marriage to be cancelled, and all the
festivities—which should have lasted for several days more—
were stopped throughout the kingdom.

This sudden stopping of the wedding celebrations gave rise
to much gossip, but nothing could be discovered: and this
sudden and unexpected change gave rise both in the city and
kingdom to various speculations and inquiries; but no other
account could be given of it, except that both the vizier and his
son went out of the palace very much dejected. Nobody but
Aladdin alone knew the secret, and he kept it most cunningly
to himself, so that neither the sultan nor the grand vizier, who
had forgotten Aladdin and his request, had the slightest suspicion
that he was the cause of all the trouble.

Three months had now elapsed since the sultan had made
his promise to Aladdin's mother, and so she again repaired to
the palace to hear his decision. The sultan at once recognised
her, and bade the grand vizier bring her to him.

Sir, said the widow, bowing to the ground before him, I have
come, as you directed, at the end of the three months, to plead
for my son. The sultan, when he had fixed a time to answer the
request of this good woman, little thought of hearing any more
of a marriage; but he was loath to break his word. Therefore
he consulted his vizier, who advised that such conditions should
be imposed that no one in Aladdin's position could fulfil them.
This suggestion seemed wise, so the sultan said: Good woman,
it is true sultans ought to abide by their word, and I am ready

202

to keep mine, by making your son happy in marriage with my daughter. But as I cannot marry her without some further valuable consideration from your son, you may tell him, I will fulfil my promise as soon as he shall send me forty trays of massive gold, full of the same sort of jewels you have already made me a present of, and carried by the like number of black slaves, who shall be led by as many young and handsome white slaves, all dressed magnificently. On these conditions I am

'Go, and tell him so.'

ready to bestow the princess upon him; go, and tell him so, and I will wait till you bring me his answer.

Aladdin's mother prostrated herself a second time before the throne, and retired. On her way home, she laughed within herself at her son's foolish imagination. Where, said she, can he get all that the sultan demands? When she came home, she told her son the message she had been commanded to deliver, adding, The sultan expects your answer immediately; but continued she, laughing, I believe he may wait long enough.

Not so long, mother, as you imagine, replied Aladdin. I am

very well pleased; his demand is but a trifle to what I could have done for her. I will at once provide these things.

Aladdin promptly withdrew and summoned the genie, to whom he made known his wants. The genie told him his command should be immediately obeyed, and disappeared. In a

'. . . each bearing on his head a heavy tray full of precious stones . . .'

very short time the genie returned with forty black slaves, each bearing on his head a heavy tray of pure gold, full of pearls, diamonds, rubies, emeralds, and every sort of precious stones, all larger and more beautiful than those presented to the sultan. Mother, said Aladdin, let us lose no time; before the sultan and the divan rise, I would have you return to the palace with this

204

present as the dowry demanded for the princess, that he may judge by my diligence and exactness of the ardent and sincere desire I have to procure myself the honour of this alliance.

So magnificent was this procession that as it passed through the streets crowds of people came out to look in wonder. The splendour of the dress of the slaves, which glistened with precious stones, made the people think that they were so many kings or princes. They walked sedately, Aladdin's mother at their head, towards the palace, and were all so much alike that the spectators marvelled.

As the sultan, who had been informed of their approach, had given orders for them to be admitted, they met with no obstacle, but went into the divan in regular order, one part filing to the right, and the other to the left. After they were all entered, and had formed a semicircle before the sultan's throne, the black slaves laid the golden trays on the carpet, prostrated themselves, touching the carpet with their foreheads, and at the same time the white slaves did the same. When they rose, the black slaves uncovered the trays, and then all stood with their arms crossed over their breasts.

In the meantime Aladdin's mother advanced to the foot of the throne, and having paid her respects, said to the sultan, Sir, my son feels that this present is much below the Princess Buddir al Buddoor's worth; but hopes, nevertheless, that your majesty will accept of it, and make it agreeable to the princess, and with the greater confidence since he has endeavoured to conform to the conditions you were pleased to impose.

The sultan made no longer hesitation: he was overjoyed at the sight of Aladdin's rich present. Go, said he, and tell your son that I wait with open arms to embrace him, and the more haste he makes to come and receive the princess my daughter from my hands, the greater pleasure he will do me. As soon as the tailor's widow had retired, the sultan put an end to the audience; and rising from his throne, ordered that the princess's servants should come and carry the trays into their mistress's apartment, whither he went himself to examine them with her

205

at his leisure. The fourscore slaves were conducted into the palace; and the sultan, telling the princess of their magnificent appearance, ordered them to be brought before her apartment, that she might see through the lattices he had not exaggerated in his account of them.

In the meantime Aladdin's mother got home, and showed in her air and countenance the good news she brought her son. My son, said she to him, rejoice, for you have arrived at the height of your desires. The sultan has declared that you are worthy to possess the Princess Buddir al Buddoor, and waits with impatience to embrace you, and conclude your marriage.

Aladdin, enraptured with this news, retired to his chamber, and summoned the slave of the lamp as usual. Genie, said he, I want to bathe immediately, and you must afterwards provide me the richest and most magnificent habit ever worn by a monarch. No sooner were the words out of his mouth than the genie rendered him, as well as himself, invisible, and transported him into a saloon of the finest marble of all sorts of colours; where he bathed in scented water. And when he returned into the hall he found, instead of his own, a suit the magnificence of which astonished him. The genie helped him to dress, and, when he had done, transported him back to his own chamber, where he asked him if he had any other commands. Yes, answered Aladdin, bring me a charger that surpasses in beauty and goodness the best in the sultan's stables, with a saddle, bridle, and other caparisons worth a million of money. I want also twenty slaves, as richly clothed as those who carried the present to the sultan, to walk by my side and follow me, and twenty more to go before me in two ranks. Besides these, bring my mother six women slaves to attend her, as richly dressed at least as any of the Princess Buddir al Buddoor's, each carrying a complete dress fit for any sultana. I want also ten thousand pieces of gold in ten purses; go, and make haste.

As soon as Aladdin had given these orders, the genie disappeared, but presently returned with the horse, the forty slaves, ten of whom carried each a purse containing ten thousand pieces of gold, and six women slaves, each carrying on her head a different dress for Aladdin's mother, wrapped up in a piece of silver tissue, and presented them all to Aladdin.

Aladdin took four of the purses, which he presented to his mother, together with the six women slaves who carried the dresses, telling her to spend the money as she wished; the other six he left with the slaves, and bade them cast handfuls among the people as they walked. And after this, when all was ready,

'The sultan received him with joy.'

he set out for the palace, mounted upon the charger, three of the purse-bearers walking on his right hand, and three on his left. Although Aladdin never was on horseback before, he appeared with such extraordinary grace, that the most experienced horse-man would not have taken him for a novice. The streets through which he was to pass were filled with an innumerable concourse of people, who made the air echo with their acclamations, especially every time the six slaves who carried the purses threw handfuls of gold among the populace. The sultan, much surprised by the magnificence of Aladdin's dress and the splendour of his cortège, received him with joy, and did everything in his power to honour him. After they had feasted, the marriage contract was drawn up and duly signed, and the sultan was anxious that the nuptials should be completed at once. But Aladdin said, Sir, I beg of you to grant me sufficient land near your palace on which I may build a home worthy of the princess, before our wedding takes place. You may judge of my eagerness to claim the princess by the expedition with which the castle shall be erected.

The sultan readily granted this request; and, having embraced Aladdin, he allowed him to return home.

Aladdin withdrew with a most courtly bow, and hastened home, amid the cheers of the people, to consult the genie. And as soon as he reached his house he went to his chamber, and took the lamp and rubbed it. Immediately the genie appeared, professed his allegiance, and Aladdin said to him : Genie, build me a palace fit to receive my spouse the Princess Buddir al Buddoor. Let it be built of porphyry, jasper, agate, lapis lazuli, and the finest marble of various colours. On the roof of the palace build a large, dome-crowned hall, having four equal fronts ; and instead of bricks, let the walls be formed of layers of massive gold and silver, laid alternately ; let each front contain six windows. The lattices of these, except one, which must be left unfinished, must be so enriched with diamonds, rubies and emeralds, that they shall exceed everything of the kind ever seen in the world. There must also be an inner and outer court in front of the palace, and a spacious garden ; but, above all things, provide and fill an ample treasure-house, well supplied with gold and silver. Let nothing be lacking in the kitchens and storehouses ; and let the stables be filled with the best horses. Finally, see that there is a royal staff of servants. Go, execute my orders.

It was about the hour of sunset when Aladdin gave these orders, and the next morning, before break of day, the genie presented himself, and said, Sir, your palace is finished. At a word from Aladdin the genie carried him to the palace, and led him through all the apartments, all of which, as well as the servants, delighted him. The genie then showed him the treasury, which was opened by a treasurer, where Aladdin saw heaps of purses, of different sizes, piled up to the top of the ceiling, and disposed in most excellent order. The genie thence led him to the stables, where he showed him some of the finest horses in the world, and the grooms busy in dressing them; from thence they went to the storehouses, which were filled with all things necessary, both for food and ornament.

When Aladdin had thoroughly examined the palace, he said, Genie, no one can be better satisfied than I am. There is only one thing wanting : that is, a carpet of fine velvet for the princess to walk upon from the sultan's palace here. The genie immediately disappeared, and Aladdin saw what he desired executed in an instant. The genie then returned and carried him home before the gates of the sultan's palace were opened.

When the sultan's porters came to open the gates, they were amazed to find a magnificent palace erected, and to see a carpet of velvet spread from the grand entrance. They immediately informed the grand vizier, who hastened to tell the sultan. It must be Aladdin's palace, exclaimed the sultan, which I gave him leave to build. He has done this as a surprise for me, to show what can be done in one night.

When Aladdin had been conveyed home, he requested his mother to go to the Princess Buddir al Buddoor to inform her that the palace would be ready for her reception that evening. She at once set out, attended by her women slaves. The widow was sitting with the princess when the sultan came in. He was much surprised to see the change that had taken place in her, and was greatly pleased. Aladdin had, meanwhile, set out to his new home, being careful to take the lamp and the ring, both of which had served him in such good stead. Great were the rejoicings, and loud the sounds of music, when Princess Buddir al Buddoor set out from the sultan's palace in the evening. A wonderful procession attended her to the door of Aladdin's palace, where he stood ready to receive her with all honour. He conducted her into a large hall, the wealth of which astonished her beyond measure, and then the festivities were kept up until a late hour.

The next morning, as soon as he was dressed, Aladdin set out to invite the sultan and his court to come to his palace. The sultan willingly consented, and, attended by his grand vizier and all the great lords of his court, he accompanied Aladdin. The nearer the sultan approached Aladdin's palace, the more he was struck with its beauty. But when he came into the hall, and saw the windows, enriched with diamonds, rubies, emeralds —all large, perfect stones—he was so much surprised that he remained some time motionless. Son, said the sultan, this hall is the most worthy of admiration of any in the world ; there is only one thing that surprises me, which is to find one of the windows unfinished. Sir, answered Aladdin, the omission was by design, since I wished that your majesty should have the glory of finishing this hall. I take it kindly, replied the sultan, and will give orders about it immediately.

When the sultan rose from the repast that had been prepared, he was informed that the jewellers and goldsmiths attended ; upon which he returned to the hall, and showed them the window which was unfinished. I sent for you, said he, to fit up this window in as great perfection as the rest ; and make all the dispatch you can.

The jewellers and goldsmiths examined the three-and-twenty windows with great attention, and after they had consulted together, to know what each could furnish, they returned, and presented themselves before the sultan, whose principal jeweller, undertaking to speak for the rest, said, Sir, we are all willing to exert our utmost care and industry to obey your majesty ; but among us all we cannot furnish jewels enough for so great a work. I have more than are necessary, said the sultan ; come to my palace and you shall choose what may answer your purpose.

When the sultan returned to his palace, he ordered his jewels to be brought out, and the jewellers took a great quantity, particularly those Aladdin had made him a present of, which they soon used, without making any great advance in their work. They came again several times for more, and in a month's time had not finished half their work. In short, they used all the jewels the sultan had, and borrowed of the vizier, but yet the work was not half done.

Aladdin, who knew that all the sultan's endeavours to make this window like the rest were in vain, sent for the jewellers and goldsmiths, and not only commanded them to desist from their work, but ordered them to undo what they had begun, and to carry all their jewels back to the sultan and to the vizier. They undid in a few hours what they had been six weeks about, and retired, leaving Aladdin alone in the hall. He took the lamp, which he carried about him, rubbed it, and presently the genie appeared. Genie, said Aladdin, I ordered thee to leave one of the four-and-twenty windows of this hall imperfect, and thou hast executed my commands punctually; now I would have thee make it like the rest. The genie immediately disappeared. Aladdin went out of the hall, and returning soon after, found the window, as he wished it to be, like the others.

In the meantime the jewellers and goldsmiths repaired to the palace, and were introduced into the sultan's presence; where the chief jeweller presented the precious stones which he had brought back. The sultan asked them if Aladdin had given them any reason for so doing, and they answering that he had given them none, he ordered a horse to be brought, which he mounted, and rode to his son-in-law's palace, with some few attendants on foot. Aladdin met him at the gate, and instead of answering his question, led him to the great hall, when the sultan was much surprised to find the window finished just like the others. He fancied at first that he had mistaken the window, but, having examined all the others, he found that it had been completed in a few minutes, whereas the jewellers had spent weeks upon it without finishing the work. My son, said he, what a man you are to do such surprising things always in the twinkling of an eye; there is not your fellow in the world; the more I know, the more I admire you.

Aladdin did not confine himself in his palace, but took care to show himself once or twice a week in the town, by going sometimes to one mosque, and sometimes to another, to prayers, or to visit the grand vizier, or the principal lords of the court. Every time he went out, he caused two slaves, who walked by the side of his horse, to throw handfuls of money among the people as he passed through the streets and squares. This generosity gained him the love and blessings of the people: and it was common for them to swear by his head. Thus he won the affections of the people, and was more beloved than the sultan himself.

Aladdin had conducted himself in this manner several years, when the African magician recalled him to his recollection in Africa, and, though he thought him dead in the cave where he had left him, he resolved to find out for certain. After a long and careful course of magical inquiries, he discovered that Aladdin had escaped, and lived in great splendour, all of which he owed to the wonderful lamp.

Directly the magician found out this, he set out in hot haste for the capital of China; and when he arrived, he went to a khan, where he rested after his long journey.

He made inquiries, which revealed to him Aladdin's enormous wealth, and heard of all his charities and of the magnificent palace he had built. The magician, when he saw the palace, knew that none but genies could have erected it, and he was exceeding annoyed to think how he had been worsted. He returned to the khan, determined to find out where the lamp was kept; and by the magic knowledge he possessed he was enabled to discover what he wanted to know. When, to his great delight, he learned that the lamp was in the palace—not, as he feared, about Aladdin's person—Now, said he, I shall have the lamp, and will be revenged upon this fellow, who shall be degraded to his original mean station in life.

The magician also learned that Aladdin had set out on a

hunting expedition three days before, which was to last for eight days. This knowledge was sufficient to enable the magician to carry out his plans, which he straightway did.

'Who will change old lamps for new?'

First he went to a coppersmith, from whom he purchased a dozen lamps, which he put into a basket, and then he set out to Aladdin's palace again. As he drew near he called out: Who will change old lamps for new? The princess happened to hear the cries, though she heard not his words. Curious to learn why the people collected around him, she sent one of her women to inquire what he sold.

The slave soon returned, laughing so heartily that the princess was angry. Madam, said the slave, laughing still, this fellow has a basket on his arm, full of fine new lamps, asking to change them for old ones; the children and mob, crowding about him so that he can hardly stir, make all the noise they can in derision of him.

Another female slave, hearing this, said, Now you speak of lamps, I know not whether the princess may have observed it, but there is an old one upon a shelf of the prince's robing room, and whoever owns it will not be sorry to find a new one in its stead.

The princess, who knew not the value of this lamp, commanded a slave to take it, and make the exchange. The slave obeyed, went out of the hall, and no sooner got to the palace gates than he saw the African magician, called to him, and showing him the old lamp, said, Give me a new lamp for this.

The magician never doubted but this was the lamp he wanted. There could be no other such in this palace, where every utensil was gold or silver. He snatched it eagerly out of the slave's hand, and thrusting it as far as he could into his breast, offered him his basket, and bade him choose which he liked best. The slave picked out one, and carried it to the princess; but the exchange was no sooner made than the place rang with the shouts of the children, deriding the magician's folly.

The African magician gave everybody leave to laugh as much as they pleased; and as soon as he was out of the square between the two palaces, he hastened down the streets which were the least frequented; and having no more occasion for his lamps or basket, set all down in an alley where nobody saw him: then going down another street or two, he walked till he came to one of the city gates, and pursuing his way through the suburbs, at length reached a lonely spot, where he passed the remainder of the day. When night came he pulled the lamp out of his breast and rubbed it. At that summons the genie appeared, and said,

214

ALADDIN; OR, THE WONDERFUL LAMP

What wouldst thou have? I am ready to obey thee as thy slave, and the slave of all those who have that lamp in their hands, both I and the other slaves of the lamp. I command thee, replied the magician, to transport me immediately and the palace which thou and the other slaves of the lamp have built in this city, with all the people in it, to Africa. The genie made no reply, but immediately transported him and the palace entire to the spot whither he was desired to convey it.

The sultan was so surprised at not finding the palace upon which he was used to gaze, that he called the grand vizier to him in order that he might give his opinion. The grand vizier, who feared and disliked Aladdin, was not slow to advise the sultan to have him arrested. He would have had him put to death but that the people threatened to rebel if this were done.

The sultan in his wrath sent for Aladdin, and said to him: Where is your palace? Indeed, answered Aladdin, I cannot tell you; but pray sir, give me forty days, and if at the end of that time I do not restore it to its place, I offer my head as a forfeit. Go then, said the sultan, but forget not to return in forty days.

Aladdin went out of the sultan's presence in great humiliation, so that he durst not lift up his eyes. The

' The sultan was so surprised at not finding the palace . . .'

215

principal officers of the court, who had all professed themselves his friends, turned their backs to avoid seeing him. He was quite distraught, and wandered about the city vainly asking if any one had seen his palace.

Having spent three days in this way, he at length went into the country, determined to end his life. As he approached the river in which he intended to drown himself, he slipped and fell, and in falling rubbed the magic ring, which he still wore, but of which he had forgotten the power. Immediately the genie whom he had seen in the cave appeared, and said : What wouldst thou ? I am thy slave ; the slave of the ring. Genie, said Aladdin, agreeably surprised at this unexpected help, transport me immediately to the spot whither my palace has been removed. No sooner were these words spoken than Aladdin found himself in Africa, beside his own palace, under the princess's window.

It so happened that shortly after the Princess Buddir al Buddoor came to the window, and seeing Aladdin was overcome with joy. Come, she cried, to the private door, and hasten to me. Aladdin's joy was no less than that of the princess ; he tenderly embraced her, and then asked : Tell me what has become of the lamp that stood on the shelf in my room. Alas, replied the princess, I foolishly changed it for a new one, not knowing its power, and the next morning found myself in this place, which I am told is Africa. Then, since we are in Africa, said Aladdin, I know that this must be the doing of the African magician. Can you tell me where he keeps the lamp ?

The princess told him that the magician always carried the lamp in the bosom of his dress, for that he had shown it to her. Then, said Aladdin, we may yet punish this wicked magician. Let the private door be opened to me directly I return : for the first thing is to secure the lamp.

Aladdin set out and soon descried a wayfarer who was over-joyed to change clothes with him, and went to a druggist's and asked for a certain powder, which was very costly. The druggist looked askance, but Aladdin showed him a purse full of gold and demanded half a dram, with which he returned quickly to the palace. He entered by the private door; and hastening to the princess's apartment he said to her : When the magician comes to visit you, you must be most gracious to him. Entertain him as becomes you, and ere he leaves request him to drink to you. Then give him this cup, in which there is a powder that will send him to sleep. While he sleeps we can secure the lamp whose slaves will do our bidding, and we shall be restored to China once more.

The princess most carefully performed all that Aladdin had directed, and when the magician came as usual to pay her a visit, he was agreeably surprised to find her waiting to receive him with a smile. He spent some time with her ; and then, at her request, drank the cup of wine before leaving. Immediately he had swallowed it he fell back on the sofa dead, and the princess gave the signal which she had arranged with Aladdin.

'. . . . a *wayfarer who was overjoyed to change clothes with him.*'

As soon as Aladdin entered the hall, the princess rose from her seat, and ran over-joyed to embrace him ; but he stopped her, and said, Princess, it is not yet time ; oblige me by retiring to your apartment ; and let me be left alone a moment, while I endeavour to transport you back to China as speedily as you were brought from thence.

When the princess and her women were gone out of the hall, Aladdin shut the door, and going directly to the dead body of the magician, opened his vest, took out the lamp—which was carefully wrapped up, as the princess had told him—and unfolding and rubbing it, the genie immediately appeared. Genie, said Aladdin, I command thee to transport this palace instantly into China, to the place from whence it was brought hither. Immediately the palace was transported into China,

'. . . he fell back dead.'

and its removal was only felt by two little shocks—the one when it was lifted up, the other when it was set down, and both in a very short interval of time.

The sultan, who rose early, looked, as was his wont, in sorrow over the empty space; but perceiving that the palace had been replaced, he was overjoyed. He at once called for his horse and rode over to the palace, to welcome the return of his daughter and Aladdin. Aladdin, who had foreseen this visit, had risen early, and was ready to receive the sultan in the hall, clothed in a most magnificent garment. He led the sultan straight to the princess's apartment, where the happy father fondly embraced his child. Son, said he, turning to Aladdin, forgive the harshness of my conduct towards you, which was inspired by paternal affection. Sir, replied Aladdin, you are not to blame ; that base magician was alone the cause of all my troubles.

Although the African magician was dead, he had a younger brother who was equally skilful as a necromancer, and even surpassed him in villainy and pernicious designs. These two brothers did not live together, but each year they communicated by means of their magic arts. Not having received any tidings of his elder brother, the younger one made an astrological inquiry, by which he discovered that he had been poisoned ; and, by a further investigation, he discovered that he was buried in the capital of China, near the dwelling of the man who had murdered him : who, he learned, was married to the sultan's daughter.

He at once set out to the capital of China to avenge his brother's death, and after a long and fatiguing journey reached the city, where he soon discovered that Aladdin was the poisoner whom he sought. He took a lodging in a khan, where he heard of the virtue and piety of a woman called Fatima, who was retired from the world, and of the miracles she wrought. As he fancied that this woman might be serviceable to him in the project he had conceived, he requested to be informed more particularly who that holy woman was, and what sort of miracles she performed.

What ! said the person whom he addressed, have you never seen or heard of her ? She is the admiration of the whole town, for her fasting, her austerities, and her exemplary life. Except Mondays and Fridays, she never stirs out of her little cell ; and on those days on which she comes into the town she does an infinite deal of good; for there is not a person but is cured by her laying her hand upon them.

That very night the magician went to Fatima's cell; and, having murdered her, he put on her clothes and went to the palace of Aladdin, bent upon revenge.

As soon as the people saw the holy woman, as they imagined him to be, they presently gathered about him in a great crowd.

'Put on her clothes and went to the palace.'

Some begged his blessing, others kissed his hand, and others, more reserved, only the hem of his garment; while others stooped for him to lay his hands upon them; which he did, muttering some words in form of prayer, and, in short, counterfeited so well, that everybody took him for the holy woman.

Though the progress was slow the magician at length reached the square in front of the palace. The princess happening to hear that the holy woman was there, and being desirous of seeing her, sent one of her slaves to bid her enter. The people, seeing the slave approach, fell back to allow him to approach Fatima. Holy woman, said he, the princess wishes to see you. The princess does me too great an honour, replied the false Fatima. I am ready to obey her command: and at the same time followed the slave to the palace, greatly delighted at the success of his plot.

When they had conversed, the princess said: My good mother, I have one thing to request, which you must not refuse me; it is, to stay with me, that you may edify me with your way of living; and that I may learn from your good example. Princess, said the counterfeit Fatima, I beg of you not to ask what I cannot consent to, without neglecting my prayers and devotion. That shall be no hindrance to you, answered the princess; I have a great many apartments unoccupied; you shall choose which you like best, and have as much liberty to perform your devotions as if you were in your own cell.

The magician, who desired nothing more than to introduce himself into the palace, where it would be a much easier matter for him to execute his designs, said, after a pause: Princess, whatever resolution a poor wretched woman as I am may have made to renounce the pomp and grandeur of this world, I dare not presume to oppose the will and commands of so pious and charitable a princess. He accordingly followed her with tottering gait.

Afterwards the princess requested him to dine with her; but he, considering that he should then be obliged to show his face, which he had always taken care to conceal; and fearing that the princess should find out that he was not Fatima, begged of her earnestly to excuse him, telling her that he never ate anything but bread and dried fruits, and desiring to eat that slight repast in his own apartment. The princess granted his request, saying, You may be as free here, good mother, as if you were in your own cell: I will order you a dinner, but remember I expect you as soon as you have finished your repast.

After the princess had dined, and the false Fatima had been

informed by one of the slaves that she was risen from table, he failed not to wait upon her. My good mother, said the princess, I am overjoyed to have the company of so holy a woman as yourself, who will confer a blessing upon this palace. But now I am speaking of the palace, Pray how do you like it? And before I show it all to you, tell me first what you think of this hall.

Upon this question, the counterfeit Fatima surveyed the hall from one end to the other, and said, As far as such a solitary being as I am, who am unacquainted with what the world calls beautiful, can judge, this hall is truly admirable and most beautiful; there wants but one thing. What is that, good mother? demanded the princess; tell me, I conjure you. For my part, I always believed, and have heard say, it wanted nothing; but if it does, it shall be supplied.

Princess, said the false Fatima, with great dissimulation, forgive me the liberty I have taken; but my opinion is, if it can be of any importance, that if a roc's egg were hung up in the middle of the dome, this hall would have no parallel in the four quarters of the world, and your palace would be the wonder of the universe.

My good mother, said the princess, what bird is a roc, and where may one get an egg? Princess, replied the pretended Fatima, it is a bird of prodigious size, which inhabits the summit of Mount Caucasus; the architect who built your palace can get you one.

The princess often thought of the roc's egg, and it annoyed her to think that anything was lacking from her palace; so when Aladdin returned she received him coldly, and said; I always believed that our palace was the most superb, magnificent and complete in the world; but I will tell you now what I find fault with upon examining the hall of four-and-twenty windows. Do not you think with me that it would be complete if a roc's egg were hung up in the midst of the dome? Princess, replied Aladdin, it is enough that you think there wants such an ornament; you shall see by the diligence used to supply that deficiency that there is nothing which I would not do for your sake.

Aladdin left the Princess Buddir al Buddoor that moment, and went up into the hall of four-and-twenty windows, where, pulling out of his bosom the lamp which, after the danger he had been exposed to, he always carried about him, he rubbed it, upon which the genie immediately appeared. Genie, said Aladdin, there wants a roc's egg to be hung up in the midst of the dome; I command thee, in the name of this lamp, to repair the deficiency. Aladdin had no sooner pronounced these words, than the genie gave so loud and terrible a cry that the hall shook, and Aladdin could scarcely stand upright. What! wretch, said the genie, in a voice that would have made the most undaunted man tremble, is it not enough that I and my companions have done everything for you, but you, by an unheard-of ingratitude, must command me to bring my master and hang him up in the midst of this dome? This attempt deserves that you, your wife, and your palace, should be immediately reduced to ashes: but you are happy that this request does not come from yourself. Know then, that the true author is the brother of the African magician, your enemy, whom you have destroyed as he deserved. He is now in your palace, disguised in the habit of the holy woman Fatima, whom he has murdered; and it is he who has suggested to your wife to make this pernicious demand. His design is to kill you, therefore take care of yourself. After these words the genie disappeared.

Aladdin quickly resolved what to do. He returned to the princess and pretended to be suddenly taken ill. The princess, remembering Fatima's power, at once sent for her, and she came with all speed. In the meantime the princess explained how the holy woman came into the palace, and when she appeared Aladdin smiled and bade her welcome at so opportune a moment. Surely, good woman, said he, you can cure me as you have others.

The counterfeit Fatima advanced towards him, with his hand all the time on a dagger concealed in his girdle under his

'. . . genie gave so loud and terrible a cry . . .'

gown. Aladdin perceived this, and snatched the weapon from his hand, and slew him on the spot.

My dear husband, what have you done? cried the princess in surprise. You have killed the holy woman. No, my princess, answered Aladdin with emotion, I have not killed Fatima, but a villain, who would have assassinated me if I had not prevented him. This wicked wretch, added he, uncovering his face, is brother to the African magician.

Thus was Aladdin delivered from the persecution of two brothers, who were magicians. Within a few years afterwards the sultan died in a good old age, and as he left no male children the Princess Buddir al Buddoor succeeded him, and she and Aladdin reigned together many years, and left a numerous and illustrious posterity.

Adventure of the Caliph
Haroun al Raschid

ONCE as the Caliph Haroun al Raschid, with Grand Vizier
Giafer, disguised as a merchant, was proceeding across
the bridge that spans the river Euphrates, in the middle
of the city of Bagdad, he met an old man who was blind, begging
for alms. The caliph gave him a piece of gold, and was much
surprised at the old man's request. For he said: Pray, sir,
give me a box on the ears, otherwise I shall be unable to accept
your alms, without breaking a solemn vow.

After some hesitation the caliph obeyed this strange request,
and gave him a very slight blow, and continued on his walk.
When they had gone a little way the caliph said to the vizier,
Return and tell that blind man to come to my palace to-morrow
at the hour of afternoon prayer, for I would fain hear his history,
which must be strange. The vizier hastened to obey, and then
resumed his walk with the caliph.

When they came into the town, they found in a square a
great crowd of spectators, looking at a handsome young man
who was mounted on a mare, which he drove and urged full
speed round the palace, spurring and whipping the poor creature
so barbarously that she was all over sweat and blood. The
caliph was much distressed, and bade the vizier summon the

226

young man to the palace also, that he might know why he ill-treated the mare so.

They then turned towards the palace, and on the way thither the caliph espied a handsome building which he had noticed before. Who lives there? said he. The vizier made inquiries, and learnt that it was one Cogia Hassan, surnamed Alhabbal, which means rope maker, since that was his trade. The caliph was much interested, and commanded the vizier to summon him also to the palace on the morrow.

The next day, therefore, the three men repaired to the palace, where they were introduced into the caliph's presence by the grand vizier.

They all three prostrated themselves before the throne, and when they rose up, the caliph asked the blind man his name, who answered, it was Baba Abdalla.

Baba Abdalla, said the caliph, tell me why you require those who give you alms to give you a box on the ear. The blind man, having bowed low, replied: Sir, I will tell you; and then you will see the apparently strange action is but a slight penance for a great crime of which I am guilty.

The Story of Baba Abdalla

COMMANDER of the faithful, continued Baba Abdalla, I was born at Bagdad, and at an early age found myself in possession of considerable wealth, and soon began to trade with all the cities of your realm.

One of my journeys led me to Bussorah. When I was returning with my laden camels, I met a dervise, with whom, after we had each satisfied the other's curiosity, I sat down to eat.

During our repast the dervise told me that he knew of a spot close by where there were such immense riches, that if all my fourscore camels were loaded with the gold and jewels that might be taken from it, they would not be missed.

I was delighted by what I heard, and begged the dervise to conduct me to the spot, whereupon he replied: I am ready to conduct you to the place where the treasure lies, and we will load your fourscore camels with jewels and gold, as much as they can carry, on condition that when they are so loaded you will let me have one half, and you be contented with the other; after which we will separate and take our camels where we may think fit. You see there is nothing but what is strictly equitable in this division; for if you give me forty camels, you will procure by my means wherewithal to purchase thousands.

Although avarice made me loath to forego so much, I had no alternative but to accept the terms the dervise offered. When he had heard my decision he led me to the place.

THE STORY OF BABA ABDALLA

It was a valley situated between two high mountains, so secluded that there was no fear of discovery. When we arrived the dervise bade me stop my camels, and he quickly collected

'. . . revealing a magnificent palace in the side of the mountain.'

some sticks and proceeded to kindle a fire, pronouncing over it an incantation. A dense smoke arose from the fire, and when this had cleared away I perceived that the sides of the cliff opposite to us had rolled back, revealing a magnificent palace in

229

the side of the mountain, with great heaps of treasure lying about.

I was as rapacious as a bird of prey in the way I seized the gold and filled my sacks, until I perceived that the dervise paid more heed to the jewels, when I followed his example, so that we took away more jewels than gold. Among other things the dervise took a small golden vase, which he showed me contained nothing more than a glutinous ointment; and after we had loaded our camels he closed the rock by using some mystic words.

'. . . I called to him as loud as I could.'

We now divided our camels, each taking forty, and travelled together till we came to the great road, where we were to part; the dervise to go to Bussorah, and I to Bagdad. We embraced each other with great joy, and taking our leave pursued our different routes.

I had not gone far before the demon of ingratitude and envy took possession of my heart, and I deplored the loss of my camels, but much more the riches wherewith they were loaded. The dervise, said I to myself, has no occasion for all this wealth,

280

since he is master of the treasure, and may have as much as he pleases ; so I gave myself up to the blackest ingratitude, and determined immediately to take the camels with their loading from him.

To execute this design I called to him as loud as I could, giving him to understand that I had something material to say to him, and made a sign to him to stop, which he accordingly did.

When I came up to him, I said, Brother, I had no sooner parted from you, but a thought came into my head, which neither of us had reflected on before. You are a recluse dervise, used to live in tranquillity, disengaged from all the cares of the world, and intent only upon serving God. You know not, perhaps, what trouble you have taken upon yourself, to take care of so many camels. If you would take my advice, you would keep but thirty ; you will find them sufficiently troublesome to manage. Take my word ; I have had experience.

The dervise, who seemed rather afraid of me, at once made me choose ten from his forty. This I promptly did, and drove them after my forty. I was much surprised by his ready compliance, and my avarice increased. Brother, said I, thirty camels are too many for you to manage, since you are not used to the work, therefore I beg of you relieve yourself of ten more.

My discourse had the desired effect upon the dervise, who gave me, without any hesitation, the other ten camels ; so that he had but twenty left, and I was master of sixty, and might boast of greater riches than any sovereign princes. Any one would have thought I should now have been content ; but I became more greedy and desirous of the other twenty camels.

I redoubled my solicitations and importunities to make the dervise condescend to grant me ten of the twenty, which he did with a good grace : and as to the other ten he had left, I embraced him, kissed his feet, and caressed him, conjuring him not to refuse me, but to complete the obligation I should ever be under to him, so that at length he crowned my joy, by giving me them also. Then a thought came into my head, that the little box of unguent which the dervise showed me had something in it more precious than all the riches I had, and so I longed to possess it, and said : What will you do with that little box of ointment ? It seems such a trifle, it is not worth carrying away. I request you to make me a present of it ; for what occasion has a dervise, as you are, who has renounced the vanities of the world, for perfumes, or scented unguents ?

Would to heaven he had refused me that box ; but if he had, I was stronger than he, and resolved to have taken it from him by force ; that for my complete satisfaction it might not be said he had carried away the smallest part of the treasure.

The dervise readily pulled it out of his bosom, and presenting it to me with the best grace in the world, said : Here, take it, brother, and be content ; if I could do more for you, you needed but to have asked me ; I should have been ready to satisfy you.

When I had the box in my hand, I opened it, and looking at the unguent, said to him : Since you are so good, I am sure you will not refuse the favour to tell me the particular use of this ointment.

The use is very surprising and wonderful, replied the dervise : if you apply a little of it round the left eye, you will see at once all the treasures contained in the bosom of the earth ; but if you apply it to the right eye, it will make you blind.

At my request the dervise applied some of the ointment to my left eye, when I found that he had indeed spoken truly. I saw incalculable riches, and longed to grasp them all. But thinking that the dervise merely wished to hide something from me, when he said, that, if applied to the right eye, loss of sight would ensue, I bade him put some round that eye.

Pray remember, said the dervise, that you will immediately become blind.

Far from being persuaded of the truth of what the dervise

said, I imagined, on the contrary, that there was some new mystery, which he meant to hide from me. Brother, replied I,

'. . . *applied some of the ointment to my left eye.*'

smiling, I see plainly you wish to mislead me; it is not natural that this ointment should have two such contrary effects.

The matter is as I tell you, replied the dervise, taking the name of God to bear witness; you ought to believe me, for I cannot disguise the truth.

I would not believe the dervise, who spoke like an honest man. My insurmountable desire of seeing at my will all the treasures in the world, and perhaps of enjoying those treasures to the extent I coveted, had such an effect on me, that I could not hearken to his remonstrances, nor be persuaded of what was, however, but too true, as to my lasting misfortune I soon experienced.

I persuaded myself that if the unguent, by being applied to the left eye, had the virtue of showing me all the treasures of the earth, by being applied to the right, it might have the power of putting them at my disposal. Possessed with this thought, I obstinately pressed the dervise to apply the ointment to my right eye; but he as positively refused. Brother, said he, after I have done you so much service, I cannot resolve to do you so great an injury; consider with yourself what a misfortune it is to be deprived of one's eyesight: do not reduce me to the hard necessity of obliging you in a thing which you will repent of all your life.

I persisted in my obstinacy, and said to him in strong terms, Brother, I earnestly desire you to lay aside all your difficulties. You have granted me most generously all that I have asked of you hitherto, and would you have me go away dissatisfied with you at last about a thing of so little consequence? For God's sake, grant me this last favour; whatever happens I will not lay the blame on you, but take it upon myself alone.

The dervise made all the resistance possible, but seeing that I was able to force him to do it, he took a little of the fatal ointment, and applied it to my right eye. But alas! when I came to open it, I could distinguish nothing with either eye, and became blind as you now see me.

Ah! dervise, I exclaimed in agony, what you forewarned me of has proved but too true. Fatal curiosity, added I, insatiable desire of riches, into what an abyss of miseries have they cast me! But you, dear brother, who are so charitable and good, among the many wonderful secrets you are acquainted with, have you not one to restore to me my sight again?

Miserable wretch! answered the dervise, if you would have been advised by me, you would have avoided this misfortune, but you have your deserts; the blindness of your mind was the cause of the loss of your eyes. Pray to God, therefore, if you believe there is one; it is He alone that can restore it to you. He gave you riches, of which you were unworthy, on that account takes them from you again, and will by my hands give them to men not so ungrateful as yourself.

The dervise left me to myself overwhelmed with confusion, and plunged in inexpressible grief. After he had collected my camels, he drove them away, and pursued the road to Bussorah.

I cried out loudly as he was departing, and entreated him not to leave me in that miserable condition, but to conduct me at least to the first caravanserai; but he was deaf to my prayers and entreaties. Thus deprived of sight and all I had in the world, I should have died with affliction and hunger, if the next day a caravan returning from Bussorah had not received me charitably, and brought me back to Bagdad. After this manner was I reduced to beggary without resource. But to expiate my offence against God, I enjoined myself, by way of penance, a box on the ear from every charitable person who should commiserate my condition.

This, commander of the faithful, is the motive which seemed so strange to your majesty yesterday, and for which I ought to incur your indignation. I ask your pardon once more as your slave, and submit to receive the chastisement I deserve. Baba Abdalla, said the caliph, you may cease to beg publicly, for in future my grand vizier will pay you four silver dirhens, accompanied with your self-imposed penance, to show my appreciation of your remorse.

At these words, Baba Abdalla prostrated himself before the caliph's throne, returned him thanks, and wished him all happiness and prosperity.

285

The Story of Syed Nouman

THE caliph then commanded the young man to tell why
he so ill-treated the mare, whereupon he spoke as
follows: Sir, my name is Syed Nouman, and my history
is a strange one. I married a beautiful woman, named Amine,
whose strange conduct has caused my grief.

As it is the custom for us to marry without seeing or knowing whom we are to espouse, your majesty is sensible that a
husband has no reason to complain, when he finds that the wife
who has been chosen for him is not horribly ugly and deformed,
and that her carriage, wit, and behaviour make amends for
any slight bodily imperfections. The first time I saw my wife
with her face uncovered, we regarded each other with mutual
admiration. My wife never ate anything except a little rice,
which she consumed grain by grain, carrying the food to her
mouth with a silver bodkin. As I knew that this was not
sufficient to support life I became suspicious, and determined to
watch her. Therefore I lay awake at night, hoping to discover
an explanation of the mystery, and at last I was rewarded.
For one night, when she thought me fast asleep, she got out of
bed softly, dressed herself with great precaution, and went
softly out of the room. When she was gone, I arose, threw
my cloak over my shoulders, and followed her till I saw her
enter a burying-ground just by our house. There she joined
a ghoul, whose horrid feast I saw her partake. Much distressed
at this sight I returned home to bed, scarcely able to abide

286

'*There she joined a ghoul, . . .*'

my wife's presence, when she returned as noiselessly as she had gone.

The next day I went our early and remained away all day, but when I returned Amine ordered dinner to be served, and ate the rice in the same odd manner she did on previous occasions. Unable to look upon her in silence, I said : Are not my feasts as good as those provided by ghouls ? At these words Amine's face became terrible, and she cried in fury : Wretch, receive the punishment of thy prying curiosity, and become a dog !

Amine had no sooner pronounced these words, than I was immediately transformed into a dog. My wife then took up a stick and beat me unmercifully. After this she opened the door, and I rushed howling down the street pursued by a great many dogs, which snapped at me ferociously. To escape from them I ran into a shop where sheep's heads were exposed to view ; and later, seeing a lot of dogs waiting outside, I joined them and got something to eat. On the next day I went to a baker's shop, where the master received me kindly, and allowed me to stay with him.

I had lived some time with this baker, when a woman came one day into the shop to buy some bread, who gave my master a piece of bad money among some good, which he returned, and requested her to exchange. The woman refused to take it again, and affirmed it to be good. The baker maintained the contrary, and in the dispute told the woman he was sure that the piece of money was so visibly bad that his dog could distinguish it. Having called me, he said : See, and tell me which of these pieces is bad. I looked over all the pieces of money, and then set my paw upon that which was bad, separated it from the rest, looking in my master's face to show it him.

The baker was not a little surprised, and soon my fame became so great that the shop was crowded with customers. One day a woman entered, and having tested my ability, she beckoned me to follow her home. I understood what she meant, and went readily enough. We soon reached her house, when she bade me enter, and conducted me to her daughter, who was an enchantress. Daughter, said she, this is the famous dog, which I think is a man in disguise. Say, am I right? You are, replied the young lady, and I will quickly remove the enchantment.

The young lady arose from her sofa, put her hand into a basin of water, and, throwing some upon me, said, If thou wert born a dog, remain so; but if thou wert born a man, resume thy former shape, by the virtue of this water. At that instant the enchantment was broken, and I became restored to my natural form.

I thanked my deliverer, and was about to depart, when she said: Take of this water, and when you go home, throw it over your cruel wife, and say, ' Receive the reward of your evil deeds.' I did as she commanded, and immediately Amine became changed into a mare—the same you saw me upon yesterday. This is the punishment I inflict upon her. You have now heard my history, as you desired.

The caliph then said, Your wife indeed deserves her punishment, yet I would fain see you reconciled, were I sure that she would abstain from her evil ways, since I think she has suffered enough. Having spoken thus, he turned to Cogia Hassan, who told his story in obedience to the caliph's command.

The Story of Cogia Hassan Alhabbal

SIR, it is to my two friends Saadi and Saad that I, Cogia Hassan Alhabbal, the rope maker, owe all my present wealth : I will now tell you in what manner I acquired the riches. Saadi and Saad could never agree as to the chief factor of happiness. Saadi, who is very rich, was always of opinion that no man could be happy in this world without wealth, to live independent of every one. Saad was of a different opinion ; he agreed that riches were necessary to comfort, but maintained that the happiness of a man's life consisted in virtue, without any further eagerness after worldly goods than what was requisite for decent subsistence and benevolent purposes.

One day, as they were talking upon this subject, as I have since been informed by them both, Saadi said : I will make an experiment to convince you, by giving, for example, a sum of money to some artisan. And as they happened to be passing my shop, they saw me at work on my ropes. The Saad said : There is a man, pointing to me, whom I can remember a long time working at his trade of rope-making, and in the same poverty : he is a worthy subject for your liberality, and a proper person to make your experiment upon. The two friends came to me, and told me the object of their visit, after which Saadi pulled a purse out of his bosom, and, putting it into my hands, said : Here, take this purse ; you will find it contains two hundred pieces of gold : I pray God bless you with them, and

240

give you grace to make the good use of them I desire; and, believe me, my friend Saad whom you see here, and I shall

both take great pleasure in finding they may contribute towards making you more happy than you now are.

After I had duly thanked them the two friends departed, and I returned to my work to think over my good fortune. Then I began to wonder what I should do with the money, to keep it safe, for I had in my poor house neither box nor cupboard to lock it up in, nor any other place where I could be sure it would not be discovered if I concealed it.

In this perplexity I sewed up the gold, except ten pieces, which I kept out to provide for my immediate wants, in the folds of the linen which went about my turban. I then bought a fresh stock of hemp, and afterwards, as my family had eaten no meat for a long time, I went and bought something for supper.

As I was carrying home the meat I had bought, a famished vulture flew upon me, and would have taken

'. . . . a famished vulture flew upon me.'

it away, if I had not held it very fast. So fierce was the struggle that my turban fell on the ground.

The vulture immediately let go his hold, and, seizing my turban, flew away with it. I cried out so loud that I alarmed all the men, women, and children in the neighbourhood, who joined their shouts and cries to make the vulture quit his hold; but our cries did not avail; he carried off my turban, and we soon lost sight of him, and it would have been in vain for me to fatigue myself with running after him.

I went home very melancholy at the loss of my money. I was obliged to buy a new turban, which diminished the small remainder of the ten pieces; for I had laid out several in hemp. The little that was left was not sufficient to give me reason to indulge the great hopes I had conceived.

While the remainder of the ten pieces lasted, my little family and I lived better than usual; but I soon relapsed into the same poverty, and the same inability to extricate myself from wretchedness. However, I never murmured nor repined; though, when I told my neighbours I had lost a hundred and ninety pieces of gold, they only laughed at me.

When, at the end of six months, the two friends returned to my shop, I felt very much ashamed of the incredible story I had to tell them. Saadi scoffed at my word, and said: Hassan, you joke, and would deceive me. What have vultures to do with turbans? They only search for something to satisfy their hunger. Sir, I replied, I can call witnesses to prove my words. Then, to my surprise, Saad took my part, and told Saadi a great many stories of vultures, some of which he affirmed he knew to be true, insomuch that at last Saadi pulled out his purse, and counted out two hundred pieces of gold into my hand, which I put into my bosom for want of a purse, vowing to take more care of this generous present, for which he would not receive one word of thanks, but walked on quietly with his friend.

As soon as they were gone, I left off work, and went home; but finding neither my wife nor children within, I pulled out my money, put ten pieces by, and laid the rest in a vessel of bran which stood in the corner. My wife came home soon after, and as I had but little hemp in the house, I told her I should go out to buy some, without saying anything to her about the two friends.

'. . . laid the rest in a vessel of bran.'

While I was absent, a sandman, who sells scouring-earth, passed through our street. My wife wanted some, but as she had no money, she asked him if he would make an exchange of

243

some earth for some bran. This he agreed to do, and took the pot and bran along with him.

When I returned, I noticed that the vessel was gone, and I asked my wife what was become of it, when she told me the bargain she had made with the sandman, which she thought to be a very good one.

I then told her what a serious mistake she had made, and reproached her bitterly.

My wife was like one distracted when she knew what a fault she had committed. She cried, beat her breast, and tore her hair and clothes. Unhappy wretch that I am, cried she, am I fit to live after so dreadful a mistake? Where shall I find this sandman? I know him not, I never saw him in our street before. Oh! husband, added she, you were much to blame to be so reserved in a matter of such importance!

Wife, said I, moderate your grief; by your howling you will alarm the neighbourhood, and they will only laugh at, instead of pitying us.

After this I did not look forward with pleasure to the return of the two friends; in fact, when I saw them coming towards me, I could not look them in the face, but told what had happened with downcast eyes and a sorry heart. They listened in silence, and after I had finished the narration of my misfortunes I added: I see, sir, that it has pleased God, whose ways are secret and impenetrable, that I should not be enriched by your liberality, but that I must remain poor: however, the obligation is the same as if it had wrought the desired effect.

After these words I was silent; and Saadi, turning about to his friend Saad, said: You may now make your experiment, and let me see that there are ways, besides giving money, to make a poor man's fortune. Let Hassan be the man. I dare say, whatever you may give him, he will not be richer than he was with four hundred pieces of gold. Saad had a piece of lead in his hand, which he showed Saadi. You saw me, said he, take up this piece of lead, which I found on the ground: I will give it to Hassan, and you shall see what it is worth.

THE STORY OF COGIA HASSAN ALHABBAL

Saadi burst out a-laughing at Saad. What is that bit of lead worth? said he—a farthing? What can Hassan do with that? Saad presented it to me, and said, Take it, Hassan; let Saadi laugh; you will tell us some news of the good luck it has brought you one time or another. I thought Saad was in jest, and had a mind to divert himself: however, I took the lead, and thanked him. The two friends pursued their walk, and I fell to work again.

At night when I pulled off my clothes to go to bed, the piece of lead, which I had never thought of from the time he gave it me, tumbled out of my pocket. I took it up, and laid it on the place that was nearest me. The same night it happened that a fisherman, a neighbour, mending his nets, found a piece of lead wanting; and it being too late to buy any, as the shops were shut, he called to his wife and bade her inquire among the neighbours for a piece. She went from door to door on both sides of the street, but could not get any, and returned to tell her husband her ill success. He asked her if she had been to several of their neighbours, naming them, and among the rest my house. No, indeed, said the wife, I have not been there: that was too far off; and if I had gone, do you think I should have found any? I know by experience they never have anything when one wants it. No matter, said the fisherman, you must go there; for though you have been there a hundred times before without getting anything, you may chance to obtain what we want now.

The fisherman's wife went out grumbling, came and knocked at my door, and waked me out of a sound sleep. Hassan, said she, my husband wants a bit of lead to load his nets with, and if you have a piece, desires you to give it him. Remembering the piece which Saad had given me, I told my neighbour I had some; and if she would stay a moment, my wife should give it to her. Accordingly, my wife, who was awakened by the noise as well as myself, got up, and groping about where I directed her, found the lead, opened the door, and gave it to the fisherman's wife, who was so overjoyed that she promised my wife that in return for the kindness she did her and her husband, she would answer for him we should have the first cast of the nets.

The fisherman was so much rejoiced to see the lead, which he so little expected, that he much approved his wife's promise.

'. . . holding in his hand a fine fish.'

He finished mending his nets, and went a-fishing two hours before day, according to custom. At the first throw he caught but one fish, about a yard long, and proportionable in thickness; but afterwards had a great many successful casts; though of all the fish he took, none equalled the first in size.

The next morning, mindful of his wife's promise, he came to me, holding in his hand a fine fish, and said: Neighbour, my wife promised you last night, in return for your kindness, whatever fish I should catch at my first throw. It pleased God to send me no more than this one for you, which, such as it is, I desire you to accept. I wish it had been better.

Neighbour, said I, the bit of lead which I sent you was such a trifle that it ought not to be valued at so high a rate : neighbours should assist each other in their little wants. I have done no more for you than I should have expected from you had I been in your situation ; therefore I would refuse your present, if I were not persuaded you give it me freely, and that I should offend you ; and since you will have it so, I take it, and return you my hearty thanks.

After these civilities, I took the fish, and carried it home to my wife, who said that she could not cook it whole, as we had no utensil large enough. Do it as you can, said I, for any way it will be good. While my wife was preparing it, she found a large crystal, which she took for a piece of glass, and gave it to the youngest of our children for a plaything, and his brothers and sisters handed it about from one to another, to admire its brightness and beauty.

At night, when the lamp was lighted and the children were still playing with the crystal, they perceived that it gave a light, when my wife, who was getting them their supper, stood between them and the lamp. They began to squabble over its possession, so I called to the eldest to know what was the matter, who told me it was about a piece of glass, which shone in the dark. Curious to test the truth of this I put out the lamp, and found out that they were quite right.

Look, said I, this is another advantage which Saad's piece of lead has procured : we shall now be saved the expense of oil.

When the children saw the lamp was put out, and the bit of glass supplied the place, they cried out so loud, and made so great a noise from astonishment, that it aroused our neighbours, whose room was only separated by a thin partition. This neighbour was a Jew, a jeweller and very wealthy, and the next day he sent his wife to complain of being disturbed out of their first sleep. Good neighbour Rachel, which was the Jewess's name, said my wife, I am very sorry for what happened, and hope you will excuse it; you know it was caused by the children, and they will laugh and cry for a trifle. Come in, and I will show you what was the occasion of the noise.

The Jewess went in with her, and my wife, taking the diamond (for such it really was, and a very extraordinary one) out of the chimney, put it into her hands. See here, said she, it was this piece of glass that caused all the noise; and while the Jewess, who understood all sorts of precious stones, was examining the diamond with admiration, my wife told her how she found it.

Indeed, Ayesha, which was my wife's name, said the jeweller's wife, giving her the diamond again, I believe, as you do, it is a piece of glass; but as it is more beautiful than common glass, and I have just such another piece at home, I will buy it, if you will sell it.

The children, who heard them talking of selling their plaything, presently interrupted their conversation, crying and begging their mother not to part with it, who, to quiet them, promised she would not.

The Jewess being thus prevented in her intended swindling bargain by my children, went away, but first whispered to my wife, who followed her to the door, if she had a mind to sell it, not to show it to anybody without acquainting her.

No sooner had the Jewess informed her husband of the find she had made than he sent her to offer my wife twenty pieces of gold for the glass. But my wife would not part with it until she had consulted me. And as I happened to come home at that instant, my wife told me of the offer. I paused for a while, reflecting upon Saad's assurances that the piece of lead would make my fortune, but the Jewess, fancying that the low price she had offered was the reason I made no reply, said, I will give you fifty, neighbour, if that will do.

As soon as I found that she rose so suddenly from twenty to fifty, I told her that I expected a great deal more. Well, neighbour, said she, I will give you a hundred, but that is so much, I know not whether my husband will approve my offering it. At this new advance, I told her I would have a hundred thousand pieces of gold for it; that I saw plainly that the diamond, for such I now guessed it must be, was worth a great deal more, but to oblige her and her husband, as they were neighbours, I would limit myself to that price, which I was determined to have; and if they refused to give it, other jewellers should have it, who would give a great deal more.

The Jewess confirmed me in this resolution by her eagerness to conclude a bargain; and by coming up at several biddings to fifty thousand pieces, which I refused. I can offer you no more, said she, without my husband's consent. He will be at home at night; and I would beg the favour of you to let him see it, which I promised.

When the Jew himself came in the evening, I remained firm to my offer; and although he haggled, I refused to accept less than I had said. In the end he decided to pay what I asked, and deposited two bags, each containing one thousand pieces of gold, as surety, promising to pay the rest on the morrow. This he did according to our agreement, and I handed him the diamond.

In spite of my wife's request for rich clothing, I vowed not to lavish my wealth, but to lay the foundations of a great business. There I spent all that day and the next in going to the people of my own trade, who worked as hard every day for their bread as I had done; and giving them money beforehand, engaged them to work for me in different sorts of rope-making, according to their skill and ability, with a promise not to make them wait for their money, but to pay them as soon as their work was done.

By this means I obtained a monopoly of the rope trade of Bagdad, and was soon obliged to hire large warehouses. Later, wishing to have more spacious accommodation, I built that house you saw yesterday, which, though it makes so great an appearance, consists, for the most part, of warehouses for my business, with apartments absolutely necessary for myself and family.

Some time after I had left my old mean habitation, and removed to this, Saad and Saadi came to see how I had fared, and to their surprise learned that I had become a great manufacturer, and was no longer called plain Hassan, but Cogia Hassan Alhabbal, and that I had built, in a street which was named to them, a house like a palace.

They immediately set out to congratulate me upon my success; and as I happened to see them coming, I was able to receive them with a becoming display of gratitude. After we were seated, Saadi said: Cogia Hassan, pray tell us by what skill you have converted the four hundred pieces of gold I gave you into so great a fortune. Saad here interposed, saying: Why do you still doubt our friend's veracity? Let him tell us himself to which of us he owes his wealth.

After this discourse of the two friends, I told them every circumstance your majesty has heard, without forgetting the least.

My words were powerless to convince Saadi, who persisted in claiming the honour of having made me rich. And as, when the discussion was ended, it was late, they made ready to depart. But I detained them, saying: Gentlemen, there is one favour I have to ask: I beg of you not to refuse to do me the honour to stay and take a slight supper with me, also a bed to-night, and to-morrow I will carry you by water to a small country house, which I bought for the sake of the air, and we will return the same day on my horses.

They courteously accepted my invitation, and while supper was being prepared I showed them over my house and garden, which they admired. But their praises were loudest when we reached the supper-room, where everything was provided for their delectation.

The next morning, as we had agreed to set out early to enjoy the fresh air, we repaired to the riverside by sunrise, and went on board a pleasure boat well carpeted that waited for us;

and in less than an hour and a half, with six good rowers and the stream, we arrived at my country house.

I conducted my guests over the house, and afterwards into the gardens, where, at the end of the garden, was a wood of handsome trees.

As we stood watching two of my boys, whom I sent into the country, ran into the wood, and seeing a nest which was built in the branches of a lofty tree, they sent a slave up to fetch it. The slave, when he came to it, was much surprised to find it composed of a turban: and when he reached the ground, he recommended the boys to bring it to me, that I might see the curiosity. After I had examined it well, and turned it about, I said to my guests, Gentlemen, have you memories good enough to remember the turban I had on the day you did me the honour first to speak to me? I do not think, said Saad, that either my friend or I gave any attention to it;

'They sent a slave up to fetch it.'

251

but if the hundred and ninety pieces of gold are in it, we cannot doubt of it.

I am convinced that the gold is here, said I, for it is very heavy. Before I undo it, however, I beg you to notice its weather-stained appearance, showing that it has been in the tree a long time.

I then pulled off the linen cloth which was wrapped about the cap of the turban, and took out the purse, which Saadi knew to be the same he had given me. I emptied it on the carpet before them, and said, There, gentlemen, there is the money; I will count it, and see if it be right, and found it to be one hundred and ninety pieces of gold. Then Saadi, who could not deny so manifest a truth, addressing himself to me, said, I agree, Cogia Hassan, that this money could not serve to enrich you; but the other hundred and ninety pieces, which you would make me believe you hid in a pot of bran, might. I vowed that it was not so; and after that no more was said about the matter. We entered the house and had dinner, and in the cool of the evening rode back to Bagdad in the moonlight.

It happened, I know not by what negligence of my servants, that we were then out of grain for the horses, and the store-houses were all shut up; when one of my slaves, seeking about the neighbourhood for some, met with a pot of bran in a shop; bought the bran, and brought the pot along with him, promising to carry it back again the next day. The slave emptied the bran, and dividing it with his hands among the horses, felt a linen cloth tied up, and very heavy; he brought the cloth to me in the condition that he found it, and presented it to me.

I immediately recognised it, and, running to my guests, said, See, here are the other hundred and ninety pieces of gold. As further proof I sent the pot to my wife, who quickly identified it as the one she had exchanged for the earth.

Saadi readily submitted, renounced his incredulity; and said to Saad, I yield to you, and acknowledge that money is not always the means of becoming rich.

Saadi would not hear of receiving back the money; therefore

we decided to bestow it in charity.   And when the two friends, Saadi and Saad, left on the next day we had sworn eternal friendship, which has endured ever since.

The caliph then expressed his satisfaction with their story, and said that the diamond was now in his treasury, and that he valued it above all his jewels.   And, added he, bring your friends here that they may see it.

After these words the caliph gave Cogia Hassan, Syed Nouman and Baba Abdalla leave to depart, having expressed his approval of their histories.

The Story of Ali Cogia a merchant of Bagdad

IN the reign of the Caliph Haroun al Raschid, there lived at Bagdad a merchant whose name was Ali Cogia, a man of moderate means. He lived in the house which had been his father's, independent, and content with the profit he made by his trade. It happened that he had a remarkable dream for three successive nights. In it a venerable old man came to him, and, with a severe look, reprimanded him for not having made a pilgrimage to Mecca. This troubled him much, for he knew that his faith demanded that he should pay his respects to the holy city, and after this vision dared not tarry any longer without performing his duty. He therefore sold off his household goods, his shop, and with it the greatest part of his merchandise, reserving only some articles, which he thought he might turn to a better account at Mecca.

Having let his house also, he took his small savings, amounting to one thousand pieces of gold, and put them in a jar, which he filled up with olives, and deposited with a friend, who promised to take care of the jar, not knowing what lay under the olives, until he returned. He then joined a caravan which was about to set out, and started on his pilgrimage.

Ali Cogia reached Mecca in safety, and having paid a visit to the holy mosques, he thought about disposing of the goods he had brought with him. For this reason he exposed them in the bazaar for sale.

254

Two merchants passing by, and seeing Ali Cogia's goods, thought them so choice that they stopped some time to look at, though they had no occasion for, them; and when they had satisfied their curiosity, one of them said to the other, as they were going away, If this merchant knew to what profit these goods would turn at Cairo he would carry them thither, and not sell them here, though this is a good mart.

Ali Cogia heard these words; and as he had often heard talk of the beauties of Egypt, he was resolved to take the opportunity of seeing them, by performing a journey thither. Therefore, after having packed up his goods again, instead of returning to Bagdad, he set out for Egypt, with the caravan of Cairo, where he very quickly sold his goods at a large profit. With the money he bought others, with an intent to go to Damascus. It was some time before a caravan started, and in the interval he visited all the places of interest around Cairo and on the banks of the Nile. When the caravan was ready Ali Cogia joined it, and, having visited Jerusalem on the way, arrived at Damascus after a satisfactory journey.

Ali Cogia found Damascus so delicious a place, being environed by verdant meadows, pleasantly watered, and delightful gardens, that it exceeded the descriptions given of it in the journals of travellers. Here he made a long abode, but, nevertheless, did not forget his native Bagdad: for which place he at length set out, and arrived at Aleppo, where he made some stay; and from thence, after having passed the Euphrates, he bent his course to Moussul, with an intention, on his return, to come by a shorter way down the Tigris.

When Ali Cogia came to Moussul, some Persian merchants, with whom he had travelled from Aleppo, and with whom he had contracted a great friendship, easily persuaded him not to leave them till he should have visited Schiraz, from whence he might easily return to Bagdad with a considerable profit. They led him through the towns of Sultania, Rei, Coam, Caschan, Ispahan, and from thence to Schiraz; from whence he had the complaisance to bear them company to Hindustan, and then returned with them again to Schiraz; insomuch that, including the stay made in every town, he was seven years absent from Bagdad, whither he then resolved to return.

All this time his friend, with whom he had left his jar of olives, neither thought of him nor them; but at the time when he was on the road with a caravan from Schiraz, one evening as this merchant was supping with his family, the discourse happened to fall upon olives, and his wife was desirous to eat some, saying, she had not tasted any for a long while. Now you speak of olives, said the merchant, you put me in mind of a jar which Ali Cogia left with me seven years ago, when he went to Mecca; and put it himself in my warehouse to be kept for him against he returned. What is become of him I know not; though when the caravan came back, they told me he had gone to Egypt. Certainly he must be dead, since he has not returned in all this time; and we may eat the olives, if they prove good. Give me a plate and a candle; I will go and fetch some of them, and we will taste them.

'. . . by shaking the jar, some of the gold tumbled out.'

The wife tried to persuade her husband not to touch the property of another, but he would not heed, and went to get the olives.

When he came into the warehouse, he opened the jar, and found the olives mouldy; but to see if they were all so to the

256

bottom, he turned some of them upon the plate ; and by shaking the jar, some of the gold tumbled out.

At the sight of the gold the merchant, who was naturally covetous, looked into the jar, perceived that he had shaken out almost all the olives, and what remained was gold coin. He immediately put the olives into the jar again, covered it up, and returned to his wife. Indeed, wife, said he, you were in the right to say that the olives were all mouldy ; for I found them so, and have made up the jar just as Ali Cogia left it ; so that he will not perceive that they have been touched, if he should return. You had better have taken my advice, said the wife, and not have meddled with them. God grant no mischief happens in consequence !

The merchant was not more affected with his wife's last words than he had been by her former, but spent almost the whole night in thinking how he might appropriate Ali Cogia's gold to his own use, and keep possession of it in case he should return and ask him for the jar. The next morning he went and bought some olives of that year, took out the old with the gold, and filled the jar with the new, covered it up, and put it in the place where Ali Cogia had left it.

About a month after the merchant had committed this unworthy action, Ali Cogia arrived at Bagdad ; and as he had let his house, alighted at a khan, choosing to stay there till he had announced his arrival to his tenant, and given him time to provide himself with another residence.

The next morning Ali Cogia went to pay a visit to the merchant his friend, who received him in the most obliging manner, and expressed great joy at his return, after so many years' absence, telling him that he had begun to lose all hope of ever seeing him again. After the usual compliments on both sides on such a meeting, Ali Cogia desired the merchant to return him the jar of olives which he had left with him, and to excuse the liberty he had taken in giving him so much trouble.

My dear friend, replied the merchant, you are to blame to make those apologies. Your vessel has been no inconvenience to me; on such an occasion I should have made as free with you: there is the key of my warehouse, go and fetch your jar; you will find it in the place where you left it.

Ali Cogia went into the merchant's warehouse, took his jar, and after having returned him the key with thanks for the favour he had done him, returned with it to the khan where he lodged; but on opening the jar, and putting his hand down as low as the pieces of gold had laid, was greatly surprised to find none. His astonishment was so great that he stood some time motionless; then lifting up his hands and eyes to heaven, he exclaimed, 'Is it possible that a man, whom I took for my friend, should be guilty of such baseness?'

Ali Cogia, alarmed at the apprehension of so considerable a loss, returned immediately to the merchant. My good friend, said he, be not surprised to see me come back so soon. I own the jar of olives to be the same I placed in your warehouse; but with the olives I put into it a thousand pieces of gold, which I do not find. Perhaps you might have occasion for them, and have employed them in trade: if so, they are at your service till it may be convenient for you to return them; only put me out of my pain, and give me an acknowledgment, after which you may pay me at your own convenience.

The merchant, who had expected that Ali Cogia would come with such a complaint, had meditated an answer.

Ali Cogia, said he, you agree that you left a jar of olives with me; and now you have taken it away, you come and ask me for a thousand pieces of gold. Did you ever tell me that such a sum was in the jar? I did not even know that they were olives, for you never showed them to me. I wonder you do not ask me for diamonds and pearls instead of gold; be gone about your business, and do not raise a mob about my warehouse; for some persons had already collected. These words were pronounced in such great heat and passion, as not only made those who stood about the warehouse already stay longer, and create a greater mob, but the neighbouring merchants came out of their shops to learn what the dispute was between Ali

Cogia and the merchant, and endeavour to reconcile them; but when Ali Cogia had informed them of his grievance, they asked the merchant what he had to say.

The merchant owned that he had kept the jar for Ali Cogia in his warehouse, but denied that ever he meddled with it; swore that he knew it contained olives only because Ali Cogia told him so, and requested them all to bear witness of the insult and affront offered him. You bring it upon yourself, said Ali Cogia, taking him by the arm; but since you use me so basely, I cite you to the law of God: let us see whether you will have the assurance to say the same thing before the cauzee.

With all my heart, said the merchant; we shall soon see who is in the wrong.

Ali Cogia carried the merchant before the magistrate, where he accused him of having, by breach of trust, defrauded him of a thousand pieces of gold, which he had left with him. The cauzee demanded if he had any witnesses; to which he replied, that he had not taken that precaution, because he had believed the person he trusted his money with to be his friend, and always took him for an honest man. The merchant made the same defence he had done before the merchants his neighbours, offering to make oath that he never had the money he was accused of, and that he not so much as knew there was such a sum; upon which the cauzee took his oath, and dismissed him acquitted for want of evidence.

Ali Cogia, extremely mortified to find that he must sit down with so considerable a loss, protested against the sentence, declaring to the cauzee that he would appeal to the caliph, who would do him justice; which protestation the magistrate regarded as the effect of the common resentment of those who lose their cause; and thought he had done his duty in acquitting a person who had been accused without witnesses.

While the merchant returned home triumphing over Ali Cogia, and overjoyed at his good fortune, the latter went and drew up a petition; and the next day, observing the time when the caliph came from noontide prayers, placed himself in the street he was to pass through; and holding out his hand with the petition, an officer appointed for that purpose, who always goes before the caliph, came and took it to present it.

As Ali Cogia knew that it was the caliph's custom to read the petitions on his return to the palace, he went into the court, and waited till the officer who had taken the petition came out of the caliph's apartment, who told him that the caliph had appointed an hour to hear him next day; and then asking him

'. . . holding out his hand with the petition, . . .'

where the merchant lived, he sent to notify to him to attend at the same time.

That same evening, the caliph, accompanied by the grand vizier, Giafer, and Mesrour, captain of the guard, went disguised through the town, as he often did; when, on passing through a street, the caliph heard a noise, and mending his pace, came to a gateway, which led into a little court, in which he perceived ten or twelve children playing by moonlight.

The caliph, who was curious to know at what play the children

were engaged, sat down on a stone bench just by ; and heard one
of the liveliest of the children say, Let us play at the cauzee.
I will be the magistrate ; bring Ali Cogia and the merchant
who cheated him of the thousand pieces of gold before me.

As the affair of Ali Cogia and the merchant had made a great
noise in Bagdad, it had not escaped the children, who all accepted
the proposition with joy, and agreed on the part each was to
act. Not one of them refused him who made the proposal to be
cauzee ; and when he had taken his seat, which he did with all
the seeming gravity of a judge, another, as an officer of the
court, presented two boys before him : one as Ali Cogia, and the
other as the merchant against whom he complained.

The pretended cauzee then directing his discourse to the
feigned Ali Cogia, asked him what he had to lay to that merchant's charge. Ali Cogia, after a low obeisance, informed the
young cauzee of the act, related every particular, and afterwards
begged that he would use his authority, that he might not lose
so considerable a sum of money. The feigned cauzee, turning
about to the merchant, then asked him why he did not return
the money which Ali Cogia demanded of him. The feigned
merchant alleged the same reasons as the real merchant had done
before the cauzee himself, and offered to confirm by oath that
what he had said was truth.

Not so fast, replied the pretended cauzee ; before you come
to your oath, I should be glad to see the jar of olives. Ali
Cogia, said he, addressing himself to the boy who acted that part,
have you brought the jar ? No, replied he. Then go and fetch
it immediately, said the other.

The pretended Ali Cogia went immediately, and returning,
feigned to set a jar before the cauzee, telling him that it was
the same he had left with the accused person, and received from
him again. But, to omit no part of the formality, the supposed
cauzee asked the merchant if it was the same ; and as by his
silence he seemed not to deny it, he ordered it to be opened.
He that represented Ali Cogia seemed to take off the cover,
and the pretended cauzee made as if he looked into it. They

261

are fine olives, said he, let me taste them ; and then pretending to eat some, added, They are excellent : but, continued he, I cannot think that olives will keep seven years, and be so good ; therefore send for some olive merchants, and let me hear what is their opinion. Two boys, as olive merchants, then presented themselves. Are you olive merchants ? said the sham cauzee. Tell me how long olives will keep fit to eat ?

Sir, replied the two merchants, let us take what care we can, they will hardly be worth anything the third year ; for then they have neither taste nor colour. If it be so, answered the cauzee, look into that jar, and tell me how long it is since those olives were put into it ?

The two merchants pretended to examine and to taste the olives, and told the cauzee they were new and good. You are mistaken, said the young cauzee ; Ali Cogia says he put them into the jar seven years ago. Sir, replied the merchants, we can assure you they are of this year's growth ; and we will maintain there is not a merchant in Bagdad but will say the same.

The feigned merchant who was accused would have objected against the evidence of the olive merchants ; but the pretended cauzee would not suffer him. Hold your tongue, said he, you are a rogue ; let him be impaled. The children then concluded their play, clapping their hands with great joy, and seizing the feigned criminal to carry him to execution.

Words cannot express how much the caliph Haroun al Raschid admired the sagacity and sense of the boy who had passed so just a sentence, in an affair which was to be pleaded before himself the next day. He withdrew, and rising off the bench, asked the grand vizier, who heard all that had passed, what he thought of it. Indeed, Commander of the True Believers, answered the grand vizier, I am surprised to find so much sagacity in one so young.

But, answered the caliph, do you know one thing ? I am to pronounce sentence in this very cause to-morrow ? the true Ali Cogia presented his petition to me to-day ; and do you think, continued he, that I can give a better sentence ? I think

not, answered the vizier, if the case is as the children represented it. Take notice then of this house, said the caliph, and
bring the boy to me to-morrow, that he may try this cause in
my presence; and also order the cauzee, who acquitted the
merchant, to attend to learn his duty from a child. Take care
likewise to bid Ali Cogia bring his jar of olives with him, and let
two olive merchants attend. After this charge he pursued his
rounds, without meeting with anything worth his attention.

The next day the vizier went to the house where the caliph
had been a witness of the children's play, and asked for the
master; but he being abroad, his wife appeared thickly veiled.
He asked her if she had any children. To which she answered,
she had three; and called them. My brave boys, said the vizier,
which of you was the cauzee when you played together last
night? The eldest made answer, it was he: but, not knowing
why he asked the question, coloured. Come along with me,
my lad, said the grand vizier; the Commander of the Faithful
wants to see you.

The mother was alarmed when she saw the grand vizier
would take her son with him, and asked, upon what account
the caliph wanted him? The grand vizier encouraged her, and
promised that he should return again in less than an hour's time,
when she would know it from himself. If it be so, sir, said the
mother, give me leave to dress him first, that he may be fit to
appear before the Commander of the Faithful. As soon as the
child was dressed, the vizier carried him away and presented
him to the caliph.

When they reached the palace the boy was very shy, until
the caliph reassured him. He then ordered the merchants to
be brought forward. When they were introduced, they prostrated themselves before the throne, bowing their heads quite
down to the carpet that covered it. Afterwards the caliph said
to them, Plead each of you your causes before this child, who
will hear and do you justice; and if he should be at a loss, I
will assist him.

Ali Cogia and the merchant pleaded one after the other;

but when the merchant proposed his oath as before, the child said, It is too soon; it is proper that we should see the jar of olives.

At these words Ali Cogia presented the jar, placed it at the caliph's feet, and opened it. The caliph looked at the olives, took one and tasted it, giving another to the boy. Afterwards the merchants were called, who examined the olives, and reported

'Plead each of you your causes before this child,' . . .

that they were good, and of that year. The boy told them, that Ali Cogia affirmed that it was seven years since he had put them up, when they returned the same answer as the children who had represented them the night before.

Though the wretch who was accused saw plainly that these merchants' opinion must convict him, yet he would say something in his own justification. But the child, instead of ordering him to be impaled, looked at the caliph, and said, Commander of the Faithful, this is no jesting matter; it is your majesty that must condemn him to death, and not I, though I did it yesterday in play.

The caliph, fully satisfied of the merchant's villainy, delivered him into the hands of the ministers of justice to be impaled. The sentence was executed upon him, after he had confessed where he had concealed the thousand pieces of gold, which were restored to Ali Cogia. The monarch, most just and equitable, then turning to the cauzee, bade him learn of that child to acquit himself more exactly of his duty; and embracing the boy, sent him home with a purse of a hundred pieces of gold as a token of his liberality and admiration of his acuteness.

The Story of Abou Hassan or the Sleeper Awakened

IN the reign of the caliph Haroun al Raschid, there lived at Bagdad a very rich merchant, who had but one son, whom he named Abou Hassan, and educated with great strictness. When his son was thirty years old, the merchant dying, left him his sole heir, and master of great riches, amassed together by much frugality and close application to business.

Abou Hassan, whose father had always forbidden him to be extravagant, longed to spend money, and resolved to make a reputation for lavish generosity. To this end he divided his riches into two parts; with one half he bought houses in town, and land in the country, with a resolution never to touch the income of his real estate, which was considerable enough to live upon very handsomely, but lay it all by as he received it. With the other half, which consisted of ready money, he designed to make himself amends for the time he had lost by the severe restraint in which his father had always kept him.

With this intent, Abou Hassan formed a society with youths of his own age and condition, who thought of nothing but how to make their time pass agreeably. He gave magnificent entertainments, and spared neither trouble nor expense to make them celebrated throughout the city. So enormous was the outlay,

266

that in a year the money he had set apart for the purpose was spent, and he was forced to desist. As soon as he discontinued keeping this table, his friends forsook him; whenever they saw him they avoided him, and if by chance he met any of them, and went to stop them, they always excused themselves on some pretence or other.

Abou Hassan was more affected by this behaviour of his friends, who had forsaken him so basely and ungratefully, after all the protestations they had made him of inviolable attach-

'*He went . . . into his mother's apartment, and sat down on the end of a sofa.*'

ment, than by the loss of all the money he had so foolishly squandered. He went melancholy and thoughtful, his countenance expressive of deep vexation, into his mother's apartment, and sat down on the end of a sofa at a distance from her. What is the matter with you, son? said his mother, seeing him thus depressed. Why are you so altered, so dejected, and so different from yourself?

At these words Abou Hassan melted into tears; and in the midst of his sighs exclaimed, Ah! mother, I see at last how insupportable poverty must be; I am sensible that it deprives us of joy, as the setting of the sun does of light. As poverty makes us forget all the commendations passed upon us before our fall, it makes us endeavour to conceal ourselves, and spend our nights in tears and sorrow. In short, a poor man is looked upon, both by friends and relations, as a stranger. You know, mother, how I have treated my friends for this year past; I have entertained them with all imaginable generosity, till I have spent all my money, and now they have left me, when they suppose I can treat them no longer. For my real estate, I thank Heaven for having given me grace to keep the oath I made not to encroach upon that. I shall now know how to use what is left. But I will, however, try how far my friends, who deserve not that I should call them so, will carry their ingratitude. I will go to them one after another, and when I have represented to them what I have done on their account, ask them to make up a sum of money to relieve me, merely to try if I can find any sentiment of gratitude remaining in them.

Not one of his companions was affected with the arguments which the afflicted Abou Hassan used to persuade them; and he had the mortification to find that many of them told him plainly they did not know him.

He returned home full of melancholy, and going into his mother's apartment said, Ah! madam, instead of friends I have found none but perfidious, ungrateful wretches, who deserve not my friendship; I renounce them, and promise you I will never see them more. He resolved to be as good as his word, and took every precaution to avoid falling again into the inconvenience which his former prodigality had occasioned, taking an oath never to give an inhabitant of Bagdad any entertainment while he lived. He drew the strong box into which he had put the rents received from his estates from the recess where he had placed it in reserve, put it in the room of that he had emptied, and resolved to take out every day no more than was sufficient to defray the expense of a single person to sup with him, who, according to the oath he had taken, was not of Bagdad, but a stranger arrived in the city the same day, and who must take his leave of him the following morning.

'. . . told him plainly they did not know him.'

Conformably to this plan, Abou Hassan took care every morning to provide whatever was necessary, and towards the close of the evening went and sat at the end of Bagdad bridge; and as soon as he saw a stranger, accosted him civilly, invited him to sup and lodge with him that night; and after having informed him of the law he had imposed upon himself, conducted him to his house. The repast with which Abou Hassan regaled his guests was not costly, but well dressed, with plenty of good wine, and generally lasted till the night was pretty far advanced; instead of entertaining his guests with the affairs of State, his family, or business, as is too frequent, he conversed on different agreeable subjects. He was naturally of so gay and pleasant a temper, that he could give the most agreeable turns to every subject, and make the most melancholy persons merry. When he sent away his guests the next morning, he always said, God preserve you from all sorrow wherever you go; when I invited you yesterday to come and sup with me, I informed you of the law I have imposed on myself; therefore do not take it ill if I tell you that we must never see one another again, nor drink together, either at home or anywhere else, for reasons best known to myself; so God conduct you.

One day when Abou Hassan was waiting at the bridge as usual, the caliph Haroun al Raschid, attended by one slave, chanced to come by in the garb of a merchant of Moussul. Abou Hassan, taking him for such, saluted him courteously and said: Sir, I congratulate you on your happy arrival in Bagdad; I beg you to do me the honour to sup with me, and repose yourself at my house for this night, after the fatigue of your journey. He then told him of his custom of entertaining the first stranger he met with. The caliph found something so odd and singular in Abou Hassan's whim, that he was very desirous to know the cause; and told him that he could not better merit a civility, which he did not expect as a stranger, than by accepting the obliging offer made him; that he had only to lead the way, and he was ready to follow him.

Abou Hassan, little guessing the rank of his guest, treated

him as an equal, and gave him the usual good but plain supper
of which he himself partook. After they had supped and
washed their hands, Abou Hassan placed wine upon the table
and requested the caliph to drink, which he did, expressing
himself well pleased with the wine. He also listened with
satisfaction to the young man's easy and cultured conversation.
And at last, in a burst of confidence, Abou Hassan told the caliph
his history, which interested him greatly. You are indeed a
fortunate man, said he, to have been warned in time, and I
highly commend your conduct.

Thus they sat, drinking and talking of indifferent subjects,
till the night was pretty far advanced; when the caliph said:
Before we part, pray tell me if there is any way in which I can
be of service to you? Speak freely, and open your mind; for
though I am but a merchant, it may be in my power to oblige
you myself, or by some friend.

To these offers of the caliph Abou Hassan, taking him still
for a Moussul merchant, replied: I am very well persuaded,
sir, that it is not out of compliment that you make me these
generous tenders; but upon the word of an honest man, I
assure you, I have nothing that troubles me, no business, nor
desires, and I ask nothing of anybody. I have not the least
ambition, as I told you before, and am satisfied with my condition; therefore, I can only thank you for your obliging proffers,
and the honour you have done me in condescending to partake
of my frugal fare. Yet I must tell you, pursued Abou Hassan,
there is one thing gives me uneasiness, without, however, disturbing my rest. You must know the town of Bagdad is divided
into quarters, in each of which there is a mosque with an imaum
to perform service at certain hours, at the head of the quarter
which assembles there. The imaum of the division I live in is
a surly curmudgeon, of an austere countenance, and the greatest
hypocrite in the world. Four old men of this neighbourhood,
who are people of the same stamp, meet regularly every day
at this imaum's house. There they vent their slander, calumny,
and malice against me and the whole quarter. Were I but in

a position to punish them I would do so; and I wish the caliph knew of their doings, for he is just and would stop them. Would that I had the caliph's power for one day; then I would order the imaum to receive four hundred lashes, and each of the four

'*Four old men of this neighbourhood, . . .*'

men who abet his actions should receive one hundred, as the reward of their iniquities.

The caliph immediately decided upon a plan by which he could enable Abou Hassan's wish to be realised. He took the bottle and poured out a glass of wine, drank it off to his host's health; and then filling the other, put into it artfully a little opiate powder, which he had about him, and giving it to Abou Hassan, said, You have taken the pains to fill for me all night, and it is the least I can do to save you the trouble once. I beg you to take this glass : drink it for my sake.

Abou Hassan took the glass, and to show his guest with how much pleasure he received the honour, drank it off at once. Directly he swallowed it the powder took effect, and he fell into a sound sleep. The caliph commanded the slave he had brought with him to take Abou Hassan upon his back, and follow him; but to be sure to observe the house, that he might know it again. In this manner the caliph, followed by the slave with his sleeping load, went out of the house, but without shutting the door after him as he had been desired, went directly to his palace, and by a private door into his own apartment, where the officers of his chamber were in waiting, whom he ordered to undress Abou Hassan and put him into his bed, which they immediately performed.

The caliph then sent for all the officers and ladies to the palace, and said to them, I would have all those whose business it is to attend my levee wait to-morrow morning upon the man who lies in my bed, pay the same respect to him as to myself, and obey him in whatever he may command; let him be refused nothing that he asks, and be addressed and answered as if he were the Commander of the Faithful. In short, I expect that you attend to him as the true caliph, without regarding me; and disobey him not in the least circumstance.

The officers and ladies, who understood that the caliph meant to divert himself, answered by low bows, and then withdrew, every one preparing to contribute to the best of their power to perform their respective parts adroitly.

The caliph next sent for the grand vizier : Giafer, said he, I have sent for you to instruct you, and to prevent your being surprised to-morrow when you come to audience, at seeing this man seated on my throne in the royal robes : accost him with the same reverence and respect as you pay to myself : observe and punctually execute whatever he bids you do, the same as if I commanded you. He will exercise great liberality, and commission you with the distribution of it. Do all he commands; even if his liberality should extend so far as to empty all the coffers in my treasury; and remember to acquaint all my emirs and the officers without the palace, to pay him the same honour at audience as to myself, and to carry on the matter so well, that he may not perceive the least thing that may interrupt the diversion which I design myself.

After the grand vizier had retired, the caliph went to bed in another apartment, and gave Mesrour, the chief of his eunuchs, the orders which he was to execute, that everything should succeed as he intended, so that he might see how Abou Hassan would use the power and authority of the caliph for the short time he had desired to have it. Above all, he charged him not to fail to awaken him at the usual hour, before he awakened Abou Hassan, because he wished to be present when he arose.

Mesrour failed not to do as the caliph had commanded, and as soon as the caliph went into the room where Abou Hassan lay, he placed himself in a little raised closet, from whence he could see all that passed. All the officers and ladies, who were to attend Abou Hassan's levee, went in at the same time, and took their posts according to their rank, ready to acquit themselves of their respective duties, as if the caliph himself had been going to rise.

As it was just daybreak, and time to prepare for the morning prayer before sunrise, the officer who stood nearest to the head of the bed put a sponge steeped in vinegar to Abou Hassan's nose, who immediately awoke with a start. He was greatly surprised to find himself in a large room, magnificently furnished, the ceiling of which was finely painted in Arabesque, adorned with vases of gold and silver, and the floor covered with a rich silk tapestry. After casting his eyes on the covering of the bed, he perceived it was cloth of gold richly embossed with pearls and diamonds; and near the bed lay, on a cushion, a habit of tissue embroidered with jewels, with a caliph's turban.

THE STORY OF ABOU HASSAN

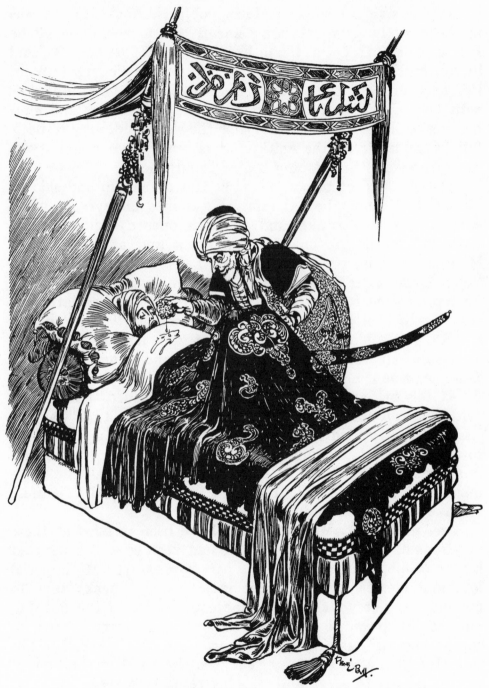

'. . . put a sponge steeped in vinegar to Abou Hassan's nose'

275

At the sight of these glittering objects, Abou Hassan was in the most inexpressible amazement, and looked upon all he saw as a dream; yet a dream he wished it not to be. So, said he to himself, I am caliph; but, added he, recollecting himself, it is only a dream, the effect of the wish I entertained my guest with last night; and then he turned himself about and shut his eyes to sleep. At the same time the slave said, very respectfully, Commander of the Faithful, it is time for your majesty to rise to prayers, the morning begins to advance.

At the sound of this voice Abou Hassan sat up and said to himself, this cannot be a dream. He rubbed his eyes, to make sure that he was awake, and when he opened them, the sun shone full in at the chamber window; and at that instant Mesrour came in, prostrated himself before Abou Hassan, and said: Commander of the Faithful, your majesty will excuse me for representing to you, that you used not to rise so late, and that the time of prayer is over. If your majesty has not had a bad night, it is time to ascend your throne and hold a council as usual: all your generals, governors, and other officers of State, wait your presence in the council-hall.

At this discourse, Abou Hassan was persuaded that he was neither asleep nor in a dream; but at the same time was not less embarrassed and confused under his uncertainty what steps to take. At last, looking earnestly at Mesrour, he said to him in a serious tone, Whom is it you speak to, and call the Commander of the Faithful? I do not know you, and you must mistake me for somebody else.

Any person but Mesrour would have been puzzled at these questions of Abou Hassan; but he had been so well instructed by the caliph, that he played his part admirably. My imperial lord and master, said he, your majesty only speaks thus to try me: is not your majesty the commander of the faithful, monarch of the world from east to west, and vicar on earth to the prophet sent of God? Mesrour, your poor slave, has not forgotten you, after so many years that he has had the honour and happiness to serve and pay his respects to your majesty.

276

He would think himself the most unhappy of men, if he has incurred your displeasure, and begs of you most humbly to remove his fears ; but had rather suppose that you have been disturbed by some troublesome dream.

Abou Hassan burst out laughing at these words, and fell backwards upon the bolster, which pleased the caliph so much that he would have laughed as loud himself, if he had not been afraid of putting a stop too soon to the pleasant scene he had promised himself.

Abou Hassan, when he had tired himself with laughing, sat up again, and speaking to a little boy that stood by him, black as Mesrour, said : Hark ye, tell me who I am ? Sir, answered the little boy modestly, your majesty is the commander of the believers, and God's vicar on earth. That is not true, you little black-face, said Abou Hassan ; then he called the lady that stood nearest to him : Come hither, fair one, said he, holding out his hand, bite the end of my finger, that I may feel whether I am asleep or awake.

The lady, who knew the caliph saw all that passed, was overjoyed to have an opportunity of showing her power of diverting him, went with a grave countenance, and putting his finger between her teeth, bit it so hard that she put him to violent pain. Snatching his hand quickly back again, he said : I find I am awake, and not asleep. But by what miracle am I become caliph in a night's time ? This is certainly the most strange and surprising event in the world ? Then addressing himself to the same lady, he said : I conjure you, by the protection of God, in whom you trust as well as I, not to hide the truth from me ; am I really the Commander of the Faithful ? It is so true, answered the lady, that we who are your slaves are amazed to find that you will not believe yourself to be so. You are a deceiver, replied Abou Hassan : I know very well who I am.

More puzzled than ever, Abou Hassan permitted Mesrour to assist him to rise, and he submitted to be dressed by the slaves without offering any resistance. When this task was completed, the grand vizier led him through the double rows of curtains to the council-hall, where he was conducted with all the splendour of royal pomp to the throne. Having reached the throne, Mesrour gave him his arm to lean upon, and another officer on the other side did the same, and by their aid Abou Hassan mounted the steps and sat down amidst the acclamations of the officers, who wished him all happiness and prosperity.

The caliph had, meanwhile, followed, and taken up his station in a place from which he could see without being seen. What pleased him highly, was to see Abou Hassan fill his throne with almost as much gravity as himself.

As soon as Abou Hassan was seated upon the throne the grand vizier came forward and, making a low obeisance, said: Commander of the Faithful, God shower down blessings on your majesty in this life, receive you into his paradise in the other world, and confound your enemies.

Abou Hassan who began by this time to believe that he really was caliph, asked the grand vizier what business there was to transact. Commander of the Faithful, replied the grand vizier, the officers of your council wait without till your majesty gives them leave to pay their accustomed respects. Abou Hassan immediately ordered the door to be opened so that the officers might enter. And he bowed to them regally as they prostrated themselves before taking their seats.

After this ceremony the business of the day was transacted, the grand vizier standing before the throne made his report, and the caliph, who watched everything, greatly admired the wit with which Abou Hassan called the cadi to him and said: Go to a mosque in a certain quarter, wherein there is an old imaum; seize him and four old men, who abet his weakness, and bastinado them; give the imaum four hundred, and each of the others one hundred strokes. After that, mount them all five, clothed in rags, on camels, with their faces to the tails, and lead them through the whole city, with a crier before them, who shall proclaim with a loud voice, This is the punishment of all those who are meddlesome. Command them also to quit the quarter for ever. The cadi bowed to the grand vizier and with-

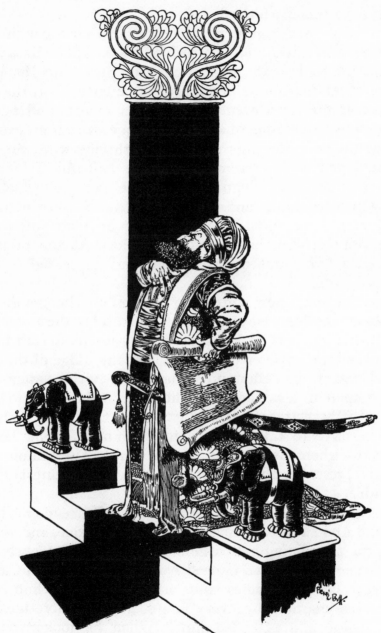

'. . . the grand vizier standing before the throne made his report.'

drew to execute the order, and in a short time returned to report that his duty was discharged.

The caliph was highly pleased at the firmness with which this order was given, and perceived that Abou Hassan was resolved not to lose the opportunity of punishing the imaum and the other four old hypocrites of his quarter. In the meantime the grand vizier went on with his report, and had just finished, when the judge of the police came back from executing his commission. He approached the throne with the usual ceremony, and said, Commander of the Faithful, I found the imaum and his four companions in the mosque, which your majesty pointed out; and as a proof that I have punctually obeyed your commands, I have brought an instrument signed by the principal inhabitants of the ward. At the same time he pulled a paper out of his bosom, and presented it to the pretended caliph.

Abou Hassan, then addressing himself to the grand vizier, said, Go to the high treasurer for a purse of a thousand pieces of gold, and carry it to the mother of one Abou Hassan, who lives in the same quarter to which I sent the judge of the police. Go and return immediately. The grand vizier, after laying his hand upon his head, and prostrating himself before the throne, went to the high treasurer, who gave him the money, which he offered a slave to take, and to follow him to Abou Hassan's mother, to whom he gave it, saying only, The caliph makes you this present. She received it with the greatest surprise imaginable.

The business of the day being finished, the council withdrew, and Abou Hassan descended from the throne, and was conducted to the dining-hall, where he fared sumptuously while the musicians played and danced before him. And all the while seven very beautiful ladies stood near and fanned him. Abou Hassan was charmed by everything; not least by the beauty of the ladies who attended him. When he looked at them attentively, he said that he believed one of them was enough to give him all the air he wanted, and would have six of the ladies sit at table with him, three on his right hand, and three on his left. The six ladies obeyed; and Abou Hassan taking notice that out of respect they did not eat, helped them himself, and invited them to eat in the most pressing and obliging terms. Afterwards he asked their names, which they told him were Alabaster Neck, Coral Lips, Moon Face, Sunshine, Eyes' Delight, Heart's Delight, and she who fanned him was Sugar Cane. The many soft things he said upon their names showed him to be a man of sprightly wit, and it is not to be conceived how much it increased the esteem which the caliph (who saw everything) had already conceived for him.

After this repast Abou Hassan was conducted into another hall, where dessert was spread, and where seven other ladies, more beautiful than the others, stood ready to fan him. Abou Hassan, however, would not suffer them to do so, but bade them sit near him that he might enjoy their society. The caliph was delighted to hear the ready wit with which he amused the ladies, and knew him to be a man of no ordinary merits.

By this time, the day beginning to close, Abou Hassan was conducted into a hall, much more superb and magnificently furnished, lighted with wax in seven gold lustres, which gave a splendid light. There he saw seven large silver flagons full of the choicest wines, and by them seven crystal glasses of the finest workmanship. Hitherto Abou Hassan had drunk nothing but water, according to the custom observed at Bagdad, from the highest to the lowest, and at the caliph's court, never to drink wine till the evening.

As soon as Abou Hassan entered the hall, he went to the table, sat down, and was a long time in a kind of ecstasy at the sight which surrounded him, and which was much more beautiful than anything he had beheld before. Taking by the hand the lady who stood on the right next to him, he made her sit down by him, and presenting her with a cake, asked her name. Commander of the Faithful, said the lady, I am called Cluster of Pearls. No name, replied Abou Hassan, could have more properly expressed your worth; and indeed your teeth exceed

281

the finest pearls. Cluster of Pearls, added he, since that is your name, oblige me with a glass of wine from your fair hand. The lady brought him a glass of wine, which she presented to him with a pleasant air. Then Abou Hassan drank with each of the seven ladies. And when he had toasted them severally, Cluster of Pearls went to the buffet, poured out a glass of wine, and putting in a pinch of the same powder the caliph had used the night before, presented it to Abou Hassan. Commander of the Faithful, said she, I beg of your majesty to take this glass of wine, and before you drink it, do me the favour to hear a song I have composed to-day, and which I flatter myself will not displease you. When the lady had concluded, Abou Hassan drank off his glass, and turned his head towards her to give her those praises which he thought she merited, but was prevented by the opiate, which operated so suddenly that his mouth was instantly wide open, and his eyes close shut, and dropping his head on the cushions, he slept as profoundly as the day before when the caliph had given him the powder. One of the ladies stood ready to catch the glass, which fell out of his hand ; and then the caliph, who enjoyed greater satisfaction in this scene than he had promised himself, and was all along a spectator of what had passed, came into the hall to them, overjoyed at the success of his plan. He ordered Abou Hassan to be dressed in his own clothes, and carried back to his house by the slave who had brought him, charging him to lay him on a sofa in the same room, without making any noise, and to leave the door open when he came away.

Abou Hassan slept till very late the next morning. When the powder was worked off, he awoke, opened his eyes, and finding himself at home, was in the utmost surprise. Cluster of Pearls ! Morning Star ! Coral Lips ! Moon Face ! cried he, calling the ladies of the palace by their names, as he remembered them ; where are you ? Come hither.

Abou Hassan called so loud, that his mother, who was in her own apartment, heard him, and running to him upon the noise he made, said, What ails you, son ? what has happened to you ? At these words Abou Hassan lifted up his head, and looking haughtily at his mother, said, Good woman ! who is it you call son ? Why, you, answered his mother very mildly ; are you not Abou Hassan, my son ? It is strange that you have forgotten yourself so soon. I your son ? replied Abou Hassan ; you know not what you say ! I am the Commander of the Faithful ! and you cannot make me believe otherwise.

Abou Hassan's mother, who was convinced that he was suffering from a mental disorder, tried to change the conversation. And to do this she related how the imaum had been punished on the previous day. Abou Hassan no sooner heard this relation, but he cried out, I am neither thy son nor Abou Hassan, but certainly the Commander of the Believers. I cannot doubt after what you have told me. Know that it was by my order the imaum and the four sheiks were punished.

His mother vainly tried to soothe his troubled mind, but her remonstrances only enraged Abou Hassan the more ; and he was so provoked at his mother, that, regardless of her tears, he took hold of a cane, and ran to his mother in great fury, and in a threatening manner that would have frightened any one but a mother so partial to him, said, Tell me directly who I am. I do not believe, son, replied she, looking at him tenderly and without fear, that you are so abandoned by God as not to know your mother, who brought you into the world, and to mistake yourself. You are indeed my son Abou Hassan, and are much in the wrong to arrogate to yourself the title which belongs only to our sovereign lord the Caliph Haroun al Raschid, especially after the noble and generous present the monarch made us yesterday.

At these words Abou Hassan grew quite mad. The circumstance of the caliph's liberality persuaded him more than ever that he was caliph, remembering that he had sent the vizier. And in his frenzy, he beat his mother with the cane, telling her the while that it was he who sent the money.

The poor mother, who could not have thought that her son would have come so soon from words to blows, called out for help so loud, that the neighbours ran in to her assistance. Abou Hassan continued to beat her, at every stroke asking her if he was the Commander of the Faithful, to which she always answered tenderly, that he was her son.

At the sound of her cries the neighbours came running in, and upon hearing Abou Hassan proclaim himself as caliph, they no longer doubted but that he was insane. They therefore seized him, and, having bound him, carried him to the lunatic asylum, where he was lodged in a grated cell, and here they left him to recover his senses. He received fifty strokes of the bastinado daily to help him to remember that he was not the Commander of the Faithful as he maintained.

By degrees those strong and lively ideas, which Abou Hassan had entertained, of having been clothed in the caliph's habit, having exercised his authority, and been punctually obeyed and treated like the true caliph, the assurance of which had persuaded him that he was so, began to wear away. He then made up his mind to think of the whole thing as a dream, and to return to his own house in peace.

When Abou Hassan's mother came to see him, she found him so much better that she wept for joy. Indeed, mother, said he, I cannot understand what has taken place, but I am resolved to regard it all as a very vivid dream. And I beg of you to forgive me for all my ill-treatment of you. My son! cried she, transported with pleasure, my satisfaction and comfort to hear you talk so reasonably is inexpressible, and it gives me much joy; but I must tell you my opinion of this adventure. The stranger whom you brought home the evening before your illness to sup with you went away without shutting your chamber door after him, as you desired, which I believe gave the devil an opportunity to enter, and throw you into the horrible illusion you have been in: therefore, my son, you ought to return God thanks for your deliverance. I believe that you are right, said he, and I beg of you to have me released from this place. His mother waited no second asking, but hurried to the keeper, who, having examined Abou Hassan, released him as she desired.

'. . . and here they left him to recover his senses.'

Abou Hassan took several days' rest after his return, and then resumed his practice of inviting a stranger to supper. The very first time he went to the bridge he perceived the merchant who, as he thought, had caused all his troubles, coming towards him. Abou Hassan turned away to avoid him, but the merchant would not be put off, and came up to him. Ho, brother Abou Hassan, said he, is it you?—I greet you! Give me leave to embrace you?—Not I, replied Abou Hassan, I do not greet you. I will have neither your greeting nor your embraces. Go along!

The caliph, who had carefully planned the meeting, since he knew that Abou Hassan had returned home, was not to be diverted from his purpose by this rude behaviour. He well knew the law Abou Hassan had imposed on himself, never to have commerce again with a stranger he had once entertained, but pretended to be ignorant of it. Ah! brother Abou Hassan, said he, embracing him, I do not intend to part with you thus, since I have had the good fortune to meet with you a second time; you must exercise the same hospitality towards me again that you showed me a month ago, when I had the honour to drink with you.

Abou Hassan would fain have sent the caliph away, but his efforts to rid himself of his unwelcome presence were futile, and at last he found himself compelled to allow him to accompany him. But, said he, since your last visit entailed so much trouble, I must tell you what happened, and beg of you to spare me a repetition. Abou Hassan then related his adventure, and concluded by making the caliph promise to form no more good intentions for his future. I am satisfied, said he, and will forgive all that is past.

As soon as Abou Hassan entered his house, he called for his mother and for candles, desired his guest to sit down upon a sofa, and then placed himself by him. A little time after, supper was brought up, and they both began to eat without ceremony. When they had done, Abou Hassan's mother cleared the table, set on a small dessert of fruit, wine, and glasses by her son, then withdrew, and appeared no more.

THE STORY OF ABOU HASSAN

After they had been drinking for some time the caliph said : Have you never thought of getting married ? No, replied Abou Hassan, I prefer to remain free. That is not right, continued the caliph. I must find you a lady who will be worthy of your love. And I am sure you will like her. Then taking Abou Hassan's glass he put into it a little of the powder, and handed it to his host filled with wine. Come, said he, drink the health of the lady I shall provide for you.

Abou Hassan took the glass, laughing, and shaking his head, said, Be it so ; since you desire it, I cannot be guilty of so great a piece of incivility, nor disoblige a guest of so much merit in such a trifling matter. I will drink the health of the lady you promise me, though I am very well contented as I am, and do not rely on your keeping your word. No sooner had Abou Hassan drank off his bumper, than he was seized with as deep a sleep as before ; and the caliph ordered the same slave to take him and carry him to the palace. The slave obeyed, and the caliph, who did not intend to send back Abou Hassan as before, shut the door after him, as he had promised, and followed.

When they arrived at the palace, the caliph ordered Abou Hassan to be laid on a sofa in the hall, from whence he had been carried home fast asleep a month before ; but first he bade the attendants to put him on the same habit in which he had acted as caliph, which was done. He then charged all the officers, ladies, and musicians, who were in the hall when he drank the last glass of wine which had put him to sleep, to be there by daybreak, and to take care to act their parts well when he should wake. He then retired to rest, charging Mesrour to awake him before they went into the hall, that he might conceal himself in the closet as before.

Things being thus disposed, and the caliph's powder having had its effect, Abou Hassan began to awake without opening his eyes. At that instant, the seven bands of singers joined their voices to the sound of hautboys, fifes, flutes, and other instruments, forming a very agreeable concert. Abou Hassan was in great surprise to hear the delightful harmony ; but

287

when he opened his eyes, and saw the ladies and officers about him, whom he thought he recognised, his amazement increased. The hall that he was in seemed to be the same he had seen in his first dream, and he observed the same lustres, and the same furniture and ornaments.

He was, however, too frightened to regain all his faculties at once. God have mercy upon me, he exclaimed, for I am possessed of the evil spirit. The lords tried to convince him that he was the victim of an unpleasant dream. Sir, cried he, see my back, are these marks, then, imaginary? I tell you I can feel the pain of the blows come still. Come hither and bite my ear, that I may feel if I am awake. One of the slaves stepped forward and obeyed, whereupon Abou Hassan screamed, but was still mystified. The band immediately struck up, and all the attendants began to dance round the sofa on which Abou Hassan sat. Seeing among the ladies some that he recognised, Abou Hassan threw off his royal robes and joined in the dance, jumping and cutting capers, with the others. So amused was the caliph that he put his head into the room and cried out: Abou Hassan, Abou Hassan, have you mind to cause my death from laughing?

As soon as the caliph's voice was heard, everybody was silent, and Abou Hassan, among the rest, who, turning his head to see from whence the voice came, knew the caliph, and in him recognised the Moussul merchant, but was not in the least daunted; on the contrary, he became convinced that he was awake, and that all that had happened to him had been real, and not a dream. He entered into the caliph's pleasantry: Ha! ha! said he, looking at him with good assurance, you are a merchant of Moussul, and complain that I would kill you. I see the whole thing now. But nay, tell me what you did to make me insensible, or else I shall always feel that I am half mad.

The caliph then told him all that had happened during the unnatural sleep, and how it was accomplished. I have a desire to know how my people live, said he, and therefore often wander about the city in disguise. It was thus that I came to your house; and hearing you express a wish to have royal power for a day, I decided to grant your wish. I never thought that my acquiescence would lead to so much trouble, but I am prepared to make every return in my power—not only as your due, but because I have proved that you are a man of high qualities. Ask what you will and I shall grant it.

Commander of the Faithful, replied Abou Hassan, how great soever my tortures may have been, they are all blotted out of my remembrance, since I understand my sovereign lord and master had a share in them. And since I may make a request, I would ask to be allowed to enjoy the happiness of admiring, all my lifetime, your virtues.

The caliph was much pleased by this speech, and ordered Abou Hassan to be given whatever he wanted, and to come to him whenever he wished. Abou Hassan suitably expressed his obligation, and returned home to tell his mother all that had taken place, and how his previous experience had been no empty dream.

The caliph was much delighted by Abou Hassan, whose society he constantly desired. He also brought him to his wife Zobeide, who was greatly entertained by the history of his adventures. She often expressed a wish to see him, and noticing that whenever he came he had his eyes always fixed upon one of her slaves, called Nouzhatoul-âouadat, resolved to tell the caliph of it. Commander of the Faithful, said she one day, you do not observe that every time Abou Hassan attends you in your visits to me, he never keeps his eyes off Nouzhatoul-âouadat. And she seems to respond to his advances. If you approve of it, we will make a match between them.

Madam, replied the caliph, if Nouzhatoul-âouadat is willing to accept Abou Hassan as a husband I see no obstacle. Let them decide at once, since they are both present.

Abou Hassan threw himself at the caliph's and Zobeide's feet, to show the sense he had of their goodness; and rising up, said, I cannot receive a wife from better hands, but dare not

'*Abou Hassan threw himself at the caliph's and Zobeide's feet.*'

hope that Nouzhatoul-âouadat will give me her hand as readily as I give her mine. At these words he looked at the princess's slave, who showed by her respectful silence, and the sudden blush that arose in her cheeks, that she was disposed to obey the caliph and her mistress Zobeide.

The rejoicings at the wedding lasted for many days, and both Zobeide and the caliph gave the newly-married couple very handsome presents. Abou Hassan found his wife all that he desired, and she was equally pleased with him—in fact, they suited each other admirably. After the feastings and merry-makings, Abou Hassan and his wife settled down to live in great luxury. They spared no expense on the entertainments they gave, and so extravagantly did they spend money that scarcely a year after the wedding they found themselves penniless.

In their need Abou Hassan said to his wife : I was sure that you would not fail me in a business which concerns us both ; and therefore I must tell you, this want of money has made me think of a plan which will supply us, at least for a time. It consists in a little trick we must play, I upon the caliph and you upon Zobeide, and as it will, I am sure, divert them both greatly, it will answer advantageously for us. You and I will both die. Not I, indeed, interrupted Nouzhatoul-âouadat ; you may die by yourself, if you please, but I am not so weary of this life ; and whether you are pleased or not, will not die so soon. If you have nothing else to propose, you may die by yourself ; for I assure you I shall not join you.

You are a woman of such vivacity and wonderful quickness, replied Abou Hassan, that you scarcely give me time to explain my design. Have but a little patience, and you shall find that you will be ready enough to die such a death as I intend ; for surely you could not think I meant a real death ? Well, said his wife, if it is but a sham death you design, I am at your service, and you may depend on my zeal to second you in this manner of dying ; but I must tell you truly, I am very unwilling to die as I apprehended you at first to mean.

Be but silent a little, said Abou Hassan, and I will tell you what I promise. I will feign myself dead, and you shall lay me out in the middle of my chamber, with my turban upon my face, my feet towards Mecca, as if ready to be carried out to burial. When you have done this, you must lament, and weep bitterly, as is usual in such cases, tear your clothes and hair, or pretend to do it, and go all in tears, with your locks dishevelled, to Zobeide. The princess will of course inquire the cause of your grief; and when you have told her, with words intermixed with sobs, she will pity you, give you money to defray the expense of my funeral, and a piece of rich brocade to cover my body, that my interment may be the more magnificent, and to make you a new dress in the room of that you will have torn. As soon as you return, I will rise, lay you in my place, and go and act the same part with the caliph, who I dare say will be as generous to me as Zobeide will have been to you.

This plan commended itself to Nouzhatoul-âouadat, and she at once acted upon her husband's suggestion and placed him as he desired, pulled off the head-dress, and went straight to Zobeide, weeping and mourning. She poured out her woes to the sympathetic princess, who was deeply grieved when she heard of Abou Hassan's death. After the two women had sorrowed together, the princess ordered her slaves to give Nouzhatoul-âouadat a purse of gold and a rich piece of brocade to cover the body, and bade her have no fear for the future, that she would take care of her.

As soon as Nouzhatoul-âouadat got out of the princess's presence, she dried up her tears, and returned with joy to Abou Hassan, to give him an account of her good success. When she came home she burst out laughing on seeing her husband still stretched out in the middle of the floor; she ran to him, bade him rise and see the fruits of his stratagem. He arose, and rejoiced with his wife at the sight of the purse and brocade. Unable to contain herself at the success of her artifice, Come, husband, said she, laughing, let me act the dead part, and see if you can manage the caliph as well as I have done Zobeide.

That is the temper of all women, replied Abou Hassan,

who, we may well say, have always the vanity to believe they
can do things better than men, though at the same time what

'. . . and went straight to Zobeide, weeping and mourning.'

good they do is by their advice. It would be odd indeed, if I,
who laid this plot myself, could not carry it on as well as
you. But let us lose no time in idle discourse; lie down in

298

my place, and witness if I do not come off with as much applause.

Abou Hassan wrapped up his wife as she had done him, and with his turban unrolled, like a man in the greatest affliction, ran to the caliph, who was holding a private council. He presented himself at the door, and the officer, knowing he had free access, opened it. He entered holding with one hand his handkerchief before his eyes, to hide the feigned tears, which trickled down his cheeks, and striking his breast with the other, with exclamations expressing extraordinary grief.

The caliph, surprised at seeing Abou Hassan in such a plight, asked the cause of his grief, and when he heard that Nouzhatoul-âouadat was dead he expressed his grief in becoming words. He also bade the vizier present Abou Hassan with a purse of gold and some rich cloth, just as Zobeide had done for Nouzhatoul-âouadat. Abou Hassan prostrated himself before the caliph and thanked him for his kindness. Then, taking the gifts, he hurried back to his house, greatly pleased by the success of his scheme.

Nouzhatoul-âouadat, weary with lying so long in one posture waited not till Abou Hassan bade her rise; but as soon as she heard the door open, sprang up, ran to her husband, and asked him if he had imposed on the caliph as cleverly as she had done on Zobeide. You see, said he, showing her the stuff, and shaking the purse, that I can act a sorrowful husband for a living wife, as well as you can a weeping widow for a husband not dead. Abou Hassan, however, was not without his fears, that this double plot might be attended with some ill consequences. He thought it would not be amiss to put his wife on her guard as to what might happen, that they might act in concert. For, added he, the better we succeed in embarrassing the caliph and Zobeide, the more they will be pleased at last, and perhaps may show their satisfaction by greater liberality. This last consideration induced them to carry on their stratagem further.

The caliph, though he had important affairs to decide, was so impatient to condole with the princess on the death of her slave that he rose up as soon as Abou Hassan was gone, and went to Zobeide's apartment. Madam, said he, allow me to express my deep sorrow for the loss you have sustained by the death of Nouzhatoul-âouadat. Commander of the Faithful, replied Zobeide, you are mistaken; it is Abou Hassan who is dead, not Nouzhatoul-âouadat. Excuse me, madam, said the caliph, you are wrong; Abou Hassan is alive and well.

Zobeide was much piqued at this dry answer of the caliph. Commander of the Faithful, replied she, give me leave to repeat to you once more, that it is Abou Hassan who is dead, and that my slave Nouzhatoul-âouadat, his widow, is living. All my women, who wept with me, can bear me witness, and tell you also that I made her a present of a hundred pieces of gold and a piece of brocade. The grief which you found me in was on account of the death of her husband; and just at the instant you entered I was going to send you a compliment of condolence.

At these words of Zobeide, the caliph cried out in a fit of laughter, This, madam, is a strange piece of obstinacy; but you may depend upon Nouzhatoul-âouadat's being dead. I tell you no, sir, replied Zobeide sharply; it is Abou Hassan that is dead, and you shall never make me believe otherwise.

The caliph at once ordered the vizier to go and find out the truth of the matter at Abou Hassan's house. When Mesrour had departed he said to Zobeide, You will see, in a moment, which of us is right. So convinced am I that I will bet my garden of pleasures against your palace of paintings, though the one is worth much more than the other. They solemnly vowed to abide by the bet, and anxiously awaited Mesrour's return.

While the caliph and Zobeide were disputing so earnestly, and with so much warmth, Abou Hassan, who foresaw their difference, was very attentive to whatever might happen. As soon as he perceived Mesrour through a window, at which he sat talking with his wife, and observed that he was coming directly to their apartment, he guessed his commission, and bade his wife make haste to act the dead part once more, as they had agreed, without loss of time; but they were so pressed that Abou Hassan had much ado to wrap up his wife, and lay the piece of brocade which the caliph had given him upon her, before Mesrour reached the house. This done, he opened the

'Mesrour hastened back to report the result of his inquiries.'

door of his apartment, and with a melancholy, dejected countenance, and his handkerchief before his eyes, went and sat down at the head of the pretended deceased.

This satisfied Mesrour, who hastened back to report the result of his inquiries to the caliph. The caliph was highly delighted, and laughed long when he heard the tidings. You hear, madam, said he, you have lost your bet.

Zobeide, however, would not accept Mesrour's unsupported testimony; and as she disputed the wager, it was agreed to send her nurse to see whether Abou Hassan was really dead. But as Abou Hassan was watching at the window, he was prepared to take his place on the couch directly he saw the nurse approaching, so that by the time she reached the apartment Nouzhatoul-âouadat had completed the task of laying him out, and stood mourning by his side.

The nurse stayed only to offer her condolences, and then started back to the palace as fast as she could. As soon as she was gone, Nouzhatoul-âouadat wiped her eyes and released Abou Hassan; they both went and sat down on a sofa against the window, expecting what would be the end of this stratagem, and to be ready to act according as circumstances might require.

The nurse's report only complicated matters, as both the caliph and the princess were convinced of the rectitude of their messengers. And as neither would give way they agreed to go together to see for themselves. Accordingly they arose and sallied forth, accompanied by their attendants.

When Abou Hassan perceived them coming he told his wife, who was very frightened. What shall we do? said she. We are ruined. Fear nothing, replied Abou Hassan. Have you forgotten already what we agreed on? We will both feign ourselves dead, and you shall see all will go well. At the slow rate they are coming, we shall be ready before they reach the door. Accordingly Abou Hassan and his wife wrapped up and covered themselves with the pieces of brocade, and waited patiently for their visitors.

Mesrour, who came first, opened the door, and the caliph and Zobeide, followed by their attendants, entered the room; but were struck with horror at the spectacle which presented itself to their view, not knowing what to think. At length Zobeide breaking silence, said to the caliph, Alas! they are both dead! You have done much, continued she, looking at the caliph and Mesrour, to endeavour to make me believe that my dear slave was dead, and I find it is true : grief at the loss of her husband has certainly killed her. Say rather, madam, answered the caliph, prepossessed to the contrary, that Nouz-hatoul-âouadat died first, the afflicted Abou Hassan sunk under his grief, and could not survive his dear wife ; you ought, there-fore, to confess that you have lost your wager, and that your palace of paintings is mine.

Hold there, answered Zobeide, warmed at being contradicted by the caliph ; I will maintain you have lost your garden of pleasures. Abou Hassan died first ; since my nurse told you, as well as me, that she saw her alive, and weeping for the death of her husband.

I will give a thousand pieces of gold to him who can tell me which of these two died first, replied the caliph.

No sooner were these words out of the caliph's mouth than he heard a voice under Abou Hassan's piece of brocade say, Commander of the Faithful, I died first ; give me the thousand pieces of gold. At the same instant Abou Hassan threw off the piece of brocade, and springing up, prostrated himself at his feet, while his wife did the same to Zobeide. The princess at first shrieked out, but recovering herself, expressed great joy to see her dear slave rise again, just when she was almost inconsol-able at having seen her dead. Ah ! wicked Nouzhatoul-âouadat, cried she, what have I suffered for your sake ? However, I forgive you from my heart, since you are not dead.

The caliph, who was very much amused, demanded the reason of the joke. Whereupon Abou Hassan replied : Com-mander of the Faithful I will declare to your majesty the whole truth, without the least reserve. The extravagant way in which my wife and I lived was beyond our means ; and finding that our money was all gone we were at our wits' end. At last, the shame of seeing ourselves reduced to so low a condition, and not daring to tell your majesty, made us contrive this stratagem, which we hope your majesty will be pleased to pardon, to relieve our necessities, and to divert you.

THE STORY OF ABOU HASSAN

The caliph and Zobeide began to laugh at the thought of Abou Hassan's scheme. The caliph, who had not ceased laughing at the singularity of the adventure, rising, said to Abou Hassan and his wife, Follow me; I will give you the thousand pieces of gold I promised, for joy to find you are not dead. Zobeide desired him to let her make her slave a present of the same sum for the same reason. By this means Abou Hassan and his wife, Nouzhatoul-âouadat preserved the favour of Caliph Haroun al Raschid and the Princess Zobeide, and by their liberalities were enabled to pursue their pleasures.

．　　　．　　　．　　　．　　　．　　　．　　　．　　　．

The Sultan of the Indies could not fail to admire the prodigious store of interesting stories with which the Sultana had whiled away the time through one thousand and one nights.

He also admired the courage which had inspired her to offer to become his wife; and for her sake his stern vow was relaxed, so that he could not bear to put her to death. I confess, most lovely Scheherazade, said he, that your wit has disarmed me. For your sweet sake I renounce my terrible vow to slay a woman every day. And for that reason you shall ever be remembered as the deliverer of the maidens who would have fallen victims to my wrath—which I now know to be unjust. The Sultana cast herself at his feet, and embraced him with the most warm affection and gratitude.

The grand vizier was the first who learned these glad tidings, which he caused to be quickly spread through every province and town of the empire, so that the fair Scheherazade won the blessing of every one throughout the country. The Sultan lived happily with his lovely Sultana, and their names were loved and respected throughout the wide territory of the Empire of the Indies.

THE END

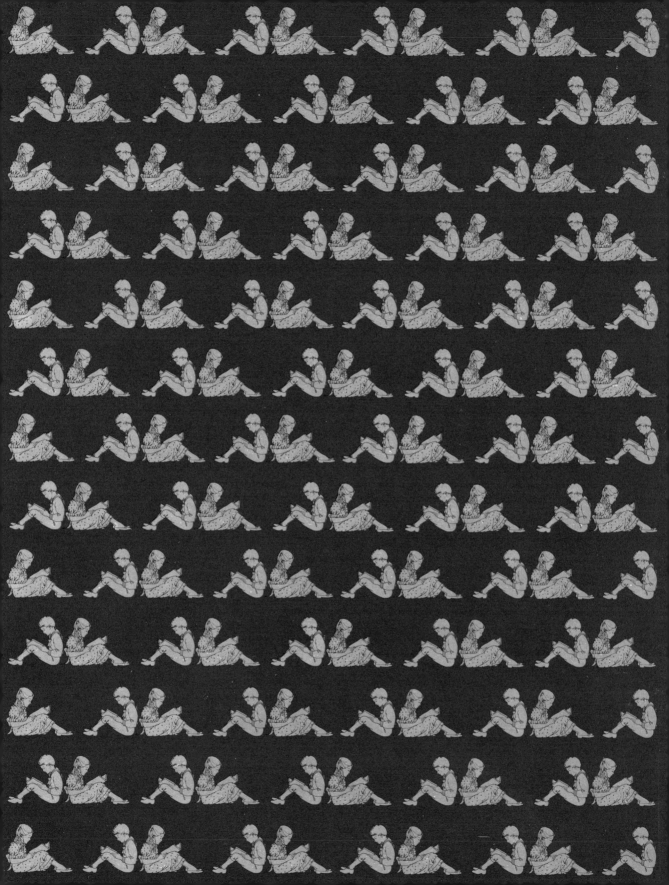